"You're here, you're here!" the little girl cried, wrapping herself around Mia's thighs, as Grant looked on.

"Aren't you forgetting somebody?" Mia whispered to Haley. "Maybe your daddy would like a welcome back hug, too."

"But I just saw him this morning!" Haley said. "And 'sides, he doesn't know how to hug."

"Then maybe," Mia said softly, "you could show him how."

Haley glanced over at Grant and then looked back at Mia. "He's the daddy. He has to hug first."

Oh, for heaven's sake. She hauled Haley up, dangling her in front of her father. "Hug, already."

As she'd hoped, Grant grabbed for his daughter, and Haley—bless her—threw her arms around her father's neck, and ta-da!

"Now, was that so hard?" Mia asked.

But when she next looked up, Grant's gaze briefly touched hers, swarming with a world of unspoken emotions, setting off a volley of a whole bunch of the suckers inside her head, as well.

Dear Reader,

Like every other five-year-old, at some point I asked my mother if Santa was real. Since the gifts were all piled in a corner of my parents' bedroom, the whole Ho-Ho-Ho Delivery Service thing was kinda shot, anyway. So Mama told me Santa Claus was a spirit (cagey woman, my mother), and off I went, satisfied. Not until much later, however, did I really appreciate the wisdom behind her response.

Because even the most secularized version of Santa is still about the message, not only behind the trappings of the season, but also beyond a particular religious belief. Santa Claus symbolizes love and generosity and joy…and, perhaps most of all, hope. So little Haley's plea to the jolly old elf isn't about asking for *stuff*, it's an unselfish faith in something beyond her small self to bring healing and happiness to the people she loves.

Leave it to a small child to really get the true meaning of Christmas…just like that long-ago kindergartner who intuitively understood her mother's off-the-cuff explanation about something far more substantial than mere myth.

Karen Templeton

DEAR SANTA

KAREN TEMPLETON

Silhouette

SPECIAL EDITION®

Published by Silhouette Books

America's Publisher of Contemporary Romance

SILHOUETTE BOOKS

ISBN-13: 978-0-373-24864-3
ISBN-10:   0-373-24864-4

DEAR SANTA

Visit Silhouette Books at www.eHarlequin.com

Printed in U.S.A.

Books by Karen Templeton

KAREN TEMPLETON,

a Waldenbooks bestselling author and RITA® Award nominee, is the mother of five sons and living proof that romance and dirty diapers are not mutually exclusive terms. An Easterner transplanted to Albuquerque, New Mexico, she spends far too much time trying to coax her garden to yield roses and produce something resembling a lawn, all the while fantasizing about a weekend alone with her husband. Or at least an uninterrupted conversation.

She loves to hear from readers, who may reach her by writing c/o Silhouette Books, 233 Broadway, Suite 1001, New York, NY 10279, or online at www.karentempleton.com.

To Tristan, my first grandbaby
Trust me—Santa will have nothing
on your grandparents!
Merry First Christmas, little one.

Chapter One

"Mr. Braeburn? Are you still there?"

"Yes, yes…" Grant released a long, strained breath, pressing his fingers into his eyelids. "I'm here." He blinked at the rain-drenched vista on the other side of his home office window, watching distractedly as sixty-foot pines cowered and shuddered under the leaden sky's relentless onslaught. "How—" He carefully cleared his throat. "How did you know to call me?"

"Mrs. Braeburn had emergency contact information in her purse. And the glove compartment." The doctor—middle-aged, still not comfortable with making these sorts of calls, Grant guessed—paused. "And her briefcase."

A humorless chuckle released the vise constricting Grant's lungs. Catching himself, he sank into a leather club chair facing the window. "I'm sorry—"

"Shock often produces seemingly inappropriate emotions," the doctor said kindly. "It's a coping mechanism. So the pain doesn't overwhelm us."

"It's not…" Outside, rivers slammed against the paned windows. Grant shook his head to clear it. "Justine and I were divorced more than a year ago."

"Ah. Yes. Of course." A pause. "I understand you have a daughter?"

Grant shut his eyes, willing his brain to assimilate… anything. "Yes. She's here. It's my weekend."

"Then…you'll tell her?"

"Of course," Grant said, even as he thought, *How the hell do you tell a three-year-old her mother's dead?* He sucked in an acid-tinged breath, then asked, "Justine…she was alone? In the car?"

"Yes."

"What happened?"

Another pause, then a measured, "She apparently took a curve too quickly, hit a patch of wet leaves and lost control. She may have been on her cell phone."

Typical, he thought bitterly. Justine would practically have a panic attack if she lost contact with the outside world for more than five minutes. With each breath, Grant's lungs eased. Slightly. "I suppose I'll need to make arrangements?"

"There's no other family, then?"

"Not to my knowledge."

"Mr. Braeburn, I could…give you some names if you, or the little girl, would like to talk to someone?"

"Thank you. But I have my own contacts. Should the need arise."

"Of course. If there's nothing else…?"

"No. No, wait…"

"Yes?"

A second's wrestling preceded, "Her face?"

The doctor hesitated, then said, "She'd been a beautiful woman, I take it?"

For some time after the call, Grant stood staring into the late day dreariness outside, the phone still clamped in his chilled hand. An odd, tight smile pulled at his mouth. He could just imagine Justine's soul—if she had one—floating over her lifeless body, wailing over losing her looks. Especially considering the megabucks she'd invested in them—

"Mr. B.? Everything all right?"

Grant turned; his housekeeper's puglike face was more deeply creased than usual, worry peering out from light brown eyes framed in drooping crow's feet. Etta Bruschetti didn't exactly fit the mold of who one generally found keeping lives and houses intact in this part of the world. But the smart-mouthed brunette kept him honest, on his toes and from believing his own press. It also didn't hurt that she cooked as though she'd been personally instructed by God.

He returned his gaze outside and said quietly, "Haley's mother was killed in a car crash a few hours ago."

"What? Ohmigod, you're not serious!" Etta pressed a broad hand to her generous chest. "God, that's awful. That poor woman!"

One side of Grant's mouth twitched. "Oh, come on, Etta...I know how you felt about Justine."

"Okay, so maybe I wasn't exactly all broken up when the two of you split. But I wouldn't wish somethin' like that on anybody, you know what I mean?"

Even though the question was rhetorical, Grant nodded anyway. Etta stuffed her hands in the pockets of the white utilitarian apron she wore over her sweatshirt and jeans, the closest she came to a uniform unless Grant entertained. Which he hadn't since the divorce. "Guess that means the baby's gonna be living here full-time now, huh?"

His thought processes hadn't gotten that far. But of course, he realized with a slug to his midsection—Justine's death made him a single father.

One who had thus far bungled this fatherhood thing like nobody's business.

"Yeah," he finally said on a stream of air. "It does."

A few minutes later, he climbed the stairs to his daughter's bedroom, where Haley would spend hours at a time playing with her extensive stuffed toy and doll collection. At first, Grant had assumed Haley simply hadn't inherited her mother's sociability gene. Eventually, however, he'd realized the child simply preferred the company of her "friends" to him.

His heart racing, he stood outside his daughter's partially open door, steeling himself as he listened to her nonstop chatter. Just like her mother, who'd never been at a loss for words, either. A good trait in a lawyer, Grant supposed. Swallowing sawdust, he knocked softly, then pushed the door open.

Instantly, the chatter stopped. A goofy-looking stuffed lion—Justine's last present to her, Grant realized with a punch to his gut—clutched in her arms, Haley glanced up at his entrance, her expression a disturbing blend of caution and indifference. Selfishly—and guiltily—Grant had often wondered if perhaps a more outgoing child would have helped him overcome his own ineptitude, would have shattered by now whatever had kept him from feeling what other fathers felt for their children.

At least, some fathers.

Still, he wasn't immune to his daughter's almost painful beauty, with her dark blond curls and enormous, thick-lashed brown eyes, her fair skin with its perpetual faint blush. She also seemed frighteningly bright for a child who wouldn't be four for another several weeks. But then, what did he know?

"Did Mommy call?" she asked with her customary directness, and his insides twisted. Without fail, Justine always called Haley during these weekend visits, even when she was away herself. Whatever had happened between him and his ex-wife, Justine had been completely devoted to their daughter.

In fact, his ex-wife had been completely besotted by Haley from the moment the doctor had laid the messy, squalling child in Justine's arms…while Grant had only been bewildered. By the baby, by the unexpected—in this case—mother-daughter bond, by the cozy, exclusive world the two of them had with each other from day one. A world to which Grant had never been able to figure out the secret password that would have gained him entrance.

Flexing his hands at his hips, Grant crossed the hooked rug covered with dozens of multicolored pastel butterflies, eternally in flight in a pale blue sky, to sit heavily on a faux-painted toy chest. Too astute by far, Haley watched him, her gaze steady. Judgmental.

Grant stared at his folded hands for a long moment, realizing he had no idea what the hell he was doing. What he was supposed to do. This was the kid who used to scream bloody murder if she lost sight of her mother for more than a few seconds—how on earth would she react to *this?*

"Daddy?"

The word was flat, perfunctory. She might as well have been calling him a plate or a chair or a tree. She kept her distance, hugging that lion, eyeing him suspiciously. "Are you mad?"

"No," Grant said, surprised she would read his hesitation as anger. "But I have something to tell you. Something sad. And I'm not sure how to go about it."

She waited, frowning, not so much trusting as curious, he thought. He took a deep breath and plunged.

"Mommy was in an accident," he said quietly, his heart punching his rib cage. "In her car. And she got hurt very badly. So badly, the doctors couldn't fix her. And… and she died."

Haley stilled, her gaze fixed on his. Then she lowered her eyes to the lion and started stroking his mane, curling her small fingers through the golden fluff. From underneath her lashes, she peered at him again. "Died? Like Grandpa?"

She'd still been a baby when Grant's father had died, much too young for Patrick Braeburn's death to have made an impact. And Justine's parents had both been gone long before she and Grant married. With a pang, Grant realized death was just a word to the little girl, a word without any real relevance or meaning.

"Yeah. Like Grandpa."

Another moment or two passed before she said, "Mommy says the doctor always makes you better."

"They tried their hardest, they really did—"

"So Mommy's coming back. She always comes back. Always."

"Not this time," Grant said over the nausea. "She can't."

Hugging the lion more tightly, Haley kept her eyes locked in his for several seconds before returning to the other side of the room, where she squatted in front of her dollhouse and began one-handedly rearranging things, as if she'd somehow sucked the news inside her. Almost light-headed with uncertainty, he wondered if he should hold her. Ask her if she was okay. Something.

"Haley? Do you…want to talk?"

She swept one hand through her curls in a gesture that was her mother to a T. "No, thank you. I'll talk to Mommy when she comes."

Oh, God.

"Haley, Mommy's not coming back—"

But she was shaking her head, the curls a blur as her movements became more and more agitated. "No, she's coming back, an' we're going to the toy store when we get home, she promised." Her eyes veered to Grant's, dry but determined. "She *promised*."

"Haley, honey—"

Grant reached for her, but she lurched backward, stumbling over a stuffed beagle lying sideways on the lacquered, honey-blond floor to land on her bottom.

"No!" she bellowed, frantically scrambling away, crab-style, to plaster herself against the wall underneath one window, between a pair of white bookcases crammed with books and games and puzzles. "I don't want you! I want *Mommy!*"

Despite the wet-clay feeling of helplessness swamping him, Grant crouched in front of his daughter, who shoved the heels of her sneakers into the floor, pressing further into the wall. "It's okay," he said as she started to whimper, "I'm going to take care of you now—"

"No!" she shrieked, launching the stuffed lion at his chest. "I wanna go home! I want to talk to Mommy *now!*"

Grant sprang to his feet and crossed to the other side of the room, ramming his hand through his hair and trying to catch his breath. Rain still slashed at the windows, pummeled the roof, the normally comforting sounds of a rainy fall Saturday barely audible over Haley's hysterics. Juggling millions of dollars of other people's money, taking risks that most human beings wouldn't dare…no sweat. How to comfort his daughter—how to even get over the first hurdle, of getting her to understand what was going on? Not a clue.

He glanced over at his little girl, huddled in her niche. She'd grabbed the lion again, clutching it to her and rocking, her face smashed into the thing's mane. After a moment, Grant lowered himself onto the edge of Haley's bed, a white four-poster smothered in yellow and white gingham ruffles. From ten feet and a world away, she glanced over, then scootched sideways to give him her back, clumsily scrubbing the back of her hand across her dripping nose.

"Go 'way."

"I can't."

"Why?"

"Because Mommy wouldn't want me to leave you alone."

Haley tossed a withering look over her shoulder, then pulled her knees closer to her chest, a tiny, stricken figure in her little corduroy skirt and sweater. And Grant, who was not by any means a religious man, found himself praying—pleading—to be shown what to do.

Etta appeared at the doorway, phone in hand, frown in place. She motioned Grant over, then whispered, "It's that friend of Justine's. Mia Vaccaro? She said she and Justine were supposed to get together this afternoon, but she won't answer her cell. Wants to know if you know anything."

With a last glance at his daughter's fragile-looking back, Grant took the phone, thinking this was why he'd never been a big fan of that whole prayer business to begin with.

Because all too often, the answer is exactly what you *don't* want.

"Where is she?" Mia tossed the question in Grant's housekeeper's direction as she catapulted herself through the mansion's open door, simultaneously unwinding her scarf and shrugging out of her tweed jacket.

"Upstairs, in her room," the older woman said, relieving her of the garments. "But—"

"Thanks."

Mia strode across the black-and-white tiled floor in the mini-rotunda that served as a vestibule, deaf to the screams of *Money, money, money!* reverberating from the high-ceilinged space. That she'd made it up here in one piece was a miracle in itself, considering all she really wanted to do was curl up in a corner somewhere until the world made sense again—

"Mia. Wait."

The deep voice hit its mark like a sharpshooter's bullet. Already at the foot of the curved staircase, Mia spun around, her gaze colliding with a pair of steely lasers, nailing her to the spot. Not until then did she realize she was panting, as though she'd run all the way from Manhattan instead of driven. Vaguely, it dawned on her that she hadn't even changed clothes after she'd talked to Grant, that she was still in the same rumpled jeans and who-gives-a-damn hoodie she'd been wearing to schlep fake fall foliage to the pier for the Chins' anniversary party the next night, that her tortoiseshell clip was hanging by maybe two teeth to her long, thick hair.

That she looked every bit the scatterbrain he undoubtedly thought she was.

"Grant! I'm sorry, traffic was a bear on the Henry Hudson, I got here as soon as I could!"

One side of his mouth ticked. Grant Braeburn's version of a smile. "Clearly. Thank you. Before you go up…?" He gestured toward a room off the entryway. His office, if she remembered correctly. She'd been in the house before, of course—for the wedding, once after that for dinner with Christopher, a night branded in her memory as somewhere between miserable and excruciating. But she wasn't here to see Justine's ex, she was here for the little girl who'd wrapped herself around Mia's heart from the first time she'd laid eyes on the baby when she was less than a day old.

"Mia!" came the imperious tone when she started upstairs. "We need to talk!"

"Later!"

She'd already reached the landing when his fingers wrapped around her arm. A lesser woman might have been intimidated—or, in other circumstances, turned on—by the man's grip. Or, at the very least, let out a soft, feminine squeal of surprise. Instead, Mia went for the severely pissed-off look. One that nicely complemented Grant's own.

"Damn it, Mia—I don't want you breaking down in front of Haley."

"Not a problem," she said, yanking out of his grasp and striding across a billion bucks' worth of oriental runner toward Haley's room. Whatever issues Grant had with her—or she, him—would have to wait. Preferably until they were both dead and buried—

The thought literally made her stumble, although she righted herself before Grant could notice. She hoped. But despite the heartburn from hell dissolving her digestive system, she wasn't about to crumple.

Not yet, anyway.

Grant loomed behind her, much too close, as, through Haley's open door, Mia could see the child sitting quietly in the middle of her bed in her teddy-bear-flecked pajamas, sucking her thumb—a habit given up months ago. And clutched to her small, far-too-fragile-looking chest, Mia realized with another fiery blast to her midsection, was the stuffed lion Justine had only just given her.

"Hey, little bit," she said softly, and the child's head shot up. A second later she'd streaked across the room to wrap her arms around Mia's thighs.

Then she tilted her head back, hope and worry and confusion tangled in her eyes. "Did Mommy come with you?"

Crap. Mia glanced over at Grant, whose glower had rearranged itself into something much more worrisome, then lowered herself to one knee, lumpy throats and heartburn from hell be damned.

"No, baby," she said softly, brushing Haley's curls off her cheek, praying she was striking the right balance between reassuring and serious. "Mommy's not here."

Haley disengaged herself to swing back and forth, clutching the toy. "Then are you going to take me back to the city?"

Slowly, Mia shook her head. "No, sweetie pie. You're going to stay with your daddy now."

The little girl frowned. "Daddy said Mommy got broken an' the doctors couldn't fix her."

"That's right," Mia said, swallowing back tears.

Soft brown eyes shifted from Mia to Grant and back again. "Like Hump-y Dump-y?"

"Yeah, baby. Like Humpty Dumpty."

"But Hump-y Dump-y's not real. Mommy said."

Bugger. "Well, that's true, but—"

"So where is she?"

Oh, brother. Mia glanced up at Grant, desperately hoping for a bone, here. Justine hadn't been particularly religious that Mia knew of, and Grant's spiritual bent was anybody's guess. However, since no bone seemed to be forthcoming, Mia decided to go with thirty years of Catholic indoctrination and let the chips fall where they may. "She's in heaven, sweetie. With the angels."

"What's heaven?"

Ah. Clearly she was introducing new material. "Someplace really, really nice where people go after they die."

"It's far away?"

"Yes. Very far."

Her brow puckered, Haley fingered Mia's loose hair. "C'n you get there in a taxi?"

"No."

"How 'bout an airplane?"

"Nope."

Almost expressionless, Haley looked at her for a long moment, then down at the lion. A second later, she held the lion out to Mia, who wagged one of the lion's floppy paws and said softly, "Who's this neat guy?"

"That's Henry. Mommy gave him to me."

"I know. I was with her when she bought him for you."

"You were?"

"Uh-huh."

After another moment's thoughtful consideration, Haley leaned over and whispered, "I have to go to the bathroom," and Mia whispered back, "Okay," and the little girl bounced off, Henry safely tucked under one arm. Mia struggled to her feet; her hands stuffed in the front pocket of her hoodie, she frowned toward the bathroom door.

"You've already gotten ten times further than I could," Grant said behind her, the words brittle as dry sticks. Mia turned her frown on him, thinking, *And whose fault is that?* From what Justine had said, the man hadn't even tried to fight for joint custody. Not that Jus would have given it to him, but still.

But this was hardly the time to call him on any of it. She walked to the other side of the room, idly poking through the little girl's collection of Dr. Seuss. "Weird, isn't it?" Mia said, sliding *Horton Hears a Who* back into the bookcase. "To think there's a time when we have no concept of what death means."

"Do we ever?" he said softly.

She had nothing to say to that.

After several excruciatingly awkward moments, they heard a flush, then the water running. A minute later, Haley emerged from the bathroom, Henry still in tow. "Henry had to go pee-pee, too," she said, climbing back up onto her bed. "He feels much better now. 'Cept he's sad."

"Oh?" Mia said, sitting beside her. "How come?"

"'Cause he misses his mommy."

Mia braced herself, even as she forced a smile to her lips. "But he has you to take care of him, right? So maybe he'll stop feeling so sad."

Haley's eyes swerved to Grant, then back to Mia. "But I'm not as good as her, she reads stories to him an' buys him ice cream and toys and stuff to make him feel better after he gets his shots. Who's gonna read to him if his mommy doesn't come back?"

Was this normal, Mia wondered, that despite "Henry's" being sad, Haley herself seemed more perplexed than unhappy? Mia reached out to smooth Henry's flyaway mane. "Well, I suppose you could read to him," she said, but Haley shook her head.

"I can't tell what all the words are yet. Mostly I just look at the pictures."

"Ah. But you know, I bet Henry would like looking at the pictures with you. Or maybe," she added with another darted glance in Grant's direction, "Henry's *daddy* could read to him? Why not?" she added when Haley shook her head again, more vigorously this time.

"'Cause I don't think he knows how, either."

"You don't think his daddy knows how to read?" Mia said, her words piercing Grant's almost palpable stillness.

Haley hugged the toy harder. "I don't think he knows how to read to *Henry*."

"Well…maybe *Henry* could show him?"

A faint crease marring her brow, Haley seemed to think this over for a second before she shrugged and said softly, "Maybe." Then she yawned and knuckled her eyes, a sleepy, overwhelmed little girl whose mother was dead and whose father, Mia uncharitably thought, had turned out to be a major disappointment.

"C'mon," she said gently, tugging the covers out from under Haley's itty-bitty butt. "Time for sleep."

Without protest, Haley squirmed underneath the covers, hugging Henry. "Will you be here when I wake up?" she asked, and Mia's heart broke.

"Oh, honey…I wish I could, but I've got work to do in the city tomorrow. But I'll be back soon."

Wide eyes searched hers. "You promise?"

Damn. But then, what were the odds of her being creamed by a semi or offed by a trigger-happy mugger or a flowerpot falling on her head within forty-eight hours of Justine's death? So Mia sucked in a huge breath that was equal parts prayer and willpower and said, "I promise, baby," she said, then bent over to wrap the little girl in her arms. "Big squeezies. No—*biiiig* squeezies!" she said again, and Haley strung her tiny arms around Mia's neck and hugged her for all she was worth. Then they rubbed noses and Mia laid her down again and gave her about twenty kisses before finally tearing herself away.

As she stood, however, she mouthed, "Your turn," at Grant. Who, after a moment's panicked eye-lock, moved toward the bed...only to pivot back to Mia with a weird mixture of sorrow and relief on his face.

"She's already asleep," he whispered, and Mia thought, *You wanna bet?*

Grant trailed her down the stairs, thinking about God knew what, Mia thinking that as much as she hated— *hated*—leaving Haley, she could not wait to blow this joint. Preferably while her guard was still firmly in place. But when she zeroed in on the curvy-legged table in the foyer where Etta had parked her stuff, Grant said behind her, "Don't go yet. Please."

She owed this man nothing. Not her time, and certainly not her emotional energy. That particular "on" switch had been disabled a long, long time ago. So more fool she for whatever it was that derailed her, made her turn back. Provoked an actual flicker of sympathy at the vulnerability in those icy eyes.

"I really have to get back—"

"Ten minutes," he said, and she sighed and dumped everything back on the table, then tromped back across the foyer, past the Jackson Pollock dominating the east wall, underneath the opera-house-size crystal chandelier suspended from the twenty-foot ceiling, over the Persian rug larger than her first apartment.

Money, money, money...

Grant stood aside to let her enter the office, gesturing for her to sit. Anywhere, apparently. At least a half dozen chairs begged for the privilege, mostly contemporary leather numbers in rich browns and tans, a tweedy club chair or two for variety. Funny, she would have expected lots of chrome and glass, assorted shades of black.

An open stainless steel casket, maybe, discretely placed in a far corner.

Mia briefly shut her eyes, picturing nuns the world over sighing in dismay. However, the only alternative to the grossly inappropriate flashes of black humor that overtook her whenever she was majorly stressed was grief-induced catatonia. And anyway, she could have sworn the casket comment had been in Justine's voice, accompanied by a burst of laughter and a lifted glass of Chablis.

Shoving aside an image of Justine as Mia last remembered her—runway beautiful and pulsing with energy, her eyes sparkling with mischief as they tromped down Madison Avenue arm-in-arm on a spur-of-the-moment shopping spree—Mia flopped down in one of the leather chairs. Still, the image, and the truth, lurked at the edges of her consciousness, waiting to pounce.

Ten minutes, she thought, her jeans rough against her palms as she scraped them over her thighs. *I can hang on for ten more minutes—*

"Were you able to eat before you came up?" Grant asked quietly, his brows slightly dipped. Mia shook her head. "Would you like something, then? A sandwich, at least—"

"No, I'm good." Except she then realized her mouth felt like she'd been French-kissing a blow-dryer. "I could use some water, though."

With a curt nod, Grant crossed to the small bar on the other side of the room, his loose-fitting black sweater (fine-gauge, she was guessing cashmere) and matching cords doing nothing to disguise the six-foot-plus package of solid, pulsing testosterone underneath. On paper, the man looked good. Okay, in person he looked good—all head-turning gorgeous with his dark hair and those eerie gray eyes, tall and fit and broad of shoulder, the way leading men used to look before somebody decided, for some inexplicable reason, that potent masculinity was overrated.

Add smart—investment whiz of the straw-into-gold variety—and insanely rich, and… Well. Mia supposed she could see the attraction. If one were into men whose beverage of choice was Type O Positive.

She shut her eyes again. *Go straight to hell, do not pass Go, do not collect two hundred dollars….*

"Here you go."

Jumping slightly, Mia opened her eyes again to see an über-masculine hand proffering a heavy, deeply etched glass and a parchment-colored cocktail napkin. "Thanks," she muttered, gulping down half the glass as Grant—still standing, still watching her—took a measured sip of his own drink. Something ambery and undoubtedly potent. And even more undoubtedly expensive.

"Are you all right?" he asked, startling her enough to make her hand jerk, sloshing water over the edge of the glass.

"I'm fine," she said, dabbing at her front with the napkin. She tried a smile, then thought, *Why?* "Although, to be frank, I don't think it's really hit yet."

Grant lifted his drink to his lips, then, inexplicably, relieved her of the damp, crumpled napkin before striding back to the bar to dispose of it. "I assume you and Justine were still close?"

"Uh, yeah. Sure." She waited out the twinge of hurt, of uncertainty. "It's been a strange couple of years," she said, fingering the glass's rim. "Lots of changes for both of us. So we didn't see each other as often as we used to. Before, you know, she married you. Especially once I left the firm."

Another image blossomed in her mind's eye, Justine hooting with unladylike laughter in the middle of the sidewalk, making strangers—in Manhattan!—smile. Deep inside, grief stirred and stretched. *Not yet!* Mia thought, swallowing it down. "But I'd never had a friend like Jus." After a moment's contemplation of her drink, she took a sip, then said, "Although I suppose that was due as much to timing and circumstance as anything. You know," she continued at Grant's speculative look, "both being the new kids at the firm at the same time, not to mention new to the city, neither of us having a sister…"

Her hand shook when she lifted the glass again. "But I always knew I could count on her. Trust her. And I can't believe…" Her eyes filled. "I can't believe she's g-gone," she whispered.

And the floodgates gave way.

Chapter Two

Grant's stomach clenched as Mia's hand slammed over her mouth, although not quickly enough to stifle either her moan or the torrent of tears that followed. Clearly horrified at breaking down in front of him, she struggled to her feet and stumbled to the other side of the room, although whether to get away from him or in some vain attempt to escape her own grief, he couldn't say.

Her meltdown came as no surprise, although her having held it together as long, and as well, as she had, did. Apparently, Mia Vaccaro was made of sterner stuff than he'd given her credit for, based on the few times he'd been in her company after he married Justine…a thought which in turn provoked the faintest whiff of memory, a brief impression, an obvious misapprehension. Rebuffing it—as well as his usual antipathy to waterworks—he snatched a box of tissues off an end table and carried them over to her.

"You'll make yourself ill," he said, softly, behind her quaking back. She jumped slightly, then turned, snatching three tissues in quick succession from the box and glaring at him through swollen eyelids.

"So s-sorry," Mia lobbed at him between sobs. "I d-don't know any other w-way to cry! If it b-bothers you—" she swatted in his direction with the tissues "—go away!"

So he did. Only to return a moment later with her forsaken glass of water.

"I'm n-not finished yet," she said, honking loudly into the tissues.

"I'm not rushing you. Come on, sit back down," he said, and she actually let him lead her back to the chair to finish her cry. In short order the sobs turned to sniffles, the sniffles to shudders, and the shudders to a small, trembly, "Sorry."

"Feel better?" he asked, picking up his drink from a small side table.

Mia blew her nose, tucked her arms against her midsection, then nodded.

He took a sip. "Now. Aren't you glad that didn't happen somewhere in the middle of I-95?" When she glared at him, he added, with extreme patience, "So sue me for guessing you were ready to blow."

After a moment, Mia sucked in a breath and sat up straighter, scrubbing her palm over first one cheek, then another. "Point to you," she said, then shivered. "God, I must look like hell."

She did, actually. Justine's tears had always been delicately executed, just enough to trickle down a flawlessly made-up cheek, to spike her eyelashes. No red-splotched cheeks or raccoon eyes, ever. "Now that you mention it, you might want to avoid mirrors for the next little while."

"Boy, you really are a gem among men, aren't you?" she

muttered, then waved away the comment. "Rhetorical question, no response necessary."

Grant looked at her for a moment, then walked back to his desk, gently swirling his drink in his glass. "You weren't at all surprised when our marriage fell apart, were you?"

"Once I got to know you? No."

"*Know* me?" Unaccountably irritated, Grant let his gaze drift back to the splotchy, puffy-eyed woman still quietly hiccupping in his favorite leather chair, one foot now tucked up underneath her backside. "How often have we been in the same room, Mia? A half-dozen times?"

"Often enough to confirm what I'd already suspected— that you and Justine weren't a good fit. But let's clear something up right now," she said, her brow pinched. "I didn't take some sadistic pleasure in your marriage breaking up. It wasn't about me being right, it was about my best friend being happy. If she'd been able to find that happiness with you, I would have been the first person to toast the two of you on your fiftieth wedding anniversary. But how we feel about each other is neither here nor there." Her expression softened. "The only thing that matters now is getting Haley through this."

Grant eyed her steadily for a moment before silently setting the glass on the desk. Facing her once more, he folded his arms across his chest. "Haley talks about you a great deal."

"We're best buds," she said quietly. "There've been nannies, of course. And Jus had her in preschool during the day. But the three of us would hang out..." Her voice broke; after a couple of deep breaths, she continued. "And I'd sit for her from time to time, when Jus had to work late." At Grant's frown, she rolled her eyes. "She was on the fast track to becoming partner, Grant, she couldn't exactly clock out at five on the dot every night. As anyone struggling for purchase in a huge law firm knows all too well." He thought he saw a slight shudder before she continued. "Although Jus did take work home with her as much as she could, to do after Haley was in bed. Your daughter wasn't neglected, if that's what you're thinking."

"Clearly," he said softly, even as he thought, *At least, not by her mother.* "Still. That was a lot to ask of you."

Mia's eyes narrowed. "She didn't ask, I volunteered. I love kids and I'm crazy about the squirt. And the nannies…well. They came and went. Even if I didn't see Haley that often, at least I was some sort of constant in her life. After her mother, I mean. And anyway—"

Grant noted her pointed exclusion of him from that equation.

"Considering everything Justine did for me…" Her eyes filled again, but she held up one hand, sucking in a steadying breath. "Babysitting was the least I could do to return the f-favor—"

At the wobbly last word, Grant plucked the box of tissues off the desk, but she shook her head. Then her words sank in. "What favor?"

"Okay, maybe 'favor' isn't the right word. Support, then. When I walked out on my law career to start my party-planning business, not only was Jus one of the very few people who didn't seem to think I'd lost it, she even got on the horn and called everybody she knew, lining up more work for me than I could have ever found on my own." She almost laughed. "In some ways, she seemed more determined to see me succeed than I did. And then…"

"What?" he prompted when she hesitated.

Mia screwed up her mouth, as though trying to decide how much to say. "Around the time of your divorce, my fiancé broke up with me. You met him once, he was out here for dinner. Anyway, it was a few weeks before our wedding. I was a mess. But even though Jus was still dealing with the aftereffects of her own…stuff, there she was, literally and figuratively holding my hand through one of the worst periods of my life."

Totally unaware that Grant's drink had turned to vinegar in his stomach, Mia unfolded her legs, stretching the previously trapped foot in front of her and wiggling it. "She'd call or e-mail me to ask how I was doing, suggest we go shopping or to the movies, or go to the museum or zoo with Haley…ouch! Damn, my foot fell asleep!"

Leaning over to rub the prickles away, her long hair tumbled free over her shoulders, framing her much-less-swollen face with exuberant, shiny waves. A moment later, she lifted her eyes to his, only to frown. "Is something wrong?"

With a sharp shake of his head, Grant abruptly returned to the window, unable to look at that trusting, loyal face a moment longer. He'd known, of course, from the moment he'd answered her call, heard the concern in her voice, that somehow, amazingly, Justine had managed to keep her betrayal under wraps. Otherwise, he seriously doubted even someone as wide-eyed as Mia would have continued babysitting for her *best friend's* daughter. Still, to hear it confirmed…

"For what it's worth," he said quietly, willing the words to quash the anger flaring inside him, "I didn't marry Justine expecting it to fail. I may be a risk taker in my professional life, but I've always erred on the side of caution about all things personal. So when things fell apart, I was definitely…disappointed."

"I don't know what to say," he heard behind him. Inhaling deeply, he spared her an almost-smile.

"No response necessary," he said, then returned his attention outside. "I don't blame you for feeling the way you do about me. From your standpoint, I made someone you cared about very unhappy. All I can say, in my own defense, is that it wasn't intentional. Although I do shoulder the blame for believing that Justine more clearly understood what she was getting when she married me. That I've never been a fun-and-games kind of guy."

"There's an understatement," he heard Mia mutter.

Grant turned, his mouth set, his gaze unwavering. Why he felt compelled to make this woman understand, he had no idea. Perhaps because Justine *hadn't* understood. But Justine had been his wife. Mia was…

Mia was very likely the only person who could help him bridge the canyonesque gap between him and his daughter.

"I can't help my nature, Mia. Even as a child, excessive shows of emotion made me cringe. However, I never promised Justine anything I couldn't, and didn't, deliver. That she still wanted more from me than I could give her…" He blew out a breath. "The marriage was a mistake. Or rather, the mistake was in my thinking I could somehow make a marriage work simply because getting married, starting a family, is what men my age, in my position, *do.*" He paused. "A mistake I won't make again, believe me."

"Yeah, well," she said finally, getting up, hanging on to the back of the chair as she hobbled around it, "I could've told both of you that at the beginning and saved everyone a lot of grief."

"Except then there wouldn't be Haley."

Her "oh, please" gaze slammed into his. Her eyes were

a strange shade of green, he realized, almost an olive. "And wouldn't that make *your* life a whole lot easier."

At her direct hit, heat surged up his neck. Irritated—with himself, with her, with the whole damn mess—he turned to spare her the satisfaction of his discomfiture. "Hard as this may be to believe," he said stiffly, "I do care about my daughter. About what happens to her. I always have. But I've never been comfortable around children."

"Including your own."

He hesitated, then said, "Especially my own. I seriously doubt we'll ever have the same sort of relationship she had with her mother. I'm simply not made that way."

"And *I* have zip tolerance for people who act like their kids are some kind of food they sampled once and decided they didn't care for! For crying out loud, Grant—have you even *tried?* You took Haley twice a month. If that—"

"Because neither Justine nor I wished to disrupt her routine any more than necessary!" he said, the excuse lame even to his own ears. "She often had playdates and birthday parties on the weekends—"

"Which you decided were more important than continuing her relationship with her father."

"That wasn't solely my decision, Mia."

Mia opened her mouth, only to press it tightly closed again. He guessed that as much as she'd dearly love to refute his statement, he doubted she could. Not if she'd been privy, as a close friend would have been, to Justine's fabricating some excuse or other to keep Haley with her on one of Grant's weekends.

Her eyes narrowed, but not enough to block what might have been the beginnings of doubt. "But you didn't exactly fight Justine on it, did you?"

One side of his mouth lifted. "Guilty as charged."

"Why not?"

And if he had a chance in hell of getting her to agree to his plan, he had to lay all his cards on the table, no matter how bad his admission made him look.

"Because Haley was barely two when we separated. A two-year-old who adored her mother and screamed whenever I tried to pick her up. Of *course* I tried to close the gap between us—contrary to popular opinion, I'm not a monster. But unfortunately Haley's appearance didn't magically transform me into one of those men who gets all sappy in the presence of babies. I suppose I hoped… well, that as she got older, I could make up for lost time, somehow."

"I don't believe I'm hearing this! Did it ever occur to you that maybe Haley wasn't going to wait until you were *ready* to be her father?"

"Every damn day since her birth," Grant said through gritted teeth, as if willing the raw fear—that he was going to fail his own child—to stay locked up where it couldn't do him, or Haley, any harm. "And it kills me, that there's a little girl upstairs who didn't ask for her mother to die and leave her with me as her father! That I'm the one who's supposed to get her through this, only I have no earthly idea how to do that!"

"Who the hell does, Grant?" Mia said. "Who *knows* how to handle stuff like this until they have to?"

"But at least Haley *likes* you."

Mia eyed him for a long moment, then sighed out a swear word, followed by, "I can't stay, Grant."

"Just for a few days. To help Haley through the transition."

"I can't," she repeated. "I have a life. And a business to run."

"I thought you said you loved her?"

Her eyes darkened. "Oh, you will *not* pull that emotional blackmail crap on me. Of course I love Haley. But she's not my daughter, she's yours. And whatever is or isn't going on between you is not my problem to solve—"

"I'm not asking you to solve anything, damn it! I'm only asking you to help *me* solve it! And I would think, given Haley's obvious affection for you, that you'd put her needs before whatever animosity you feel for me!"

Silence jangled between them for several seconds before she finally said, "I can't get out of this party tomorrow night, it's too big for my assistant to handle on her own. At least not on such short notice. But…" Long, blunt-nailed fingers dragged across her jaw for a moment before she crammed both hands into her jeans' pockets. "But I'm free for a few days after that. I suppose I could come back up the day after tomorrow for a day or two."

"Until after the funeral?" At her frown, Grant said, "Since Justine has no one else…"

"Right. Okay. Until after the funeral, then. But just so we're clear? I'm only doing this for Haley. Not for you."

"Fair enough."

He followed her when she walked out of his office, watching silently as she gathered her things off the table in the foyer and shrugged into a boxy tweed jacket at complete odds with the sweatshirt. And he couldn't resist wandering into the living room after she'd left to stand in front of one of the bay windows, listening to her peel rubber as she sped off, spitting gravel in her wake.

"Not exactly a prissy little thing, is she?" Etta said behind him.

He almost smiled. "No." Then he added, "She's coming back."

"So I heard. But she's right, you know. It's not up to her to fix whatever's wrong between you and Haley."

The smile stretched slightly. "You're not even the least bit repentant about eavesdropping, are you?"

"Hell, no," she said, and tromped off, and Grant eventually went upstairs to check on his daughter. The light from the hallway spilled across her bed, illuminating the tiny child sleeping fitfully in it.

Grant slipped noiselessly into the room to stand over the bed, releasing a long, soundless breath. He couldn't exactly grieve for Justine, but her death—the shock of it, the pointlessness—had still shaken him. More, in fact, than he'd at first realized. For what had happened—to her and between them—regret and genuine sorrow clawed at him, snarling and snapping. Once the truth sank in, Haley would miss her mother terribly.

As would Mia. Undeserved and misplaced though her loyalty to Justine may have been.

She doesn't know.

Again, the words pelted him, leaving the sting of guilt in their wake. But it wasn't his place to tell her. Relationship Neanderthal though he might be, even he couldn't bring himself to disabuse Mia of her faith in Justine's friendship. What would be the point? The woman was dead, her indiscretions—and betrayal—soon to be buried with her, God willing. Still, whatever his personal feelings about Mia, it had been no easy feat to tamp down the flash of anger on her behalf, that the woman she credited with getting her through the worst period of her life had actually been the very cause of her misery.

Oh, his ex-wife's talents had been quite extraordinary, he thought bitterly as Haley thrashed in her sleep, sending the poor stuffed lion sailing overboard. Grant bent over to retrieve the toy, carefully setting it where she could reach it. Instantly, a little arm shot out, groping for her new friend; Grant edged the lion closer, smiling slightly when Haley pulled the floppy thing back into the safety of her arms, her thumb popping into her mouth as she relaxed.

Then his forehead knotted as his thoughts strayed back to his ex. As much as Justine's infidelity had gouged his ego, at least it was understandable, given her obvious craving for more attention than Grant could give her. But to screw around with her best friend's fiancé...?

And then to have the gall to *console* Mia in the aftermath? Un-freaking-believable.

Almost as unbelievable as Mia's naiveté. Weren't women supposed to have some sort of radar about these things? Especially by their thirties? But then, how had the two women become such close friends to begin with? Considering how orderly and driven Justine had been, Mia—who'd given up a prime slot in one of Manhattan's most prestigious law firms to become a party planner, for God's sake—came across as downright flighty in comparison.

Then he thought of her when they'd been in here together, as unkempt as Justine had been fastidious, her dark brows drawn underneath a curtain of wind-blown, dark brown waves. And he had to admit, her obvious affection for his daughter, the concern trembling at the edges of her wide, bare mouth when she smiled, had suckered him into feeling a twinge of sympathy for her cluelessness.

He also had to admit, as personality traits went, cluelessness was far preferable to calculated treachery.

Feeling more weary than he ever had in his life, Grant gently tugged Haley's tangled covers from around her legs, smoothing them over her frail-looking shoulders. She stirred, her eyes never opening, trusting at least in sleep, even if not when awake.

Helplessness and hope collided inside his chest, nearly taking his breath.

Mia waited until she was back in her apartment, a cozy one-bedroom in the West Twenties, before digging out her cell phone to check her messages. At the sight of her parents' number, she groaned, executing a much-practiced spin-and-flop maneuver onto her sofa as her father's flat, blue-collar Massachusetts accent burrowed into her ear.

"Just wondering if you'd heard from your brother, or maybe you got a number for him or somethin', some way for us to reach him? Give us a call sometime."

No need to ask which brother they meant, since her four older brothers—and their families—all lived within ten blocks of the red-bricked, white-shuttered Springfield colonial they'd all grown up in. One black sheep out of six, you'd expect. Three, however—twelve years ago, her next oldest brother, Rudy, had knocked up his eighteen-year-old girlfriend, and then there was Mia walking away from a six-figure salary to start her own business—was just wrong. Still, at least Mia still touched base with her family from time to time. And Rudy lived with their parents, so their mother could watch his daughter, Stacey, while he was at work. Kevin, however…

She let out a sigh, punching the phone to retrieve her next message, thinking the kid would send them all to early graves. Except at twenty-six, he was hardly a kid anymore, was he…?

The second message was from Venus, her assistant, aka the Butt Saver.

"Girl, where the hell are *you? I've been trying to call*

you all freaking day, which is scaring the crap out of me because I know you don't go to the bathroom without taking your phone with you. If I don't hear from you by midnight, I'm calling the police. And no, I'm not kidding."

In her early fifties and the most organized human being Mia had ever known, Venus had been Mia's secretary at Hinkley-Cohen. And as eager to ditch the nine-to-five—or, in Mia's case, eight-to-whenever—grind as Mia had been. She immediately hit the callback button, spewing, "Sorry, sorry, sorry!" in the wake of Venus's "This had damn sight better be *good!*" Only as soon as she told Venus why she'd been incommunicado, she was all, "You're not serious? Oh, hell…I'm so sorry, baby! You must be a wreck, I know the two of you were pretty tight."

Yeah, that's what she had thought, too.

But now past the initial shock, Mia had to finally acknowledge the tiny flicker of doubt that had grown increasingly brighter since Justine's divorce, that Justine and she had been drifting apart. Not blatantly, and not all the time—the shopping trip again came to mind—but there'd definitely been the odd moment when Mia would catch Justine looking at her with something approaching regret in her eyes. As though she'd made a pact she now wished she could break. Sometimes Mia would even wonder if her babysitting availability had been the only reason Justine bothered to keep their relationship going.

"Yeah, we were," she now said to Venus, tears stinging her eyes. "Even if you didn't understand why."

"Oh, I suppose I did, if I thought hard enough about it. The two of you being new at the same time, and Justine being all flashy and glittery and worldly and whatnot, and you this subdued little thing when you first got there. What were you, twenty-one?"

"Twenty-two. And I was never subdued! And I haven't been *little* since kindergarten!"

"Okay, unpolished, then. Those sorry, clunky shoes you used to wear—"

"Hey. I paid big bucks for those shoes."

"Then more fool you. And that pitiful thing you called a suit… Honey, I had ancestors from the plantation days who were better dressed. So it was no wonder you gravitated toward her. But you know something? I never did think the friendship was real balanced. That one of you was getting more out of it than the other."

Mia frowned. "Meaning me, I presume?"

"Hell, no. Miss Justine definitely got the better end of that deal. Flash and glitter might be real pretty to look at, but you were the one with the substance. The solid one. Even if you were younger. She needed you a lot more than you ever needed her." She paused. "She needed somebody to worship her, to make her less like the little butt-wipe associate she was."

If Mia hadn't been lying down already, her knees would have given out from under her. "First off, we were both butt-wipe associates. Secondly, why didn't you ever say anything before?"

"None of my business? Wouldn't have made any difference? You seemed to be happy enough the way things were? Take your pick. And the difference was, you took your butt-wipe status in stride. She didn't." Her tone softened. "To tell you the truth, mostly I just felt sorry for Justine. She was one insecure chick. And I truly hope she finds whatever it was she was looking for on the other side, since she clearly didn't here. But I always admired you for sticking by her. The world needs more people like you, baby. And I know you must be hurting right now. So, listen, you want to pull out of the Chin party tomorrow, you go right ahead—"

"No! No, that's why I came back." One of the reasons, anyway, the other one being she could only deal with so much masculine brooding intensity at one time. That she'd actually agreed to put herself in the path of that brooding intensity for three or four entire *days*...

"You sure?" Venus said. "Because everything's under control from my end, and we've got Cissy, Armando and Silas lined up, they could practically handle things without either one of us—"

"I'm sure, Vene. Anyway, it'll do me good to focus on something else. But I did agree to go back for a few days, after the party. For Haley's sake."

"Oh, that's right, I forgot about the baby. Poor little thing. But at least she still has her daddy."

"Yeah, you'd think, wouldn't you?" Mia briefly explained the situation, which got another huge sigh from the older woman.

"Why is it you have to get a license to drive a car or serve booze or sell a house, but any idiot with a functioning joystick can have kids? Explain that one to me."

Mia smiled. "I wish I could. Not that I know what I'm doing, either, but I promised to at least give it a shot. So anyway, I'll meet you at the Chins' at noon...?"

After she'd squared everything away with Venus, she called her parents, breathing a sigh of relief when the machine picked up. Over at one of her brothers' houses, no doubt. Once again, she gave a quick rundown of events, that she'd be going back up to Connecticut the day after tomorrow, that, no, she didn't have a number for Kevin, she hadn't heard from him for months, when he'd called from Albuquerque.

Immediate obligations dispatched, Mia hauled herself off the sofa to forage in her Lilliputian-size kitchen, thinking perhaps she'd been a bit too hasty turning down Grant's offer. Now, glowering into the vast wasteland that was her refrigerator, she almost rued that steely resolve—read: stubbornness—that had seen her through high school, college, those first harrowing years as a Hinkley-Cohen butt-wipe.

As she was flipping through the smeared, dog-eared takeout menus tacked up by her phone, her doorbell rang. A quick glance through her peephole revealed the distorted visage of Mrs. Epstein, the self-appointed leader of the tenants' group hoping—slim though those hopes might be— to stonewall the landlord's bid to take the building co-op.

Under normal circumstances, Mia liked Mrs. Epstein well enough, her tendencies toward gossipmongering notwithstanding. Tonight, however, she was not in the mood. But alas, the moment she turned to tiptoe away, she heard, "It's no good pretending you're not home, sweetheart, I heard the floorboards creak."

Damn prewar joists.

On a sigh, Mia threw the trio of dead bolts and swung open the door, hanging on to the two-inch-thick (a half-inch of which was paint) slab for support. She smiled. Then frowned. Under a maroon bob, every wrinkle the old woman possessed screamed "bad news."

"We lost, bubelah. The slimeball can't kick us out until our leases are up, but there's no renewing them. We either have to buy or leave. The lawyer said we could contest it, drag it out a little longer, but the legal fund's all used up already. And the longer we wait, he says, the more it's gonna cost to buy in."

It was just as well Mia hadn't eaten yet, because God knows her stomach's contents would have made a reappearance. All over poor Mrs. Epstein. She muttered a not-nice word, which got a nod and a "You said it, sweetheart" from the old woman before she shuffled off to spread the joyous news.

Mia shut the heavy door, sliding down onto the floor with her head in her hands.

No way could she afford to buy her apartment. She'd used up nearly her entire savings as seed money for her business; only in the last few months had she been able to start repaying herself, but it would be a good year or two before she'd brought her reserves back up to what they once were. So forget the odd twenty or so grand necessary for a down payment. She didn't even have the thinnest of cushions to keep her from starving if for some reason she couldn't work. And mortgage companies didn't exactly welcome the self-employed—especially when the self-employed were, for all intents and purposes, dirt poor—with open arms.

And the best part of all this? Her lease was up in two weeks.

Two weeks.

She was one seriously screwed chick.

Chapter Three

"For heaven's sake, Grant—it's freezing out here!"

Even though they were in the sun—and it was in the mid-fifties, to boot—Grant's mother clutched the suede-trimmed collar of her plaid wool blazer, shivering up a storm as they stood at the edge of the circular drive fronting the house. "Of course Haley misses her mother," Elizabeth "Bitsy" Braeburn said, her voice far chillier than the temperature. Sunlight glinted coldly off her severely pulled-back blond hair. "That doesn't give her license to rule the roost. And if you don't exercise some control over the child now, God help us all when she gets to be a teenager."

"She's not even four, Mother," Grant said in a low voice, his hands balled in the pockets of his leather bomber jacket, thinking, *You should only know how much control I'm exercising right now.* "She doesn't even understand yet that Justine's dead."

"Then tell her again."

"I have. Repeatedly. As has Etta. The concept means nothing to her." He tore his gaze away from his daughter— all bundled up in sweaters and fleece-lined everything, sitting cross-legged in the leaf-cluttered grass with Henry in her lap as she kept an eagle eye on the ten-foot-tall entry gate—to look at his mother. Who, for reasons not yet clear, had shown up uninvited a half hour before, impeccably coiffed and tastefully accessorized, as always. "And according to the psychologist, there's not a damn thing I, or anyone, can do to force things." He looked back. "When she's ready to accept Justine's death, she will."

The vigil had begun yesterday morning, when Haley announced she was going outside to "wait for Mommy." Both Etta and Grant had patiently repeated the whole heaven thing, only to be met with an unsettling "Have you ever seen heaven?" When he had to admit that, no, he hadn't, a tiny chin went up in the air, followed by "Then how do you know it's real?"

A particularly thorny question to ask someone who didn't, in fact, "know" anything of the sort. But what was the alternative? At the moment, letting Haley believe her mother was somewhere else seemed a far better option than trying to explain that Justine no longer *was*.

But who knew the "somewhere else" would prove to be the sticking point, that in Haley's bright but still developing mind, being somewhere else meant that, at some point, a person could return. Clearly convinced—and rightly so— that her mother would never simply leave her, she simply couldn't comprehend that Justine wasn't coming back.

Hence the vigil. And since Grant couldn't see letting a three-year-old sit outside by herself for hours on end, here he, and his trusty BlackBerry, were. Never mind that, when he asked Haley if she'd like company, her only response was a "suit yourself" shrug.

At least this morning there really was someone to wait for: Mia. Who should be arriving any minute. Hell. His mother hadn't exactly taken to Justine; he could only imagine what she thought of Mia, with whom she'd only dealt with in the context of the wedding, five years before.

"For God's sake," Grant said as his mother's shivering increased. "Go inside and get warm. I'm sure Etta's got the coffeepot on—"

"Who on earth is that at the gate?" Bitsy said, shielding her eyes from the sun.

Speaking of the devil. Or—loath as Grant was to admit it—more likely a godsend, he thought as he caught sight of Mia's old minivan, growling impatiently as it waited for Etta to buzz the gate open.

"That can't be right," his mother said as the gates slowly groaned apart. "Grant, you simply *must* speak to Etta—she can't go letting in every Tom, Dick and Harry who wanders down the drive by mistake!"

"It's not a mistake." Grant said quietly, ignoring his mother's flummoxed expression as Haley scrambled to her feet, showing her first signs of enthusiasm in two days. "Stay on the grass!" Grant yelled when the little girl started running toward the drive, almost amazed when she actually stopped. As the van passed, Haley spun around, her small legs pumping as she raced it up to the house. A minute later, Mia and his daughter were a tangle of arms and kisses, and his mother—being possessed of a one-hundred-gigabyte memory—said, "Why is *she* here?"

"Did you bring Mommy?" Haley asked, trying to peer around Mia to see inside the van.

After the briefest of glances in Grant's direction, Mia

crouched in front of the child, shaking her head. "No, sweetie," she said softly. "Remember? Mommy's not alive anymore." She gently tugged a curl. "So you can't see her. Nobody can."

Haley regarded Mia for a moment or two before her thumb went into her mouth, her other arm strangling the poor stuffed toy around its neck. Then she settled into Mia's arms again, her curls flattened against Mia's bulky sweater, and Grant's throat tightened.

"That's why she's here," he pushed out. When, however, he noticed Mia's struggle to stand with Haley clinging to her, he strode over to relieve her of the child, in a move both unpremeditated and instinctive.

Now on her feet, and clearly oblivious to the bits of leaves and dirt on the knees of her jeans, Mia's eyes darted from Haley—who, while not exactly relaxed in his arms, wasn't squirming to get down, either—to Grant. A small smile toyed with her mouth before she turned to Grant's mother, who'd joined them. The smile stretched a little further.

"Mrs. Braeburn," she said smoothly, extending her hand. "It's been a long time. How are you?"

A moment passed before his mother apparently decided it wouldn't kill her to remove her hand from her pocket to shake Mia's. "All right, I suppose. Considering the circumstances." She withdrew her hand, readjusting a large tourmaline-and-diamond ring that had shifted sideways over her protruding knuckle.

If his mother's imperiousness bothered Mia, she didn't let on. But then it occurred to Grant that, in her line of work, she must deal with women like his mother every day.

"Yes, of course." Sadness flickered across her face, but the smile never wavered. "You look fantastic, though. I love your jacket!"

Eyes that had seen their share of tweakings over the past few years widened almost imperceptibly—point to Mia, for catching the old girl off guard.

"Um…thank you, dear." Bitsy's gaze remained on Mia for a long moment. "Thank you," she repeated, then turned to Grant. "*Now* can we go inside before I freeze my assets off?"

"I'm here to tell you," Etta said, hanging the vintage, black silk dupioni dress Mia planned to wear for the funeral in a white-washed armoire that, in any other house, would have dwarfed the room, "I have never seen that woman at a loss for words. I don't know if that makes you an angel or a witch, but whatever you are, keep it up! You need me for anything else, hon?"

"I didn't *need* you at all," Mia gently pointed out, shoving shut the drawer to a small Bombay chest by the bed. "Please, *please* don't wait on me, Etta—it makes me hugely uncomfortable."

Her red lips pulled down at the corners, the older woman crossed her arms under her bosom. "Well, get over it, because that's what Mr. B. pays me for. And besides…" She glanced furtively toward the bedroom's open door, then lowered her voice. "I can't tell you how nice it is to have somebody *normal* to talk to, for once."

Mia turned, a smile twitching at her lips. "You don't like Mr. Braeburn?"

"Oh, please…I got Mr. B.'s number a long time ago. He's not so bad, once you get past all the crap. But that mother of his…" Etta shook her head as Mia wondered what "number," exactly, Etta meant. "Talk about a piece of work. Thank God you're here, is all I have to say. For the baby's sake, I mean. If Dragon Lady had her way…ohmigod, can you imagine the amount of therapy the poor kid would need down the road?"

"Etta! That's terrible. And anyway, I'm only here until after the funeral. Which you know. Besides, Grant said he's already taken Haley to see somebody, right?"

After a *hmmph* meant to sum up her entire opinion on modern psychology, Etta said, "So. There's already two blankets on the bed, but if you need more, they're in the chest there at the foot of the bed, along with more pillows…. What're you lookin' at?"

The panorama outside the window had drawn Mia like a fashionista to a sample sale. "Everything," she said on a sigh, sinking onto the window seat. Although she knew there were other houses close enough to see from here, a miniforest of autumn-tinged trees obliterated all semblance of civilization. In the distance, the sun glanced off a sliver of the Long Island Sound, like a diamond tennis bracelet nestled amongst the foliage. "It really is spectacular, isn't it?"

Etta crossed the thick-piled white carpet—with the room's pale, lemon-yellow walls, it was like being inside a meringue pie—to join her at the window. "It is that. And thank God Mr. B. didn't tear the house down and replace it with one of those McMonsters like a lot of them have. Who the hell needs a forty-thousand-square-foot house?"

It was true. So many of the older houses in the area, erected at the turn of the century as testaments to their owner's position and wealth, had been replaced in the past decade or so by dozens of insanely overpriced, oversized mansions as testaments to *their* owner's overblown egos. Bowling alleys, home theaters larger than your average Manhattan art house, heliports, thirty-car garages… Amazing, how Grant managed with *only* seven bedrooms and eight baths, the formal dining room that easily sat twenty, the pool and the tennis court and the six-car garage. Still, the place—with its slump rock exterior and traditional floor plan—exuded an aura of settledness that somehow precluded pretension.

It was, quite simply, a lovely house. The kind of house that engendered fond childhood memories, that called scattered siblings back year after year for Christmas and Thanksgiving and wedding anniversaries....

Frowning, she angled her head to get a better look at the pool, now covered, and guesthouse. "He fixed it up?" she asked Etta.

"The guesthouse? Yeah, about two years ago. Before the divorce. You should see it inside, it's really something. All new kitchen and bath, the works. Listen, I made chowder for lunch, is that okay? Or I can put deli stuff out for sandwiches...?"

Mia turned to her, smiling. "Chowder's fine." Then she frowned. "Is Haley eating?"

Etta shrugged. "Not really. But then, she never really ate before, as far as I could tell. How the kid is still alive, I have no idea." She started toward the door, then twisted back, as if weighing whether or not to say whatever she was thinking. When she finally said, "Lunch is at twelve-thirty," Mia doubted that was it.

Well. Her clothes put away, her laptop set up on a small desk near the window, she might as well make herself useful and go look for Haley. Who she found—along with her father—out in the park that passed for a backyard. Haley and Henry shared a low-slung swing on a shiny new set, under the watchful eye of her father, seated on the flagstone patio in a white, cast-iron chair, his ankle crossed at the knee. At Mia's "Hey, there," he looked up, his frown—permanent, from what she could tell—easing somewhat.

"All settled in?" he asked, his attention drifting back to his daughter.

"Yeah." Her hands in the pockets of her down vest, Mia lowered herself into a matching chair a few feet away. "Your mother left?"

"Yes, thank God." He spared her a glance. "I don't think she quite knows what to make of you."

"I seem to have that effect on people." When he didn't reply, she said, "You know, since I'm here now, if you need to get back to work…?"

"Thanks," he said, his eyes never leaving his daughter. "But I'm fine."

Mia followed his gaze. "How's she been?"

Grant's shoulders hitched in a semblance of a shrug. "Quiet. Keeping to herself. Except for asking us where Justine is every five seconds. Which the doctor said to expect." He leaned forward, his hands between his knees. "I went online, did some reading up."

"Yeah. Me, too. Late last night, after I got back. From the anniversary party?" He nodded, a slight breeze ruffling his hair. Either he hadn't shaved this morning or he had a seriously overachieving five-o'clock shadow.

"I suppose it's at least somewhat reassuring," he said, "to know her reaction is normal."

"Yeah," Mia breathed out. "Kinda hard to react to something you don't understand." She sank back into the chair, her hands still in her pockets. The breeze picked up, rustling the leaves, sending a few hang gliding onto the grass. "Um…not that I'm trying to horn in or anything, but if you need help with the arrangements…?" When the frown deepened, she said, "It's what I do, remember?"

"Help?"

"No. Well, that, too. But I meant pulling food and whatnot together for two hundred out of a hat. It's why God created delis that make up platters of artfully arranged cold cuts."

"I take it you don't generally do funeral receptions, though."

"I have. They can be parties, too, depending on the deceased."

"Not in this case."

"No. Not in this case."

His eyes drifted back to Haley. "I'll pay you for your time."

"Don't be an idiot," she said, earning her a puzzled glare. Interesting combination. "Just sign a check for the food and we'll call it square."

Another nod. Then he said, "I know it's probably nuts, asking people to trek all the way out here after the service. But I thought it might help Haley. If she could say good-bye here."

"Makes sense to me," Mia said, and his shoulders seemed to relax, just a fraction, and it hit her how hard this was on him, navigating these completely uncharted waters with nothing to guide him except, she supposed, a basic desire to do the right thing by his daughter. Well, that, and the best therapy money could buy.

"I also shouldn't have strong-armed you into this," he said suddenly.

"This?"

"Coming back," he said, not looking at her as he slowly ground his knuckles into the palm of his other hand. "You've got that pained look people get when they're forced to be someplace they don't want to be. It's just I was so desperate the other day, I reacted without thinking.... I apologize."

Mia blinked, then laughed softly. "Believe me, Grant—if I didn't want to be here, I wouldn't be. No apology necessary."

Under hooded lids, his eyes slid back to hers...and her

stomach flipped. Nothing had prepared her for the full force of that probing gaze, riddled with concern. It was almost as if…

Never mind, she told herself as, knocked flat on her mental butt, she looked away until she could right herself again. When she didn't reply fast enough to suit him, he probed further.

"Then what's wrong?" he probed further. "Is it work?"

"No!" she said, a knee-jerk reaction to the presumption implicit in the question. "Business is great, O ye of little faith."

"Then what?"

She messed with a thread dangling from the hem of her sweater, then crossed her arms. "Not that you'd care, but…my building's going co-op." Her mouth pulled down at the corners. "I have to either move or buy when my lease is up. In two weeks."

"They can't give you only two weeks' notice, for God's sake!"

"They didn't. It's been in the plans for more than a year. But I've been so busy with work…and I kept holding out this tiny hope that we'd win the battle and the landlord would back down."

"Never mind that that almost never happens."

"I know," she said on a stream of air.

"I take it you can't afford to buy?"

She let out a dry little laugh. "Everything I have—had— is tied up in the business."

"You used *personal* capital as seed money?"

"It's not unheard of, Grant. Especially since I couldn't get a loan to save myself. So you can stop looking at me like that."

"Like what?"

"Like I'm some dumb cluck who had no idea what she was getting into."

"Did you even *have* a contingency plan?"

Tamping down the urge to slug the man, she said, "I left Hinkley-Cohen on very good terms. I could have gone back anytime."

"But you didn't."

"Okay, Grant? Hard as this might be for you to believe, I did know the risks going in. I also knew, given time and a long enough lever, I could make it. And I did. *Am.* But I was already in up to my eyeballs when the whole co-op ball started to roll. Moving then wasn't an option. So I took another risk, that the landlord's plan would fall through. Since it didn't," she said, turning back, "I suppose I'll figure something out."

"In two weeks."

"Twelve days, actually…. Hey, cookie," she said softly as Haley approached. "What's up?"

As much as it warmed Mia's heart when the little girl wriggled up into her lap, she didn't miss Grant's scowl at having not been chosen. *Well, bud,* she thought, wrapping her arms around Haley's waist, *you're the only one who can fix that.*

"How's Henry doing today?" she asked, her lips close to the little girl's ear.

A shrug. "His mommy still hasn't come back." A pause. "He's getting scared," she said, ruffling the thing's increasingly matted mane. "He says everybody keeps telling him she's gone to heaven and she can't come back, ever. That makes his heart hurt."

As it did Mia's. She hugged Haley more tightly. "I know," she whispered, laying her cheek against the soft curls. "I know it does. So you have to hug Henry lots and lots to make him feel better."

"I am. But he said it doesn't help."

"It will, lamb chop," Mia said, her eyes burning, not caring if Grant's were boring holes in the side of her face. "Eventually, it will."

"Promise?"

"I promise. You just have to keep reminding Henry how much you love him."

"Like you love me?"

Mia thought her own heart would break. "Yep. Like I love you. And Etta and your daddy and your grandma—we're all going to love you and love you until it doesn't hurt anymore."

A moment later, Haley cocked her head, as if listening to the stuffed toy. Then she slid off Mia's lap and turned to her. "Henry wants to know if you'd push us on the swing."

"I think that can be arranged," Mia said, getting up and holding out her hand.

"Mia."

Grant's low voice brought her head back around. He'd stood, his hands in his pockets, his mouth a straight line.

"If you want to buy your apartment, I'd be happy to co-sign for your loan."

Her eyes popped open. As did her mouth. When the buzzing stopped, however, she leaned over to Haley and said, "Go on back to the swing, I'll be there in a sec." When she was sure the little girl was out of earshot, she looked back up at Grant, standing there looking like the Daddy of all Immovable Objects.

"Why on *earth* would you do that?"

"To say thank you?"

"Then you can send me flowers. Or give me a gift certificate to Bloomie's. But I wouldn't dream of letting you take that risk. Or myself. I really can't predict my cash flow right now—"

"Not a problem."

"For you, maybe not. For me, yes. Thank you," she said softly, when he blew an obviously frustrated breath through his nose. "That's incredibly generous. But no." A piece of hair blew into her face; she pushed it back, angling her head. "My mommy always told me never to take financial favors from strangers."

"We're not strangers, Mia."

Man, this dude did not give an inch, did he? "Uh, yeah. We are."

Apparently accepting that they'd reached a stalemate, he said, "Then I suppose you'll be looking for another apartment when you get back to the city."

"That's the plan, yep."

"In less than ten days."

"Rub it in, why doncha?"

The corners of his mouth twitched. "There is one more option. If push comes to shove." He nodded toward the guesthouse. "It's sitting empty, anyway."

"Oh! Oh, no, I couldn't—"

"Think about it," he said, then turned and strode back inside.

"I take it we're not talking some rickety old shack you wouldn't keep your dog in?"

Mia could count on Venus not to mince words, about this or anything else.

"Uh, no." After Haley went down for her nap, Mia got the key from Etta to check out the guesthouse. Not that she was even remotely considering taking Grant up on his offer, but she figured she might as well know what she was turning down. "Two bedrooms," she said into her cell. "Wood floors—well, carpet in the bedrooms—a kitchen big enough for a table and more than half a person in it at once—"

"Get *out*."

"I know, I *know*. Of course, compared with the main house, it *is* a shack. Compared with what I'm likely to be able to afford in Manhattan, however, it's a palace. But come on—it's in Connecticut!"

"Uh-huh."

"And you're in Washington Heights?"

"Uh-huh."

"And what's with the 'uh-huhs'?"

"Think back. *Way* back. To the way you nearly broke something trying to get a better look when Grant walked by your office on his way to his appointment with that tax attorney—what was his name again?"

"I did not!" At yet another "uh-huh," Mia sighed. "Okay, but that was temporary insanity by reason of immaturity. And anyway, my reservations have nothing to do with… that."

"Uh-huh."

"Venus. I've met warmer cadavers."

"Girl, you have *got* to get out more."

"You know what I mean."

"Unfortunately, I do. But may I remind you that particular cadaver just offered to co-sign a sizable loan for you? Not to mention save your sorry butt so you don't end up out on the street?"

"Oh, please…this is a man who invests millions without batting an eye. And what skin would it be off his nose to let me live in this house?" Her gaze skimmed over the skuzz-free stove, the gleaming stainless steel refrigerator with a freezer large enough to hold more than a two frozen dinners, a pint of Ben & Jerry's and a single ice cube tray.

"You're tempted, I can tell," Venus said.

"Of *course,* I'm tempted. I'm not made of stone."

"We're both still talking about the house, right?"

"And you so don't want to give me a reason to rethink the raise I was going to give you."

"He didn't *have* to offer," Venus said, completely unconcerned. "But he did anyway. And it's been more than a year since that dirtwad dumped you and as far as I know you haven't even looked at a man since, and here's this good-looking dude being all generous and kind—"

"*Kind* might be stretching it," Mia said. "And it's not as if there's no ulterior motive. And besides…"

"Yeah, I know—after what happened between him and Justine, blah, blah, blah. And a girlfriend doesn't mess around another girlfriend's man, never mind that they'd been divorced for more than a year and it's not like she's gonna know, anyway. And you know something else? It takes two, baby. Meaning I know you're being loyal to Justine and all, but maybe she had something to do with the marriage falling apart, too. I'm just saying. Because you do have a problem with letting friendship blind you to who somebody really is. Take ours, for instance—you probably think I'm actually *nice.*"

"In general or at the moment?"

Venus snorted, then said, "But as far as the you-in-Connecticut-me-still-in-Manhattan thing…first off, seeing as half your clients are already up there, anyway, I'm not sure what difference it makes whether you're schlepping up there from Manhattan, or down to Manhattan from there. And think of how much you'll save in garage fees."

She had a point there. Mia needed the van for her work, but she could support a medium-size developing country for what she paid to berth her car every month. Hey, maybe she could live in her car, skip paying rent altogether...?

"I don't know, Venus. It sounds good on paper, but...I don't know. Look, I need to get back. Etta and I have to figure out what we're doing for this reception, since I seriously doubt people are going to show up with funeral food. As far as I know, I'll be back in the city on Friday."

"Yeah, but for how long?" Venus said, then hung up.

Leaving Mia standing in the middle of a puddle of brilliant fall sunshine gilding the living room's polished oak floor, feeling very conflicted indeed.

Chapter Four

In his foyer, just outside the living room—where mourners alternately chatted and gorged themselves on Mia's and Etta's impressive spread—Grant stood sentry, almost daring Christopher Schofield to walk through his front door. Of course, Grant had seriously doubted the man would have had the *cojones* to show his face at his lover's funeral reception—especially as he had to know Mia would be here—but he hadn't been about to take the chance.

Not that Mia needed Grant's protection, if one could even label his concern as such. Haley, however, did, and damned if Grant was about to let his child get inadvertently caught up in something that had nothing to do with her.

Sitting through the service, between him and his mother in a lace-collared dark-green dress she'd nearly outgrown, Haley had silently fidgeted through the proceedings with little outward reaction. Since Justine had been cremated, there'd been no casket, which—now that Grant thought about it—probably made it all even more confusing for the child. A suspicion borne out when, after they'd returned to the house, she'd begun running from room to room, upstairs and down, clearly looking for something.

Or someone.

For the past half hour or so, however, Haley had been settled in Mia's lap, her brow occasionally puckering in response to this or that person's awkward condolence. Now, watching those dark eyes solemnly taking it all in, Grant wondered if she was finally beginning to understand what had happened.

As much as any of them were, at least.

His attention drifted back to Mia, nicely cleaned up for the occasion in a full-skirted black dress that hugged her torso and pleasantly showed off black-stockinged calves, ending in very high heels. Assorted clips and things half-heartedly held her hair up off her neck, leaving assorted, shiny bits of silky brown floating around her face. She hugged Haley's waist from behind, her chin resting on the child's head, her placid expression belying the stress of the last few days. As much of a bulwark as she'd been for Haley—and Etta, when it came to pulling everything together for the reception—Grant wasn't unaware of how often she'd slipped away, only to return a few minutes later with those telltale red-rimmed eyes and splotchy cheeks.

In some strange way, part of him envied her ability to feel things so strongly, even if he couldn't completely tamp down the irritation that, in this case, her grief was misplaced. The other, saner, part was profoundly grateful to have been spared that particular character trait. How on earth did those tenderhearted sorts get through life?

And what on earth had possessed him to offer her the

guesthouse? Indefinitely, no less? Especially since her presence would only serve as a constant reminder of his gross miscalculation. His failure.

Then there was the challenge of keeping his mouth shut about Christopher and Justine. Not that he was particularly comfortable with that option, but the alternative—hurting her all over again before she'd had a chance to completely heal—was untenable.

And why was it bugging him to no end that she hadn't yet made up her mind whether to stay or not?

"Grant."

Squelching a sigh, he smiled down into pale blue eyes.

"Mother." Noticing her hands were empty, he offered to get her a drink.

She shook her head. "No, thank you, if I'd wanted a drink I could have gotten it myself." The archetype of the fit, privileged Connecticut matron in her slim-skirted charcoal-gray suit and double strand of pearls, she frowned in Mia's direction. At least, as much as her chemically enhanced epidermis would allow.

"I still don't understand why you're fostering that relationship."

"Because Mia has a way with Haley that I don't." Grant took a sip of his own tepid, watered-down Scotch and soda, lifting his other hand to ward off his mother's inevitable protest. "And right now, she needs people around who are only thinking of her."

"And I'm not? Honestly, Grant—she's so…pedestrian. Who are her people?"

"Nobody you'd know, Mother," he said quietly, his mother's snobbery, misplaced though it may have been, the least of his concerns at the moment. "I believe her father's a retired policeman. In Springfield."

"That accounts for the accent, I suppose."

"Yes, the Kennedys found their Massachusetts drawl a terrible handicap."

His mother smirked, snagging a soft drink from a passing waiter. How Mia had managed a waitstaff on such short notice, he had no idea. "Be that as it may, she's no Kennedy." As Grant put a hammerlock on the comeback begging to be let loose, she said, "I mean, I know she graduated from one of the top schools—she'd have to for Hinkley-Cohen to hire her, wouldn't she?—but has she made partner yet?"

"Actually, she left the firm. A couple of years ago. To start her own business."

"Really? Doing what?"

Grant swallowed the sip in his mouth. "Planning parties."

"Parties?" His mother snorted a dry, delicate laugh, then set her unfinished drink down on a nearby table. "Ivy League degree or not, the girl clearly doesn't have a grain of common sense."

"It's her life, Mother," Grant said, the heat in his words taking him by surprise. "What she does with that life is no one's business but hers. And not only has she worked wonders with Haley over the past few days, but if it hadn't been for Mia coming to the rescue with this reception, I'm sure Etta would have walked out the front door, never to be seen again."

"Not that that would have been much of a loss," Bitsy muttered. "And besides, it doesn't exactly take a law degree to order a few cold cut trays from Katz's." Bitsy checked her watch, then patted him on the arm. "I need to get back, I'd invited the Hendersons for dinner weeks ago, it would have been beyond rude to cancel on them this late in the game. But if you need anything, let me know."

How about a do-over on my childhood? Grant thought irritably as he watched her leave.

Although it wasn't yet fully dark by the time the last guest left, Grant could tell the day had taken its toll on his daughter. In fact, when Mia asked her if she was ready for her bath, she'd given a nod that had clearly used up her last ounce of reserve. Mia—once divested of her Grace Kelly outfit that his mother clearly saw as just a thrift shop rag and back in her customary baggy jeans and sweatshirt—volunteered to do the honors. But a half hour later, she came downstairs and strongly suggested that Grant tuck Haley in.

Over the panic slicing through him, she added, "Especially since I've done it the past two nights."

"I know, but…she's more comfortable with you."

"For the love of Pete, Grant—who put her to bed all those nights she spent with you?"

"Etta, usually."

"That's beyond sad. You know, my father drives all his kids crazy on a regular basis, but at least he *tries* to communicate with us. Even if half the time we're not exactly thrilled with the message. Well, bud, you've got to start the bonding process sometime. And four years late is better than never." Then she startled him by adding, "There's a good father in there somewhere, Grant. It's okay to let him out."

Their eyes locked for an unsettling moment or two before, on a not-very-squelched sigh, Grant headed upstairs to Haley's room. She was lying on her back in her bed, the toy lion propped on her tummy. From what he could tell they were having quite the conversation. When she noticed Grant, however, her head whipped around, a small wrinkle marring the space between her brows.

"Where's Mia?"

"Downstairs. I'm doing the honors tonight."

"What's that mean?"

"Tucking you in."

She clutched the lion more tightly, her eyes—skeptical, wary—never leaving his. "I want Mia."

Grant tamped down the spurt of annoyance. And, he realized, jealousy. "Sorry, I'm your only option."

"What about Etta?"

"She's busy, honey."

Even at her age, the child's expression said she clearly knew a load of bull when she heard it. "No, *you're* busy," she said. "You're always busy."

"Not tonight," Grant said over the flare of guilt.

Haley eyed him for another few seconds, then said, "When's Christmas?" and Grant felt as though he'd been hurled into another dimension.

"Why on earth are you asking about Christmas?"

"Because Etta said everything would be okay by Christmas. So how long is it?"

Vowing to have a word with his housekeeper, he said, "Months, yet."

"How many sleeps?"

"I don't know. A lot."

"More than this?" She held up her hands, fingers spread.

"Many more than that."

"Will I be four then?"

"Yes."

Haley looked back at the lion. "Mommy was busy, too, but she useta spend lots and lots of time with me. An' Krissy an' Ming Ha an' Amy get to see their mommies *and* their daddies all the time."

The barb hit its mark. Feeling like a world-class schmuck, Grant walked over to his daughter's bed, carefully lowering himself onto the edge of the mattress. "I know we haven't seen each other very much, Haley. My fault. But that's going to change. Starting right now." When her gaze swung to his, he added, "I promise."

She shrugged—very disconcerting, that—then clamped her arms over the lion. After a moment, she said, very softly, "Henry told me his mommy's not coming back."

Grant's heart spasmed. "He did? And...how does he know that?"

"Because there was a party, an' lots and lots of people were there, and they all talked about his mommy, and they were all sad, but she never came. And he said that's 'cause she couldn't. 'Cause she's dead. An' dead means you can't go back and see anybody, ever again. Is he right?"

Swallowing past a dry throat, Grant watched his little girl as she alternately smashed down and fluffed up the lion's mane, her eyes steady on his face. But only seeking information, he realized, not comfort. Over the unfamiliar stab of hurt, he nodded. "It's true. When somebody's dead, they can't come back and see the people who are still alive."

"Like when you leave the movies and can't go back inside?"

A tight smile pulled at Grant's mouth. "Something like that, yes. And how does Henry feel about that?"

"Sad." Smash...fluff...smash...fluff... "'Cause he still wants to see her. Like I still want to see Mommy," she said, her voice getting softer and softer. "So I guess she can't leave heaven, huh?"

"I'm afraid not."

"And I can't go to heaven to see her."

"No, you can't. Because you're alive. Only dead people go to heaven."

"Does it hurt when you're dead?" she said to the lion.

"No. Because you can't feel anything anymore."

"But can Mommy still see me? Or hear me?"

Although the room was cool, Grant's sweater felt as though it was becoming one with his skin. "I don't know, Haley. I really don't."

Her eyes veered back to his, that tiny wrinkle dug into her brow. "Etta says she can. Mia, too."

"Well, maybe they're right. Maybe she can. But nobody knows for sure."

"How come?"

"Well, because nobody's ever come back to tell us, have they?"

More frowning. "Mia says Jesus did."

Setting aside his own skepticism for the moment, Grant simply said, "That was a long time ago. And as far as I know, nobody has since."

Haley seemed to consider this for a moment, then said, "Does Mommy still love me?"

"I'm sure of it." Although at the moment he wasn't sure of anything.

Haley lifted Henry over her head, wiggling him around for a second or two before she said, "Henry says he doesn't want Mia to go away. That he wants her to stay here forever an' ever."

At the moment, Grant was tempted to agree with Henry. "I'm afraid she can't do that."

"How come?"

"Because this isn't her home. She lives in the city."

"But Henry and me had two houses, so why can't Mia?" She wiggled the lion at him. "Henry says."

On impulse, Grant reached out to touch the lion's electrified mane. "Henry likes Mia, I take it?"

"Uh-huh. Me, too. She…" He saw the lower lip tremble

for a second. "She fills up the hole inside me where Mommy used to be."

The pain that sliced through Grant was the worst he'd ever felt, far worse than when he realized Justine had been unfaithful, a hundred times worse than several years ago when he realized he'd made a catastrophic error in judgment about an investment that had cost him, and his investors, millions. From both of those, however, he'd eventually recovered. Somewhat shell-shocked, perhaps, but infinitely wiser. From this, however… He wasn't so sure.

Still, he had to try, didn't he?

"Maybe…maybe there's room for me in there, too?"

Haley shrugged, then rolled away. And although Grant knew hurting him hadn't been his daughter's intention, the snub was no less painful for its innocence.

"Do you need anything?" he asked, fighting desperately to keep his head above the bone-chilling, soul-sucking tsunami of failure. "A drink of water? A kiss good-night?"

"No, thank you," floated back to him, and Grant thought he might die, himself.

Mia beat a hasty retreat away from Haley's open bedroom door, not stopping until she skidded to a stop in the kitchen, where Etta was putting away the last of the food.

"What on earth…?" the older woman asked when Mia threw herself into the booth seat on one side of the breakfast nook.

"Quick! Hand me a cup of something, anything, so it looks like I've been here all along."

Etta poured her a cup of decaf from the pot on the counter and set it in front of her. "Don't tell me. You've been eavesdropping."

"Damn straight."

"I always knew you and me would get along good," Etta said, handing her a carton of half-and-half. Mia dumped three spoonfuls of sugar into the brew, a giant dollop of the white stuff. "And?"

"And Haley told Grant she knows Justine isn't coming back."

The older woman let out a sigh of relief, then joined Mia on the other side of the table. "Well, thank God for something." Then she frowned. "How's she doing?"

"Hard to tell. Since I couldn't exactly stick my head in the door to look."

"Then I take it no hysterics or nothing?"

Mia shook her head. "Not then, at least."

"And how did Mr. B. do?"

"Not bad, considering I'm sure he would've rather been almost anywhere else but in his daughter's bedroom at that moment. What?" she said when Etta gave her a funny look.

"I like you, okay? You're a good kid. But it bugs the hell outta me that you got no compunction about judging Mr. B. when you don't even know him."

"I can only go by what I see, Etta."

"Then maybe you should think about goin' deeper than that." Her eyes narrowed. "You got any idea how I came to work here?" When Mia shook her head, Etta said, "It was pure whaddyacallit—serendipity. I hadn't lost my husband Johnny but maybe four or five months before. I couldn't find work to save myself, except for waitressin' in some diner or bein' a hotel maid. Cookin' and cleanin', that's all I knew how to do—which is what happens when you get married at eighteen and don't ever do nothin' but keep house—but no domestic agency would give me the time of day. Said I wasn't 'right' for their clients, whatever the hell that means. And Johnny, God love him, he had a heart of gold but a head like a whiffle ball. Come to find out, after he died, he was in debt up to his butt.

"So this day I'm tellin' you about, I'm in Grand Central, right? And I'm feeling like crap, like the world's about to cave in on me, and I start crying. Right there in the middle of the concourse, I'm blubbering my eyes out. And Mr. B., he stops and asks me what's wrong—"

"Wait, wait, wait—" Mia's chin had been propped in her hand; now she jerked upright. "Grant stopped to ask a total stranger why she was crying?"

"That's right. All those people, nobody even looks at me, but Mr. B. stops. And the look in his eyes...yeah, like my cryin' was makin' him uncomfortable, but you never saw such compassion, neither. Long story short, he asks me, would I like to be his housekeeper?" She shrugged. "And here I am, six years later. So I *know*," she said, pressing her hand to her bosom, "what kind of man he really is. What's underneath. No, he don't like to show it, but if you think he don't love that little girl—"

"I don't think anything of the sort!" Mia said, startled by her own vehemence, and Etta smiled. "But what I don't understand is why he's so afraid to let his feelings out. Yeah, yeah, I know he says *he can't, it's not in his nature*," she said, mimicking his low-pitched voice, "but I don't buy it." Especially in the light of his reaction to her when she'd lost it the night of Justine's death, that look in his eyes when he'd asked her what was wrong a few days before. No, somebody was definitely in denial, here. "But what *is* his problem?"

The big woman shrugged her shoulders. "Damned if I know. Although if that she-devil mother of his is any indication, my guess is his childhood wasn't exactly somethin' out of a Christmas movie. So…you takin' him up on his offer or what?"

"Oh, God, Etta…I don't know. I have no idea when I'd find the time to look for a place in the city before my lease expires—I've got work out the wazoo over the next two weeks. So believe me, it's very, very tempting."

"But?"

"But I'm worried that the longer I'm around, the longer Grant and Haley will put off making any sort of real connection."

"Don't flatter yourself," boomed Grant's voice from the kitchen doorway, making both women jump. As Mia did her best rabbit-caught-in-the-hunter's-sights imitation, Grant calmly crossed the kitchen to the coffeemaker and poured himself a cup. Then he turned, his gaze fixed on hers. "I know what I have to do, Mia. Have known since well before you took such pains to point out my gross deficiencies as a father. Whether you stay here or not won't make a shred of difference on that score. But you need someplace to stay, at least until you figure out what your next move is. And maybe it wouldn't be such an awful thing for Haley to have someone to fall back on while I bungle my way through these next few weeks. Someone she can trust."

"So what am I?" Etta piped up. "Chopped liver?"

Grant's gaze swung to the housekeeper's, a slight smile touching his lips. "Haley doesn't associate you with her mother, Etta. She does Mia. Yes, I know—if there was no Mia, we'd manage. Somehow. But since there is…"

His eyes touched Mia's again. "If you're worried about my abdicating my responsibilities to my daughter while you're here…I promise you, that won't happen. In any case, I'll be coming into the city within the next few days to pick up the rest of Haley's things from the apartment. I could easily help you move up here at the same time."

"Just like that."

"I've always been a fan of the direct approach."

Mia stopped just short of rolling her eyes. "Still. I find it hard to believe you'd really want me around."

"I don't. But Haley does. And if my making that happen gives me a leg up with my daughter, I'll do whatever it takes to get you to agree. And besides," he said calmly, "you and I both know you're up the creek. So why go through this charade when we both know you're only going to say 'yes,' anyway?"

Of course, the sad thing was Grant was right. Mia *was* up the creek. And only an idiot would turn down a free place to stay that didn't involve roaches, rats or a trade-off of a far more dubious nature than this one. She also knew she didn't have it in her to turn her back on Haley until this rift between father and child was at least somewhat on the mend.

"Fine," she said at last. "You can pick me up on Thursday."

And Grant smiled.

Chapter Five

Mia might be borderline insane, Grant mused as he slammed shut the door to the U-Haul parked in front of Mia's van, but he had to give her high marks for being organized. In fact, by the time he'd arrived, she, her partner, Venus—who looked vaguely familiar—and a pair of college guys had pretty much carted most of her stuff downstairs. Not that there was much—a dismantled double bed, some shelves, a swivel rocker, the assorted mismatched boxes and luggage and sound system, a few plants. That was it.

Bundled up in a bulky turtleneck and down vest, the lush-figured Venus grinned at him, long gold earrings like upside-down exclamation points shivering beside full, slightly freckled cheeks. An inch of hair, if that, reddish-brown flecked with gray, hugged her skull.

"I'll take pity on you," she finally said, grinning. "We have met before. Briefly. I was Mia's secretary. At the firm."

Unbidden, Grant's gaze drifted to the woman of the hour, who, huddled against the damp, frigid breeze blowing off the Hudson, was joking with the kids as she handed each of them an envelope, her cheeks flushed from umpteen trips up and down four flights of stairs, her hair tumbling where it would around her face in the wind....

Grant turned back to Venus, his hands shoved in the pockets of his leather jacket, ignoring the speculative look in her assistant's eyes as Mia's laughter burrowed inside him like a kitten seeking warmth.

"So how's the baby doing?" Venus asked, as, the kids having loped off toward Seventh Avenue, Mia joined them.

"As well as can be expected, I suppose." His eyes caught in Mia's, wide and weary under her frown. "But she keeps to herself, for the most part. And as far as I know, she still hasn't cried."

"As far as you know?"

"I've had to get back to work, at least part-time. But I'm sure if there'd been a problem, Etta would have said something."

Venus gave him a sympathetic smile. "When my mama died, my youngest brother was only five. He kept to himself, too, for a long time. Months, as I recall. Then one day, it was like a dam burst, and everything he'd been holding in came roaring out. But I guess, up to that point, he was working things out inside his own head as best he could."

"And he was okay? Eventually, I mean?"

"Yeah, he was fine. In many ways it was harder on me and my other brothers and sister, since we were older and had been leaning on her a lot longer. I guess it hurts more when you know what it is. Anyway." She turned to Mia. "Since you're in the midst of this *move,* Miss Party Gal,

I've got a list a mile long to take care of, so I best be getting on with it."

"You're sure you don't need me to come back once we've dumped off the stuff—"

"And we have been through all this." The look Venus gave Mia was equal parts affection and exasperation. "I've got everything under control, you take all the time you need. As long as we're not talking longer than twenty-four hours."

"Okay, but you call me tonight and give me a report."

"Now that's the megalomaniac I love!" Venus said, laughing, before she turned and sashayed up the street. Grant watched her for a moment, then turned to catch Mia looking up wistfully at her apartment windows.

"You okay?"

As if coming out of a trance, she focused back on him. In an instant, her demeanor had done a complete one-eighty, from cheerful to somber. Even for Mia, this was an abrupt shift.

"I just moved out of my first real grown-up apartment, Grant. The first place that was all mine. Really, truly mine. On top of losing Justine..." She looked away, her eyes following a taxi bumping down the rutted side street, then back at him. "It's been a rough week, okay? I'm allowed to feel crappy. So," she said, turning toward her car, "are we ready?"

"No. Wait." When she twisted back, frowning slightly, he said, "Do you mind if we grab a bite to eat before we go to Justine's? I had to work through breakfast."

She almost smiled. "How on earth do you work *through* breakfast?"

"By getting up at four in the morning."

"Ouch. Okay. Now that you mention it, after all that exercise, I could probably use a snack myself. Any preferences?"

"The diner up on the corner?"

He saw the tiny, sharp intake of breath. Then she grinned. "You? Slumming in a *diner?*"

"Stranger things have happened."

"I sincerely doubt that."

A few minutes later, surrounded by steam heat, cheap vinyl, the scents of bacon and coffee and the first burgers and fries of the day, they gave the Greek waitress their orders—although, upon reflection, Grant realized it would have been easier to simply tell the overly made-up redhead to bring them one of everything on the breakfast menu. Then he noticed that wistful look had settled again in Mia's eyes, now edged in something sharp and achy.

When her gaze met his, she sat up a little straighter, smiling slightly. "Christopher and I came here a lot. This is the first time I've been in here since…" She blushed.

Grant reached for his jacket. "Come on, we can go somewhere else—"

"No, no, it's okay. It's just a restaurant, right? And it would be totally stupid and childish to stay away simply because of some dumb association with the man who shredded my heart into about five million pieces."

"Not that you feel strongly about it or anything."

"Sorry. In case you haven't noticed, my emotions sometimes go straight from heart to mouth without checking in with my brain first."

"Now that you mention it, I have noticed the phenomenon once or twice." Although actually it had been the complete and utter lack of self-pity in her voice that had sucker-punched him. Far more than he'd have ever thought possible. Grant took a sip of the surprisingly decent coffee, carefully setting the thick crockery cup back in its saucer, even more carefully considering what he was about to ask. His gaze touched hers. "You want to talk about it?"

A question that put her expressive face through its paces—surprise, wariness, bemusement…disgust. "About as much as I want to have my gall bladder removed without anesthesia," she said as the waitress brought enough food for twelve people. "Sorry about the walk-up, by the way," she said, slathering butter on her bagel.

Grant decided to take the subject switch in stride. "No problem. My cardiovascular system thanks you. Although I have to say you don't seem to have accumulated very much for having lived there as long as you had."

She shrugged, chewing. "There were a few other pieces of furniture—I use the term loosely—but I gave them away. Junk my parents foisted off on me when I moved down here, mostly. And anyway, I'm not much of a pack rat. Besides which I was never there very much. Between twelve- to fourteen-hour days at Hinkley-Cohen, then pulling all these parties together…" She shrugged again, then forked in a bite of omelet. "Basically, it was just a place to crash and keep my clothes. That's why I never bothered to upgrade."

"Upgrade?"

"To a bigger place. With an elevator. And a doorman. And a laundry room. Rather than blowing my salary on a mortgage and maintenance fees, I decided to stay there and stash my cash in a mutual fund."

"Really?"

Her eyes twinkled in the bright light blasting through the window, igniting a small, but potent, flame inside his chest. Flames were not good. Even small ones. Flames… eventually burned out. "Yeah," she said. "Sorry to blow your image of me as an airhead who can't handle her finances."

"I never said—"

"Uh, yeah. You did. It's okay, I didn't take offense."

Grant decided to chalk up his heated face to the building's overachieving furnace. "Still. To risk everything on a business that could have gone belly-up—"

"Oh, come on, Grant—*life* is risk. And anyway, isn't that a tad condescending coming from a man who risks gobs of money on a daily basis?"

"First off, I've never invested a dime my clients couldn't have afforded to lose. And secondly, I only take calculated risks."

"So do I," she said softly, looking out the window, and he wondered if they were still talking about money. Although that had been the first time she'd mentioned her former fiancé since the day Justine died, there was no mistaking the lingering hurt. Another kind of heat flared inside him, which he quickly doused by changing the subject.

"Your apartment brought back memories," he said, cutting his Canadian bacon. "Of my first apartment in the city, my senior year at Columbia. Up in Spanish Harlem," he added, just to see her eyes pop. "My parents nearly croaked."

"I bet they did." Her gaze never leaving his face, she knocked back the rest of her shot-glass-sized serving of orange juice. "Huh. I would have pegged you as the type to let Mommy and Daddy buy you a cute little one-bedroom in one of those new high-rises in the upper 90's. Or at least a brownstone near Riverside Drive."

"You would think. Oddly, once I got out on my own, I discovered I wanted to make it on my own, too. Well, within reason. I let them pay my tuition."

"Big of you."

"I didn't have much choice. My trust fund didn't come

due until I was twenty-one, and they made too much for me to qualify for financial aid."

"Poor baby."

"If it makes you feel better, I waited tables all through school."

She burst out laughing.

"What's so funny?"

"Sorry, but I'm just not seeing you doing the whole 'Let me tell you about today's specials' spiel."

"I didn't say I was particularly good at it," he grumbled, and she laughed again.

"It's good to hear you laugh," he said, surprising himself. Mia, too, judging from her gobsmacked expression. "Well, it is," he said, almost defensively. "I know the past few days have been hard on you. And oddly enough, I don't get off on seeing—or making—people around me unhappy."

She shoved the last bite of bagel into her mouth—God, the woman ate like a linebacker. She chewed for several seconds before saying, "Do *you* ever laugh? I mean, *really* laugh? I'm not talking about one of those desiccated little chuckles, but so hard your stomach hurts?"

"No."

"*No?* Just like that? Don't even have to think about it, maybe dig around in your brain for a couple of seconds…?"

"I said *no.*"

"How come?"

Grant sat back in the booth, glowering at her. "How the hell should I know? Maybe I'm not as easily amused as…some people."

"Meaning you don't have a sense of humor."

"Of course I have a sense of humor—" And he couldn't believe she'd snared him into this ridiculous argument.

"Oh, dear." Her mouth twitched. "Now I've offended you."

"Are you always this aggravating, or do I bring out the worst in you?"

"I don't know…some people might say you bring out the best."

"Can we change the subject?"

"Sure thing, *Mein Herr*."

He sighed, then said, "I know you were helping Justine plan a big fourth birthday party for Haley—"

"But you don't think it's a good idea."

His gaze bore into hers. "Do you ever let people finish their sentences?"

"Sorry. Continue."

More staring. Then he said, "Actually, if you'd said that two weeks ago, I would have agreed with you." When she threw her hands up in the air, he almost smiled. "My parents never believed in big, gaudy celebrations—"

"Now *there's* a surprise." He glared. "Sorry," she muttered.

"So I wasn't wild about the idea for my own daughter. Justine and I went more than a few rounds about it, too."

"I know," Mia said. "She told me."

Grant sighed. "Anyway, now that she's gone, and with Haley so miserable…I'm thinking maybe it's not such a bad idea. Although then I think, is it really appropriate, considering her mother will only have been dead for a little over a month?"

"You really want my opinion?" When he nodded, she said, "For good or ill, Haley's expecting a party. Justine had been making a huge deal of her turning four for months. If she doesn't get something, she's liable to feel as though she's somehow being punished for her mother's death. And that's not fair. Especially to a four-year-old. Justine was the one who died, Grant. Not Haley. Don't you think she deserves to celebrate her own milestones?"

He gave her a tight smile. "Of course, you could simply not want to be out your fee, too."

She made a sound as though trying to squelch the squeak of indignation, but then she leaned forward, eyes slitted, and said in a low voice, "You know, if I were the kind of woman to make a scene in a public place, I'd be very tempted to pour this waffle syrup over your head right now. I can't believe you'd even say that. Of course I'd waive my fee, the party was going to be my gift, anyway—"

"Goad easily, do you?"

She sat back. "You are such a jerk."

"And here I thought we were getting on so well."

"A trick of the light. Don't take it personally."

"I never do," he said, then sighed. "I don't know, Mia. A big bash—"

"Isn't appropriate for *any* four-year-old, which was a point I tried desperately to get across to Justine. If it had been up to her, she would've rented out FAO Schwartz for the afternoon. Or at the very least the skating rink at Rockefeller Center. And invited Haley's entire preschool." She shook her head. "Not that I'm above throwing an insanely overblown birthday party for the under-six set from time to time—hey, *I'm* not the one who has to deal with a batch of cranky, overstimulated kiddos at the end of the day—but a huge party would have been nuts for Haley in any case."

"Because?"

"Because she would have been completely overwhelmed." Mia hesitated, then said, "Take this any way you want, but Haley's a lot more like you than she is like Justine."

"Meaning?"

"Introspective, I suppose. Content to live inside her own head, much of the time."

"Is that what you think of me? That I prefer to live inside my own head?"

"You sure as hell don't seem terribly interested in living outside of it."

Oddly, there was nothing particularly accusatory in her tone, even if her observation was almost eerily accurate. And unsettling. "What would you suggest, then?"

She shrugged. "I haven't had two minutes to think about it. Something personal, though. Four is hugely older than three."

"If you say so."

"It *is*. I remember four. I don't remember three at all."

Stomping down the bubble of laughter threatening to erupt, Grant picked up the check. "Ready?" he said, pulling out several bills.

With a nod, Mia folded her napkin and stuffed it under the rim of her empty plate. Forty-five minutes later, after hitching Mia's van to the back of the truck and navigating insane crosstown traffic, Grant unlocked the door to Justine's twentieth-floor two-bedroom York Avenue apartment, slightly startled to realize Mia had probably been here more than he had.

They'd bought the apartment shortly after their marriage, so Justine would have a place to crash on those nights she had to stay late because of her work. He'd often come into town to join her for a late dinner, in the beginning. Or even on the occasional weekend, when she had a particularly heavy-duty case. Or so they could throw a party for their city friends to show off both the exquisitely decorated apartment—Justine had done it all herself, down to the jewel-toned silk cushions on the white sofa and the fringed tie-backs on the puddled, persimmon-colored moire draperies—and their marriage.

Until he finally realized, shortly before Haley's second birthday, that his wife and child were returning home less and less frequently; that even when he and Justine were in the same house, they were rarely in the same room, clearly finding their work far more fascinating than each other.

In the beginning, he'd thought that's what he'd wanted.

In the end, he was surprised to discover that wasn't what he wanted at all.

"I'm almost done packing up Haley's things," Mia said, preceding him into the child's room, which indeed was filled with boxes, some of which still gaped open. "I've had a key for some time," she offered in response to his undoubtedly perplexed expression. "In case of an emergency, Justine said. Funny how you think, what on earth emergency could there be?" She grabbed a packing tape dispenser off the empty bookcase and taped up the nearest box.

"But when did you have time?"

One shoulder shrugged. "I managed." She nodded toward a stack of already closed boxes, her unaffected movements, her grab-whatever's-available clothing, at such odds with the almost museum-like feeling in the apartment. Unbidden images shuddered into focus inside his head, of her in that torso-hugging black dress, the clingy, rose-colored silk number she'd worn as Justine's maid of honor. He remembered his grudging acknowledgment of her good looks, the way her dark, loose hair and deep-hued dress had been such a marked contrast to Justine's blond etherealness in her full-skirted white gown. He supposed he'd always found her physically attractive, albeit in a distracted, impersonal, decidedly nonsexual kind of way. Perhaps he hadn't been truly in love with his wife, but neither had he wanted anyone else in his bed.

Far more disturbing were the feelings trying to get a toe-hold now, feelings a long, long way from impersonal and God *knows* anything but nonsexual. Feelings the seeds of which had been sown a long time ago, that he'd assumed had withered and died. Lying dormant had not been part of the plan.

"You might as well start piling the taped ones by the door, I guess," she said, "while I finish up these. And, um…there's Justine's clothes and personal items. I didn't know what you wanted to do with them."

Grant hefted the first boxes into his arms. "I hadn't even thought about it. Any ideas?"

"Well, obviously, keep the jewelry for Haley. But there's this organization that takes gently used business clothes and distributes them to underprivileged women entering the workforce for the first time. If that's okay…?"

"Yes. Yes, that's an excellent idea, thank you."

"Good. We can take them with us, drop them off on our way out of town."

After another half hour or so of loading boxes, they came back upstairs for one final sweep. Although he frankly couldn't wait to get out of there, Mia was clearly having a harder time. She sighed, stroking the back of a starkly contemporary, cobalt-blue armchair in the living room. "Justine loved this place."

"Which is why I gave it to her. She always preferred the city, anyway."

Mia seemed to think that over for a moment before she said, "For what it's worth, she never complained about the settlement. In fact, she said you were very generous."

"She could afford to say that, considering the prenup she'd signed."

Mia's eyes cut to his. "You made her sign a prenup?"

"No, she made *me* sign one. She was the lawyer, remember?"

"Right," she said, smiling slightly. Her arms folded under her breasts, she scanned the room, chock full of furniture and artwork and more accessories than you could shake a stick at. "What are you going to do with all of this?"

"I'm selling the apartment furnished. Although, if there's anything you'd like—"

"No! I mean, thank you, but…no. It wouldn't feel right. So you're putting it on the market?"

"I've already talked to an agent, in fact. She'd suggested I hang on to it, lease it long-term, but…" He shrugged. "There didn't seem to be much point. By rights, it's Haley's, I know. But I can make more investing it for her. And I have no burning desire to be a landlord."

"Good point. Still, don't you want to keep a place in town?"

"I'm not here that often. When I am, I'll stay in a hotel. And who knows if Haley will even want to go to school or live here?"

"And if she does," Mia said, grinning, "she can continue the tradition in her own fourth-floor walk-up."

The very thought of his tiny daughter as a college student, on her own in the city, made his blood run cold. He checked his watch. "We'd better go," he said softly.

She let her gaze wander over the apartment one last time. Then she turned, a sad smile barely curving her lips as she preceded him through the door.

Chapter Six

By the time they finally left Manhattan, the sun was already hunkered down at the horizon, drenching the landscape in gold. As hard as packing up her own apartment had been, walking away from Justine's for the last time had done a serious number on her head. Why hadn't she simply confronted Justine with her doubts when she'd had the chance, when a simple conversation at least *might* have cleared everything up?

Her head propped in her hand as she watched the scenery zip past the passenger-side window, Mia felt her mouth scrunch. She knew damn well why: because, after Christopher's vanishing act, losing Justine as well would have killed her. Ignorance being bliss and all that. Now, though, that Jus was gone—

"So explain this party business to me."

Jerked out of her melancholy, it took Mia a moment or

two to click in. Her brow puckered, she lifted her head and turned to Grant. "Excuse me?"

"I know what it takes to even be invited to join Hinkley-Cohen," he said, as though annoyed that she had to be brought up to speed. "That they don't take people who aren't at or near the top of their class. And only from a handful of schools. So obviously you're smart. More than smart, possibly even brilliant. And yet you threw it all away to, what? Serve punch and blow up balloons?"

"Been thinking about this for a while, have you?"

He tossed her one of those endearing glares, and she laughed. She couldn't help it, no self-respecting depression stood a chance in the face of such rampant incredulity. "There's a bit more to it than that," she said, good-naturedly. "And my goodness, do you win the award for left-handed compliments or what? I don't know about how *brilliant* I am, but my IQ's up there, I suppose."

"Then how could you simply write off such an incredible opportunity? Let your brain go to rack and ruin?"

A week ago, she would have found his questions impertinent, if not downright rude. Now, though, she heard a genuine curiosity—and, weirdly, concern—in his voice that amused more than annoyed her.

"You mean, because what I do now is totally frivolous and unnecessary?"

"Some people might see it that way, yes."

"Like, for example, you." Lifting a hand to cut him off, she sighed. "Hey. At least you're honest. And my parents said basically the same thing. Only with more hand gestures and yelling. I knew my leaving law would kill them, considering how proud they were that their only daughter graduated from a freaking Ivy League school, for God's sake. So believe me, I didn't change course on a whim. And it's not as if I didn't give it my best shot—I was at Hinkley-Cohen for six years, don't forget. But the longer I was there, the more I hated it."

"You must have liked law at some point."

"I did. Although, looking back, I suppose the seeds for my early burnout were already planted by the time I graduated from law school. And I was so young, barely twenty-two, because I'd sliced off a year of high school, another year of undergrad. Starting my professional career already exhausted was not, I decided, a particularly good sign," she said, suddenly appalled to realize she liked the way Grant smelled.

"No, but—"

"The thing is," she said, turning away, as if that was going to make a difference, "I soon discovered that being good at something doesn't mean you've got the killer instinct necessary to keep up the requisite enthusiasm. I was bored, Grant. Out of my ever-lovin' skull. And becoming increasingly unhappy. I wasn't sleeping well, I was putting on weight, my blood pressure was up…and one day I thought, *Screw this*. Why should I spend the only life I've got—assuming the nuns weren't feeding me a line about reincarnation being totally bogus—doing something that's making me miserable and sick?"

"But…giving parties?"

Then again, who the hell cared what the man smelled like? Or even that, so, okay, nobody had twisted his arm about giving her a place to live, or driving down to the city to help her move? He was still a judgmental pr…une.

"I am running a business, Grant. Complete with bookkeeping and cash flow projections and filing taxes and all that fun stuff. Not to mention networking and negotiating prices and lots and lots of feather de-ruffling. Hell, I even have a business plan. Today, Long Island. Tomorrow, the entire middle Atlantic." When he grunted, she added, "But the difference is, I actually enjoy this. Coming up with a theme, planning the food, the decorations, the music, the works. But more than that…"

She paused, her mouth screwed to one side. She could still smell him. Judgmental or not, the dude had some seriously kickass pheromones.

"What?"

"What I do…it's about celebrating all those milestones in life that keep the human race from drowning in despair. The anniversaries and the coming-out parties and the birthdays and the graduations… Happy times, for the most part, the occasional wigged-out bride or certifiable mother notwithstanding. And about as far from frivolous and unnecessary as you can get. Except these days, few people have the time and energy to sit down to family dinners, let alone pull off a full-out party. So they willingly pay people like me to save them the wear and tear on their nerves, leaving them with nothing to do but enjoy themselves."

She let her gaze rest on the side of his face, because where else was she gonna let her gaze rest? It was a nice face, as faces went. Even if the jaw could use some serious loosening up. Then again, who wants Gary Cooper with a wimpy jaw? "I'm good at this, Grant. *Damn* good. And *I'm* proud of me even if nobody else is."

Not surprisingly, he had nothing to say to that. Well, tough noogies, she thought, again palming her cheek, watching the sky ahead succumb to dusk as the truck plowed through the rippling vortex of shadows stretched across the highway. Sure as hell she did not need this man's—or anyone's—approval for her choices.

No matter how yummy he smelled or how Gary Cooperish his face was.

Or how much she'd begun to ache, from time to time, when she stopped long enough to hear the obnoxious little voice yakking in her ear, that she was nearly thirty with no husband-type-person in sight. Because heck, yeah, she wanted one of those. Not to take care of her or anything like that, just someone who was *there*. For her. With her. *Because* of her.

She thought, when she'd met Christopher, he'd be her "there." When he'd walked away, she'd been sure he'd taken "there" with him. So she'd wrapped herself up tight, in her work and a chronic loneliness and grief she'd eventually grown to accept as a natural part of her, like the dull backache that came with her period every month. It had seemed so much easier to simply deal with the pain—it wasn't that bad, really, and anyway, wasn't that just part of being a woman?—than actually do something about it.

Now she wasn't so sure.

A good five minutes passed, the only sounds the hum of tires on the road and the low engine's steady rumble. Then, suddenly, Grant said, "For what it's worth, I don't particularly like being the way I am."

"Man," she said, frowning at him again, "are you the king of the non sequitur or what? Being what way?"

He waved one hand. "Unconnected to anything. Or anyone."

Mia wedged herself into the corner of her seat, her arms crossed. "And you're telling me this, why?"

His gaze flashed to hers, then back out to the highway. "No idea. Other than perhaps being tired of feeling as if I'm being judged all the time."

"Hah!"

"I know, I know. Bad habit."

"*Terrible* habit." When he spared her another brief look,

she averted her eyes. "On both our parts." After a pause, she said, "I assume you've, uh, talked to someone about this? About why you don't like people, I mean."

"Trust me, I helped put more than one therapist's kids through college. Didn't help. And it's not that I don't like people, it's more that…" He blew out a breath. "They're like bananas."

"Bananas?"

"Yeah. I can take them or leave them. But I'm not passionate about them."

"Stands to reason, what with you not being a monkey and all." She folded her arms. "So what are you passionate about? If anything?"

The jaw tightened as he seemed to mull this over. "Art, I suppose. Music, sometimes. Money. Making it, anyway."

"There's a difference?"

"Absolutely. It's all about the hunt, not the quarry. The thrill of conquest, when the risk pays off."

"Yeah, about that…kind of an odd choice of career, doncha think, for someone with control issues?"

In the deepening shadows, a flicker of light from a reflector glanced off his smile. "I prefer more cerebral forms of risk-taking, I suppose. Although I briefly flirted with the idea of race-car driving, back in my early twenties."

Unbidden, Mia's eyes drifted to Grant's hands, graceful and sure on the truck's steering wheel, and she imagined him handling something with much more speed and power than a U-Haul and got a head rush so strong she had to grab the dashboard to steady herself.

"Everything okay over there?"

"Uh, yeah, sure. So…about this banana thing." She glanced back at his profile, which, sad to say, was beginning to grow on her. "You feel that way about your own daughter?"

Big sigh. "Justine and I…" He shot her a look, then returned his gaze front. "We hadn't planned on having children."

"Yeah. I know. Jus was sure becoming a mother spelled the end of her career." She paused. "She'd said you weren't exactly thrilled, either."

"I wasn't."

"Which was why, frankly, I was surprised she went through with the pregnancy."

Grant was silent for a few seconds, then said, "Turns out I changed my mind."

"Then what the hell happened?" Mia said, throwing discretion out the window. "If you wanted Haley—"

"Why am I in such deep crap now? I don't know, Mia. I don't…" His hands flexed around the wheel as he shook his head. "God, we shoehorned our daughter's birth around our schedules the same way we might have made reservations at an Upper East Side restaurant. But there I was, right there with Justine, fully prepared. Or so I thought. For the all of it. Then they put Haley in my arms, and she opened her eyes and looked at me as if to say, 'Don't you *dare* screw this up.'"

He turned to Mia. "But that's exactly what I did, didn't I? I mean, for the love of God—what's wrong with me that my own child scares the living hell out of me?" She saw him swallow. "That I obviously scare her, too?"

The anguish in his voice tore her up inside. Without thinking, Mia reached over and laid her hand on Grant's arm. "I don't think Haley's afraid of you, Grant," she said, gently squeezing tensely corded muscles through his sweater. "Leery, maybe, because she's not used to being around you, but not afraid. And rumor has it that *all* kids scare their parents."

"Still, Justine rose to the occasion, didn't she? The woman who didn't even want the kid turns out to be the perfect mother, while I…"

"Grant. Stop it." She squeezed again, this time the sensation traveling from fingertips to brain, where a small electric shock registered. She let go. "Justine wasn't perfect. No parent is. They all screw up. Even the good ones."

"She won't let me touch her, Mia," he said thickly, and a small, stupid part of her wanted to touch *him*. Again. "Even after a week. And damned if I'm going to let her grow up the way I did."

Mia frowned. "The way you did…? Oh," she said quietly, getting it. "Let me guess—your mom's not exactly the touchy-feely type?"

"You might say. Apparently I was handed off to a nanny as soon as I was born. And not one of those surrogate types that filled the void left by my in absentia parents. And yes, I know, it sounds like something out of a nineteenth-century novel. *I* sound like something out of a nineteenth-century novel." At her squeak of protest, he smirked. "It's okay, I know that's what you're thinking. Justine used to say the same thing. She even called me Darcy from time to time."

"Oh, Darcy was okay. Just…misguided. And he got it together in the end." On a sigh, Mia looked back out the windshield. "And I'm probably going to hate myself in the morning for saying this, but…but I think Haley is very lucky to have you for a father. Because underneath those fifty or so layers of crap, there's a good man in there."

"So you think there's hope?"

"Yeah, but if you tell anybody, I may have to kill you. You've just got to be patient. It's like Venus said, Haley'll come to terms with Justine's death at her own pace. Shutting you out may be her way of coping until she's ready to let someone else in."

One of those long, angst-filled silences followed. Then Grant said, very softly, "Do you know what she said? The night of the funeral?" He glanced at her, then away. "That *you* fill the place in her heart where her mother used to be."

Struck speechless, Mia simply sat there, staring in front of her, acutely aware of every bump and rattle and squeak as they sped along, until she finally said, "I'm so sorry, Grant."

"Why?" He almost sounded perturbed. "It's not your fault."

"I'm sorry Justine's dead, too," she snapped, "but that wasn't my fault, either."

"No. I see your point."

"No, what you don't see is that…hearts aren't finite, Grant. Not even little girls' hearts. Especially little girls, who come hardwired to love their daddies. To trust them. Heck, I'm still crazy about mine, even though we drive each other nuts. So maybe you need to stop thinking so hard about it and just…let the two of you happen. Not that I know what I'm talking about or anything, but—"

"No, no, what you're saying…it makes sense." Something like a smile flashed across his face when he glanced over at her. "Thank you," he said, and she shrugged, half-pleased, half-embarrassed. Half wondering if maybe she was beginning to like this guy.

Naaah…

They drove in silence for another several minutes or so, until Grant said, "Since Haley's birthday is so close to Halloween, how does the idea of a costume party strike you?"

Mia stared out the windshield for several seconds, then

said, "That could certainly work. But only if you promise to wear a costume, too."

Beside her, Grant let out a groan that made her glad to be alive.

When they arrived back at Grant's house, Haley burst through the front door before Grant had cut the engine, twitching impatiently beside Mia's door until she opened it and climbed out. "You're here, you're here, you're here!" the little girl cried, wrapping herself around Mia's thighs for a second before grabbing her hand and tugging her in the direction of the guesthouse. "Etta and me put flowers in it an' everything! It's so pretty, you hafta come see!"

By this time, Grant had alighted from the truck and gone around to unlock the back. Her face burning from both Haley's uncharacteristically animated greeting and the child's completely ignoring her father, Mia tugged back, then crouched in front of Haley to look the clearly puzzled child in the eye. She knew prompting wasn't the ideal way to provoke a response, but if part of the reason she was here was to get these two together, then get them together she would, no matter what it took.

"Aren't you forgetting somebody?" she whispered. "Maybe your daddy would like a welcome-back hug, too."

"But I just saw him this morning!" Haley said, wriggling out of her grasp. "You were gone for *days!* And 'sides, he doesn't know how to hug."

"Why would you think that?"

"'Cause he never does."

Honestly. She was going to pop the man one. "Then maybe you could show him how."

That got a skeptical look. "What if he doesn't want me to?"

"Sometimes, grown-ups don't know what they want until it happens. So it couldn't hurt to try, right?"

Haley glanced over at Grant, who was stacking the boxes to go to her room on the driveway. She looked back at Mia, her brow crinkled. "He's the daddy. He has to hug first."

Oh, for heaven's sake. Funny how she'd always assumed Haley's stubborn streak had come from her *mother.*

Blowing out a gust of air, Mia stood, took Haley by the hand and marched over to Grant.

"Okay, listen up, you two," she said, taking no small pleasure in Grant's startled expression. "Here's how it works—when two people love each other, they give hugs when they part, and they give hugs when they see each other again. So, here—" She hauled Haley up by the armpits, dangling her in front of her father. "Hug, already."

As she'd hoped, Grant grabbed for his daughter before Mia dropped her—not that she would have, but he didn't know that—and Haley, bless her, threw her arms around her father's neck, and ta-da!

"Now, was that so hard?" Mia asked, then tromped back to the truck to get another box.

But when she next looked up, Grant's gaze briefly touched hers, swarming with a world of unspoken—and, she was guessing, unfamiliar—emotions, setting off a volley of a whole bunch of the suckers inside her head, as well.

A scant half hour later, she was all moved in. Even her bed was set up, Grant turning out to be far handier with a screwdriver than she would have thought. Once done, they stood in the middle of her (mostly bare) living room, arms folded, scanning the (echoing) space. With its single chair on the bare floor—upon which Haley lay curled up, fast asleep—the room looked like the set for some existential, one-character play about the pointlessness of life.

"It's okay," Mia whispered, frowning. "Less to dust."

"You could have brought the sofa—"

"No," she said, vehemently shaking her head. "You gotta cut the ties sometime, otherwise the stuff follows you for*ever.* Well…thanks." She crossed the room to grab her purse off the floor, there being no table by the door on which to set it. "Guess I'll make a food run before dinner—"

"Don't be absurd," Grant said. "You're having dinner with us."

Mia turned. "Okay, I know this is a guesthouse, but since I'm paying rent—" at her insistence "—I'm technically not a guest. So feeding me is definitely not part of the deal."

He frowned. Ah, there was the big old meanie she knew and loved.

No, not *loved.* For goodness' sake, of course not *loved,* how ridiculous was that? Knew and…expected. Yeah, that'd work. Phew.

Loved? Yeesh.

"I'm not inviting you to eat with us out of pity," he growled. Yes, growled. And damned good he was at it, too. "Or obligation. I simply thought it would be…nice. But if you'd rather not, if you're still convinced I'm subhuman or whatever it is you think I am, then forget it."

Her mouth dropped open, the resulting cavity mirroring the huge void where her brain should have been. "I don't think that!" she said. After about a hundred years. "Okay, maybe I did think that, a little, sort of, once upon a time, but…" She pushed out a sigh. "I'm sorry, Grant. You have the totally wrong end of the stick here. I did think you were only being polite."

"I don't hang out with people I don't want to be around, Mia," he said, doing the steely-eyed staring thing. Except, suddenly, she saw the loneliness trapped inside the steely eyes, silently screaming for release, like that famous Edvard Munch painting. "So shall we try this again? I say, 'You're welcome to have dinner with us,' and you say, 'Thank you, that would be lovely, when should I be there?', and I say, 'Six,' and you say, 'Great, see you then.'"

Then he scooped his snoozing daughter out of the chair, and she thought, *Can things get any weirder?*

The next day was busy, busy, busy, filled with five million errands and an afternoon spent scouting out locations for Erin Liebowitz's late-winter bat mitzvah party. Mama L. wanted elegant, Papa L. wanted "nothing too flashy"—i.e. cheap—and little Erin basically wanted a cross between a rock concert and Cirque du Soleil. Too bad Madison Square Garden was already booked. At seven, Mia pulled up in front of the guesthouse, exhausted but hopeful—she'd short-listed a half-dozen venues, she'd present them to the Liebowitzes tomorrow—got out, walked up to the door, opened it and let out a soft shriek.

A second later, her cell rang.

"I took the liberty of bringing down a few things from the house," Grant said in her ear. "Mother's house, that is. She redecorated some time ago and the stuff was just sitting piled up in a spare room. If you don't like it, however—"

"No! No, it's lovely." Mia set her purse and keys down on the hall table that hadn't been there when she'd left that morning, taking in the overstuffed, gold brocade sofa, the floral wing chair and footstool, the drop-leaf dining table and four matching chairs. The thickly piled, richly patterned rug.

A little chichi for her taste, but gift horses in the mouth and all that. Even if the gift horse had snob cooties... Oh. Wait.

She sank onto the sofa. And continued to sink for several seconds. Down cushions would be her guess. Nice. "Bitsy doesn't know, does she?"

"Not a clue."

"Who knew you were so devious?" She sagged back, letting the cushions do their thing to her weary, grateful body. "Of course, I should probably at least give lip service to the whole what-gives-you-the-right-to-barge-in-here-and-furnish-my-living-space thing."

"But you're not going to."

"Not on your life." She looked around. "Is this, like, you know, the kind of stuff those dudes on the *Antiques Road Show* would wet their pants over?"

"Only the rug. It's early nineteenth century."

She lifted her feet. "So I probably shouldn't walk over it in muddy boots, huh?"

"Probably not."

"Thank you," she said after a moment, even though her poor little Ikea bed and bookshelves were going to feel like poor relations.

"You're welcome. And we're holding dinner for you, so get your butt over here, pronto."

He clicked off and Mia frowned at the phone.

Pronto?

Then she keeled over into the deliciously poufy cushions, thinking maybe, just maybe, she could get used to *weird.*

Chapter Seven

"May I be 'scused?"

Squirming in her chair, Haley pinned Grant with her puppy-dog eyes. As far as he could tell she'd eaten two bites of chicken, a single broccoli floret and a baby carrot. Mice had larger stomachs. But Mia—who'd eaten dinner with them four nights out of the last seven—said she'd never eaten as a child, either. Since she didn't seem in imminent danger of wasting away anytime soon, Grant decided to shelve at least that worry for later.

He nodded his permission and Haley slid out of her booster seat; Grant watched her as she scampered off.

"Give it time, Grant," Mia said softly from across the table in the breakfast nook tucked inside a windowed alcove at one end of the kitchen. Grant's gaze slid back to Mia, and he didn't like what he saw. As kind as the candlelight was, it didn't banish the exhaustion in her eyes.

He picked up his wineglass. "I know the therapist said to be patient, but I still can't help feeling as though I'm waiting for the other shoe to drop." He swallowed, then added, "And you've been working too hard."

Her brows lifted. "Not that it's any concern of yours."

"Merely an observation. What's so funny?"

"'*Merely* an observation'?"

One side of his mouth lifted, as warmth stirred inside him that had nothing to do with the wine, or the leftover heat from the oven, still held captive in the room by the new triple-paned windows he'd had installed when he'd bought the old house six years ago. How the woman managed to amuse and aggravate him at the same time, he had no idea. But when she wasn't around, he actually…*missed* her. Her, and her smart mouth, and the way she'd look directly at him while giving that smart mouth free rein.

Some recluse he was.

"Not all of us were lucky enough to be brought up with the nasal New England twang," he said, his own mouth twitching.

"Ain't that the truth. But you're an investment geek, for God's sake. Not a character out of *Masterpiece Theater.*"

"Blame my father," he said quietly, sitting back, swirling the half inch left in the single glass he allowed himself each evening. "He had a thing for the English language. Couldn't abide sloppy grammar or slang." He shrugged. "It was a way to get closer to him. Or so I thought."

Her expression softened, as it always did whenever something moved her, and Grant felt another twinge of something not nearly as unpleasant as he might have once thought. Not so much his reevaluation of who Mia was, but of who he could be, might be, given half a chance.

His father would have pegged her, and rightly so, as one

of those poor fools who were ripe for manipulation. And heaven knows there were times when it was beyond tempting to deliberately play on her emotions, just so she'd look at him the way she was now. But the more they were together, the more he saw the steel underlying the velvet-soft sympathy in her strange green eyes. Kindhearted she was, absolutely, and patient beyond belief—especially with Haley—but he'd heard her on the phone going head-to-head with suppliers and caterers, with errant servers who'd left her hanging. The woman could be downright scary, Grant thought with a slight smile.

"Most kids would have rebelled," she observed, sitting back as well, her wineglass cradled in her hand. "Used slang on purpose, just to be ornery."

"I wasn't like most kids."

"Clearly."

Nobody had ever kidded him, kidded with him, before. God knows Justine hadn't. Or his parents. And the people he worked with—his "quants," mostly, the number-crunchers who supplied him with the endless flowcharts and spreadsheets that helped him minimize the risks attendant to a business predicated on uncertainty—weren't a particularly jovial bunch, on the whole. And everybody else…well, he supposed he did tend toward the intimidating side. Things were generally easier on everybody that way.

A modus operandi completely lost on Mia, who clearly didn't give a rat's ass about any of the things that impressed other people.

Which could be a problem, if he let it be. Because there was something entirely too unsettling about being around someone who not only wasn't out to make points, but who saw completely through you. Okay, maybe not completely, but enough. Too much. The best he'd hoped for, going in, was that she wouldn't get under his skin. Now it seemed she was doing exactly that.

Without even trying.

"So about this party…" Eyes sparkling, she'd leaned forward, her voice lowered in case Haley popped up, and he reminded himself that many "skin" conditions were psychological in origin, brought on by stress or worry or other mental agitations. "I'd love to do it outside, but the weather's too iffy at the end of October. So I was thinking the dining room's big enough for what I have in mind, and with all those French doors it'll still give an outdoorsy feel…."

"You can set up the party anywhere you like," he said, trying to staunch the ripple of unease that had nothing to do with his skin problem and everything to do with the devilish smile flashing at him from across the table.

"I cannot *wait* to see you in a Prince Charming getup. The question is…tights or no tights?"

"I don't do tights," he growled. "For anybody. Not even my daughter."

Mia's laugh was interrupted by her cell phone's irritatingly cheerful salsa ring. At her frown when she checked the number, Grant asked, "Problem?"

"I have no idea, it's Venus." She opened the phone, tucking it up underneath her loose hair. "Hey, what's up…?"

Grant got up to clear the table—Etta was out for the evening—to give Mia some privacy, his thoughts wandering back to this "quiet, low-key" party for his daughter. He and Mia had both realized that a typical kids' Halloween party—with its emphasis on ghouls and zombies and skeletons and graveyards and such—probably wasn't the wisest route to take after all, considering the situation. So Mia had steered Haley toward nonscary themes for her party. Natch, the kid said she wanted to be a fairy princess, with a wand and a glittery dress and a *crown,* and she wanted everybody who came to be a fairy princess, too. Except for the boys, she'd said, with a pointed look at Grant. *They* had to be *princes.*

With swords and everything.

At least she hadn't requested anybody arrive in a horse-drawn coach.

Yet.

But all-in-all, Haley seemed to be adjusting pretty well. She liked her new preschool, rarely woke during the night, hadn't done many of things the therapist had warned him she might, such as reverting to bed-wetting or becoming clingy.

Still, there was a wariness about her that kept him on alert. She'd blow hot and cold with him, affectionate one minute and aloof the next. But whatever her mood, she was always in control—far more so than seemed normal for an almost-four-year-old—

"Crap," he heard from the dining table. He turned to see Mia sitting with her head in her hands, breathing hard.

"Mia? What is it?"

A second passed before she lowered her hands, tightly crossing her arms over her chest. "Venus picked up our mail earlier from our P.O. box. There was a NSF notice from the bank. One of our clients stiffed us. For a five-figure balance."

Grant swore, provoking a tiny smile across the room. He knew better than to suggest that maybe it was a mistake, that maybe the client used the wrong checking account. Instinct told him that wasn't the case. As it clearly did Mia, who got up, her movements jerky as she gathered the few remaining dishes from the table. "Small potatoes to you, I'm sure, but to me—"

"Stealing is stealing, Mia. You have every right to be mad as hell."

The dishes clattered as she set them on the counter. "No, what I feel right now is *stupid*." She yanked open the oven door to retrieve the half-eaten chicken. "I *know* better than to accept personal checks for anything over a grand," she said, opening and closing cupboard doors until she found the aluminum wrap. "Especially from new clients. But it was right after Justine's death—" she yanked off a length of foil "—and I wasn't firing on all cylinders, and the guy's down-payment check had cleared just fine…."

He grabbed her hand, more to stop her incessant movement than anything else. But he couldn't deny the split second of awareness before he said, "Stop it. Right now. You're not the bad guy here. So call him up—"

"Venus already did," she said, plucking her hand from his. "Phone's no longer in service. And there's a For Sale sign in front of his house—he just lived up in Riverdale so she already checked." At his frown, she sighed. "She didn't want to worry me before she knew for sure. The woman's got serious mothering issues. Damn it!" Tears welled in her eyes. "*When* am I going to learn that liking people isn't a good enough reason to trust them?"

And wasn't there a world of meaning behind *that* comment? Grant cocked his head. "Are you going to cry?"

"No!" she said, scrubbing tears off her cheeks. "And *don't* touch me!" she snapped, backing away when he tried to put an arm around her shoulders. "I d-don't need to be coddled, I just need to let off steam so I can think cl-clearly. Figure out what to d-do. *Oooooh!*" She started to pace. "If I ever get my hands on that dirtwad, he can kiss his gonads goodbye."

Grant had to smile. "Okay, don't take this the wrong way…" She glared at him. "But if you need anything to tide you over…?"

She stopped pacing. Shut her eyes. Shook her head.

"No," she said on a long exhale. "It's the holiday season, I've got a lot more coming in. And I make a healthy profit—and if you so much as breathe a word of that to anybody, you can kiss *your* gonads goodbye. And you don't have to worry about the rent, either."

A frown bit into his forehead. "Why on earth would I *worry* about the rent when you're the one who insisted on paying it?"

"Sorry, it's just not in me to be a moocher. But man, I feel like such an *idiot.*"

"Because you got screwed over? Or because your business took a hit? The same way every business has had to occasionally eat losses since the first man hawked his mastodon-hunting or cave-painting skills?"

"Yeah, I know, but—"

"You just said you keep your profit margins high enough to absorb the occasional loss, right?"

"Well, of course, but—"

"And how many times have you been stiffed since you started?"

"Okay, so this is the first time, but—"

"The *first* time. Out of how many jobs?"

Some of the steam seemed to seep out. "Sixty-three."

"In two *years?*"

Normally, he wasn't big on showing his hand, but the shock of discovering the extent of her success had shorted out his brain. Still, when Mia's shoulders sagged, he realized his reaction had produced the desired effect, anyway. Except she almost immediately straightened again, meeting his gaze dead-on.

"Fine. So maybe I was due. But I swear, if I *ever* find that dude—"

"Are you two having a fight?"

Grant swung around to see Haley standing in the kitchen doorway, clutching Henry. Her eyes were huge with apprehension, as though she'd unwittingly stumbled onto a painful memory. Who had she heard fighting? Certainly not Justine and him—what few "discussions" they'd had leading up to the divorce had been excruciatingly civil, Justine being less enamored of histrionics than he. Or perhaps she'd simply refused to give him the upper hand, by losing control in his presence.

Before he could say anything, Mia swooped down on the little girl, swinging her up into her arms. "No, no, no, sweetie…I'm just mad because I found out somebody took something that belonged to me."

Whatever relief Mia's words might have brought was immediately swallowed up by the uncompromising reproach of a young child. "Oooh, that's bad," she said, her little frown almost comical. "'Cause you're never, ever s'posed to take something that's not yours. Mommy said."

Grant's lungs seized. And when, exactly, had Justine imparted this bit of wisdom to their daughter? Before or after she'd appropriated Mia's fiancé?

"That's right, you're not," Mia said, plopping Haley on a bar stool. "Hey, want some ice cream?"

"Uh-huh. 'Nilla with choc'late sauce. *Please,*" she added before Mia could prompt her. She wriggled into a more comfortable position, shot Grant an unreadable glance, then dropped her chin in the V made by her hands. "I don't like it when people fight."

"I don't blame you a bit. Although sometimes…" As Mia set the child's ice cream in front of her, her eyes touched Grant's, and something told him to brace himself. "Sometimes, when people feel strongly about something— like when they're worried or scared—they get loud. Or angry. Or they wave their arms around a lot. Like this," she said, demonstrating, and Haley giggled. "Fighting doesn't always mean people don't love each other."

The little forehead crumpled even more. "It doesn't?"

"Nope. Take my family, for instance. None of us hold anything back. If we feel something, we say it. As loudly as we want to. Then it's out of our systems and we go back to what we were doing. What's not good," she said with another pointed glance at Grant, "is keeping your feelings locked inside, where they get trapped and make you feel all icky."

"Like a burp?" Haley said, and Mia burst out laughing.

"Exactly! You feel so much better after you've let it out, right?"

"So it's okay to show if I'm mad or sad?"

"Absolutely," Mia said. Now *refusing* to look at Grant.

As well she should. In fact, the entire time Haley ate, Mia kept up a nonstop conversation with her while Grant loaded the dishwasher, his gut churning. With things he couldn't—wouldn't—say in front of Haley.

But sure as hell would, the minute he and Mia Vaccaro were alone again.

The instant Mia's "advice" to Haley had left her lips, she knew she was in biiig trouble. Something about the steam coming out of Grant's ears. That, and his clipped request, before he left the room to put his daughter to bed, that Mia stay put until he returned.

Half of her wanted to catch the next flight out to anywhere. The other half, however, figured whatever was about to hit the fan was way overdue, anyway. Because although Grant's shell had definitely begun to crack open, it was seriously irking her that this good man, this *kind* man, seemed hell-bent on only letting it open so far.

So she plopped herself in a kitchen chair, checking her e-mail on her PalmPilot while she waited, not even aware Grant had returned until his low, "I'd appreciate it if you didn't give my daughter lessons in how to be a drama queen," behind her made her jump three feet.

Mia twisted around, heart pounding, eyebrows raised. That wasn't quite what she'd expected. "A drama qu— For heaven's sake, Grant—Haley's the least likely candidate for that title I know! What on earth are you talking about?"

"I don't see how your telling her it's okay to throw a fit every time something bothers her is exactly in her best interest."

And she might have been tempted to smack him upside the head if it hadn't been for the barely disguised fear in his eyes. Still, he needed to get over it. And since she was the only other person in the room, the task to alert him to that fact fell to her. "You know, just when I think there's a real human being under there somewhere, you go and say something like that and blow it all to hell. I *never* said anything about throwing a fit—"

"You certainly implied it!"

"No, Grant," she said, slipping her PalmPilot into her hoodie pocket as she stood, "all I said was that it's okay for her to tell somebody when she's troubled or sad or upset. That it's okay to cry. Or yell. Or, heck, even throw something, as long as it's not the fine china."

"And you don't think that sends the wrong message?"

"No, frankly, I think *you're* the one sending the wrong message."

Naturally, his brows slammed together. "What's that supposed to mean?"

"It means, if you want me around to help the two of you through this, then I'm gonna call 'em as I see 'em. And what I see is a little girl who's been given the idea that showing emotion is wrong. Maybe not in so many words, but by example. You, her grandmother, even Justine, who'd never let Haley see when she was upset. So where does all that leave Haley? With a whole mess of scary feelings bottled up inside her she has no idea what to do with! Or even what they are! God, Grant—no wonder she's never cried over her mother! How can she, when nobody's ever told her it's okay?"

Realizing she was shaking, Mia turned again and yanked open the back door. "How can she," she said softly, not looking at Grant, "when her own father is so damn afraid of his *own* emotions?"

When there was no response, she said, "As I was saying," and got the hell out of there.

"Where's Mia?" Haley asked Grant as he crouched in front of her, buttoning up her quilted jacket.

"Working." An engagement party, he thought. Maybe. He hardly kept track of Mia's comings and goings. "All ready? You're sure you don't need to go to the bathroom?"

"I just went. Etta made me. I wish Mia could come, too," she said as they headed out the front door. It had been raining nonstop for the past three days; today, however, the sky was a sharp, achy blue, the air crisp but windless, and when Haley had appeared in his office, asking—not pleading, not whining, simply asking—if he'd take her for a walk, how could he say no?

"Maybe Mia can come with us another time," Grant said, his breath barely visible around his mouth as they set out. The lot was set far enough back from the main road that there would be little traffic, even once they'd left the property. Especially on a late Saturday afternoon. Squealing at the sight of a drift of scarlet maple leaves next to the drive, Haley scampered ahead, leaving Grant with his hands tucked into his bomber jacket's pockets, his thoughts a muddle inside his head.

A hundred times over the past week, Mia's words had returned to torment him. Especially after the initial flare of defensiveness died down, leaving him with the charred remains of acceptance. Because she was right, of course, about his keeping his own emotions so tightly under wraps. How could he argue the point when he'd admitted as much the day of Justine's death? When he'd given her little reason to think he'd changed?

Except he had changed, was changing, inside. Since Mia's arrival—or more to the point, since being so frequently subjected to Mia Vaccaro's Philosophy on Life—everything had begun to matter more than it ever had before. Letting his feelings out, however...

Not so easy.

Especially since he had no idea how to change a habit of more than thirty-five years' duration. His parents' examples had taken with a vengeance. But was it right to saddle his little girl with a trait that, if he were being honest, hadn't served him nearly as well as he'd once thought—

Haley's scream of dismay knifed through his thoughts. Grant sprinted over to where she stood, staring at something at the edge of the leaf pile.

"What is it, honey?"

She pointed to a large, and very dead, robin, partially buried in the leaves. "What's wrong with the birdie?" she said. "Why won't it wake up?"

Grant knelt beside her, wrapping one arm around her waist. "It's not asleep, honey. It's dead."

She looked at him, brow furrowed. "Dead?"

Grant nodded. And waited. After a moment, Haley leaned heavily into him, focused again on the bird. "Then how come it's not in heaven?"

Grant uttered both a silent curse and something close enough to a prayer to count, he hoped, for the right words. "Well…it's not the body that goes to heaven. It's…what's inside."

"Like your guts?"

"No," he said, struggling to keep a straight face. "It's…the part of a person—or an animal, I suppose—you can't see, or touch, but makes them who they are. Some people call it the soul." He looked into those trusting eyes and nearly lost it. "It's what's in here," he said, pressing one hand to her chest, and she nodded, the wrinkle leaving her brow.

"I get it now," she said, and he thought, *Good, then you can explain it to me*. Then she squatted, fingers curled around knees, to get a better look at the robin. "But why'd the birdie die? Did somebody hurt it?"

"I don't know, but I don't think so." Actually, the bird looked quite peaceful. "Everything dies at some point," he said gently. "Bodies get worn out. They stop working. Just like…like those old shoes of yours Etta threw out yesterday."

"And that's when people die?"

"Most of the time, yes."

Haley's gaze met his again. And yes, the frown was back. "Will I die?"

"One day," Grant said, cupping her head, feeling such a rush of love for her he lost his breath. "Probably not for a long, long time, though. After you're all grown-up, and have children of your own, and they have children of *their* own. Lots of people live to be more than a hundred years old."

"How long's that?"

He smiled. "More sleeps than you can even imagine."

Haley contemplated that, and the bird, for another several seconds; Grant guessed what she was thinking. "Would you like to come back later and give the bird a funeral?"

She nodded, then stood, tucking her hand in his as they walked away, the sensation painful and sweet and frightening, all at once. And *Grant* finally got it, that Haley was never going to fully heal until, somehow, *he* gave her permission to grieve. He swung her up into his arms, relishing the feel of that tiny body against his, as she laced her hands around his neck, regarding him with a calm, but eerie, intensity.

"You still miss Mommy?" Grant asked softly, and her grip tightened. After a moment, she nodded. "Do you still feel sad?"

She averted her eyes, toying with the back of his collar, her breath soft against his temple. "It hurts. Inside. I don't like it."

"Nobody does, honey. But like Mia said, it's okay to feel that way when something bad happens." They came to a wooden bench installed by some previous owner, like a lanky, soft gray cat huddled in front of a mass of somewhat overgrown bushes. Grant lowered Haley, then himself, to the worn, weathered seat, encouraging her to snuggle close. "It's even okay to cry."

"Nana says big girls don't cry."

Grant's jaw clenched. *Thank you, Mother.* "Oh, yeah? Mia cried and cried when she heard about Mommy."

"She did?"

"Buckets. She loved Mommy," he said, tamping down the burst of irritation, "and she felt terrible when she died. So it's okay for you to feel terrible, too. No matter what Nana says."

Haley planted a poker-chip-sized palm into his thigh to pull her legs up underneath her. "Do boys ever cry?"

"Depends on the boy. But sure, sometimes."

"Do you?"

"Not often, no." After a moment's vicious struggle, he added, "But I did cry the day you were born."

Her eyes settled in on his. "How come? Were you sad?"

He laughed softly. "Not at all. I was…well, I was scared, if you want to know the truth. You were so wonderful and perfect, and I was so afraid I wouldn't know how to take care of you. And because I was scared, I made some mistakes. A lot of mistakes." He swallowed. "I'm sorry, Haley. I'm afraid I haven't been a very good daddy."

When she didn't say anything, Grant thought, *Good going, dumb-ass—the kid's not even four yet, she probably has no idea what you're yammering about.* Only then she reached over and patted his knee.

"You're not a bad daddy now."

His heart cracking, Grant hauled her onto his lap. "Really?"

"Really," she said, nodding against his chest. Then she added, oh-so-seriously, "But do you *promise* to be a good daddy forever and ever?"

Grant held her close. "I promise. If you'll help me."

"Okay," she said, then wriggled off the bench, clearly ready to resume their walk. Except she quickly grew bored with walking and started to skip, with the occasional hop thrown in for good measure. "Know what?" she said.

"What?"

"I like you a lot better than Uncle Matt."

"Who's Uncle Matt?"

"Mommy's friend. But Mommy and him had a big fight one day an' Mommy told him he couldn't come over anymore."

Grant caught himself before he crushed her hand. "Do you remember what this Uncle Matt looked like?"

Haley's shoulders hitched. "He wore funny glasses. Like this." She tilted her head back, her fingers circled around her eyes.

The one time Grant had seen Mia's fiancé, he'd been wearing glasses with round tortoiseshell frames. Of course, it could just be a coincidence, but...

"Did he have dark hair like me? Or was it lighter? Like Mommy's?"

"Like Mommy's. An' he had a beard."

"A beard? Like Santa Claus?"

"Littler. An' it wasn't white. I didn't like him very much. He made me feel funny. Like it made him mad if I was there. C'n we have s'getti for dinner?"

Although Grant itched to ask more questions, he doubted he'd get much more out of someone who still had all her baby teeth. Still, he'd bet the bank that "Matt" and Christopher were the same person. But did that mean he and Justine had broken up? And if so, when?

"We had spaghetti last night," he said at Haley's "Daddy?"

"I know, but Etta always makes lots, so could we have it again? Please?"

"If Etta says it's okay, sure," he said, and at the huge grin splitting the elfin face, he thought, *Nobody's ever going to make you feel bad for existing, ever again.*

They kept walking until Grant noticed Haley's hops and skips had given way to measured plodding and increasingly pronounced yawns. He picked her up again; within seconds she'd slumped against him, fast asleep, and for the rest of the way back he wondered how on earth he could have willingly given this up.

What on earth was so scary about simply loving somebody?

Then Grant rounded the last bend before the house and

saw Mia, sitting outside on the stone steps, her hair luscious and whiskey-colored around her shoulders, her hands linked around one knee, and some strange, unfamiliar emotion jolted him, so intense as to make him slightly dizzy, shattering the peace he'd seized not moments before.

It was joy, he realized. At seeing her, at anticipating talking to her, being with her. Yes, even though the woman pushed every button he had and then some. None of that mattered. At all.

What did matter, however, was that, amidst all this rushing of emotions—identified and otherwise—had come the answer to his not-so-hypothetical question. What was so scary about loving somebody? The responsibility, that's what. A painfully renewed awareness that one's thoughts and actions could profoundly impact other person's happiness and well-being.

Unconsciously, he tightened his hold on Haley, a move which produced a sleepy yawn in his ear. God knew Grant would never again let anything—especially his own idiocy—come between him and his daughter. But even as he acknowledged the first scary signs of deepening feelings for Mia—who'd gotten to her feet and was now approaching them—he was far too much of a realist to trust that those feelings were enough to wrap around, to fill, a heart the size of Mia's.

A heart still obviously tender from some jerk's mishandling of it.

"Mia!" Haley said on a quivering yawn, squirming to get down. Launching herself into Mia's open arms, she told her all about the dead bird, and Grant felt a ripple of panic, that she'd tell her about the other part of their conversation, too. About "Uncle Matt."

Before the child got a chance, however, Mia whispered

something to her, then patted her gently on the backside, directing her inside. When she'd gone, she lifted her eyes to Grant. Then she took a moment, as if making up her mind, before saying, "I've got news."

Chapter Eight

"I wanted to tell you first," Mia said, her hands fisted inside her jacket pockets. Not surprisingly, she couldn't *quite* read Grant's expression. "Before I—we—said anything to Haley."

"Of course, but..." His eyes narrowed slightly. "Did I miss the memo about your looking for a new place to live?"

"I wasn't. Not actively, anyway. It's just something that came up. Out of the blue, actually."

And truthfully, until five minutes ago she hadn't actually made up her mind about whether or not to accept Esme Abrams's offer, that perhaps Mia could apartment sit—a gorgeously furnished, one-bedroom garden apartment near NYU, in point of fact—while Esme and her husband were away in Turin for a year?

Any sane person would have said "You betcha" before the words had cooled in the air. Not "Could I think about it for a minute?"

"You know you're under no pressure to leave?"

She smiled. "I do. And my decision has nothing to do with that."

But it had everything to do with seeing Haley in Grant's arms, his cheek pressed against the child's hair as they walked, his hand protectively splayed across her back...with the flash of something in his eyes, when he'd noticed her. A flash that was over before it began. A sign, she decided, for her to get the hell out of there before her growing admiration for Grant turned into something far harder to resist. She hadn't even realized—or at least, admitted to herself—how close to the edge she'd been until that conversation in his kitchen the other night, when it suddenly hit her how desperately she wanted Grant to see the light.

And not simply for Haley's sake.

Sure, Grant had come a long, long way with Haley. But as far as Mia could tell that that been simply a matter of adjustment. A tweak here and there. Deep down, though, Grant was still Grant—not as cold as she'd once thought, no, but still reserved and controlled and pretty damned stingy with his emotions. Because people *don't* change, not that much, and certainly not simply because you want them to. And expecting them to leads to certain disappointment.

She also knew she was vulnerable, that it would be all too easy to mistake kindness and generosity for something more. And if she didn't protect her heart, who would?

"I know my decision seems sudden," she said calmly, "but the longer we leave the arrangement open-ended, the harder it's going to be on Haley. And me." When Grant's eyebrow lifted, Mia said, "I was already attached to her. Seeing her nearly every day... The kid's been through enough changes without perpetuating something that was never supposed to be long-term to begin with."

"You think your work here is done?"

"Oh, Grant…when I first got here, the two of you couldn't even talk to each other, let alone act like father and daughter. Now…" She swallowed, remembering the tenderness of the earlier scene. "You definitely don't need me anymore. In fact, I'm not sure you ever really did. I'm flattered that you think I had something to do with your healing, but my guess is the two of you would have figured this out whether I'd been around or not."

"You honestly believe you didn't make a difference?"

"Not really, no."

His mouth set, he stared at her for a long moment, before, on a short, dry laugh, he walked a few feet away. "Of all the bizarre things I've heard come out of your mouth," he said softly, his head wagging, "that one tops the list." He turned back, his gaze tangling with hers. "Because I thank God every day that you *are* around. We *wouldn't* have made it without you, and it seriously pisses me off that you seem to think otherwise."

O-kay—mixed messages time. Stuffing hope back down in its burrow where it couldn't get hurt, she tentatively asked, "My bizarreness notwithstanding?"

His mouth actually twitched. "I meant that in the best possible way."

"Of course you did. Still. If it hadn't been for this crisis, I wouldn't be here. And anyway, one day you're going to want to remarry and give Haley a mother, and how would you explain the crazy lady out in the guesthouse?"

He visibly flinched. "I can assure you the thought never even crossed my mind. Especially after what I went through with Justine…" His mouth flatlined. "I said before I have no intention of going down that road again, and I meant it."

"Maybe not," Mia said over the ringing in her ears. "But

I think maybe it really is better if I have a base in the city."
A lie, but a convenient one. "As much as I love it out here."
Not a lie at all.

"This isn't working?"

She almost laughed at his words' double meaning. "Not really, no."

His arms crossed, he again angled slightly away, seeming to focus on a curious squirrel who'd ventured onto the drive, its tail twitching as it balanced on its haunches, begging. Finally, Grant turned back and said, simply, "When?"

"Not until after the New Year. So Haley has plenty of time to get used to the idea."

Grant stared at her for a long moment, said, "Sounds like a plan," then disappeared inside the house, leaving her standing there with nothing but her own ambivalence to keep her company.

"Well, that's good news, isn't it?" Grant's mother said, pouring a thimbleful of skim milk into her after-dinner coffee. Delicately holding the fine china cup with both hands, she took a tentative sip, then looked at Grant over the rim. "I was beginning to worry she'd planned on staying forever."

Grant waited until Rosie, his mother's gray-polyester-uniformed maid, left the dining room before frowning at the blond iceberg who had given him life. Such as it was. "She's only been here a month. That's hardly forever."

Bitsy pulled a careful face, then noiselessly lowered her cup to its saucer. "Still. At some point you're really going to have to think about replacing Haley's mother—"

"And you can stop right there. As I told Mia, I have no intention whatsoever of 'replacing' Haley's mother, as though Justine was some...some broken electronic device—"

"Excuse me? As you told Mia?"

"Yes. Because clearly all the women in my life are determined to see me wed before the year is out. To anyone *but* Mia."

Although curiosity flared in her eyes, all she said was, "Surely you don't mean you'll never marry again?"

"For the sole purpose of providing my daughter with a mother? No. Although if you're thinking she needs a woman's influence, I suppose you could fill the gap." When his mother's face froze, he added, "Then again, maybe not."

On a sigh, Bitsy's gaze swung toward her living room, where Haley lay on her stomach, silently turning the pages of a new book Bitsy had given her. "All I have to say is, you'd better hope like hell Haley *doesn't* become any more attached than she is now," Bitsy said in a low voice. "Oh, I suppose Mia's a sweet enough girl, but she's too…flaky. Unpredictable. And Haley's just beginning to get over Justine…." Her hair glinted in the flickering candlelight as she shook her head.

Grant had long since learned to choose his battles where his mother was concerned. This was not one of them. At least, not yet. Not while his brain still felt scrambled, even after more than a week, from both Mia's news and his reaction to it. After Justine—hell, even before Justine—Grant had never thought himself capable of losing his heart to a woman. Nor was he certain that was what was happening now. Let alone what to do about it if that was indeed the case.

Of course he'd known, intellectually, that Mia would leave, sooner or later. But it wasn't until after she'd made her announcement, when he'd felt as though he'd been shot, that he realized he'd been far less ambivalent about that eventuality than he'd thought. That her being around mattered.

That *she* mattered. That the thought of no longer seeing

her smile and hearing her laughter every day made him feel hollow inside.

But because she mattered, Grant wasn't about to do anything rash. Such as declaring feelings he wasn't even sure were real. Not to Mia, who deserved someone in her life she could trust without reservation.

Assuming, of course, he thought with a smirk, she'd even be interested.

"Grant?" Dragged up from the abyss of his thoughts, Grant let his gaze slowly focus on his mother's marginally concerned features. Her lips pursed. "I don't think you've heard a word I've said in the past five minutes."

"Sorry. You were saying?"

"Two things, actually. One, I decided to go to Cancun over Thanksgiving." When he frowned at her, she waved one hand, setting a trio of thin gold bangles to tinkling. "Oh, don't look at me like that, we've both always detested going through the motions over the holidays and you know it. Even when your father was still alive. So this year I decided, screw the charade, I'm going to enjoy myself, damn it." Her mouth curved. Barely. "And don't try to tell me that's not relief I see on your face."

Grant leaned back in his chair, his arms folded over his chest, trying his level best to figure out why, if his mother would go to such lengths to avoid spending the holidays with him and her only grandchild, there was hell to pay if he didn't show up for these semimonthly command dinners. "Did it ever occur to you there's something very wrong with this family?"

"There's something *wrong* with every family, Grant. I simply got tired of pretending there isn't with ours."

At that moment, Haley's soft voice as she "read" the story to herself cut through the morass clogging the dining room. Grant looked over at his daughter, nearly overcome with feelings for her. Of course all families had problems, and crises to sort through, and personality conflicts that made holiday gatherings a challenge, to say the least. He suspected, however, that his family's dysfunction level ranked well above the eightieth percentile.

How could he even consider inviting another person into this mess?

Then again…maybe Mia was the one person who could steer them all out of it. He shook his head. "Fine," he said. "Haley and I are on our own. Got it. But I assume you'll at least put in an appearance at her birthday party?"

Bitsy's hand lifted to toy nervously with the black pearl necklace lying helplessly at her throat. "Oh, I don't know, Grant…a child's birthday party? You know I'm not a kid person…"

"Not *a* child's birthday party, Mother," he said, getting to his feet. "Your granddaughter's. Who's specifically asked if you're going to be there."

Stunned eyes lifted to his. "She *wants* me there?"

"She loves you. Go figure."

Color tinged his mother's cheeks. "I'll…think about it."

Grant suppressed a smile, deciding against warning her that paper crowns and wands would be handed out at the door.

Loathing procrastination even more than she did canned peas, Mia hadn't meant to leave pulling together the decorations and favors for Haley's party until the last minute. But who knew the week leading up to the extravaganza would be insanely busy, that everything that could go wrong with her other events would? Admittedly, not entirely a bad thing, since being crazed and distracted had kept her from thinking about Grant and his moodiness—

clearly brought on by her telling him she was leaving—for more than ten seconds at a time, tops.

However, it was now inching past midnight of the day of, and a dining table laden with feathers, glitter and cardboard crowns awaited her. Thank God Etta knew how to sew and had been amenable to stitching about five thousand yards of pink glitter sheer into panels and swags and drapes that would—Mia fervently hoped—transform Grant's unused formal dining room into a fairy princess wonderland.

Mug of superstrong coffee in tow, the CD player on full-blast, she planted her butt on a dining chair, sucked in a fortifying breath and grabbed the first of many, many foil stars…only to jump five feet when her cell launched into its new samba ring.

"Mia?" came her mother's still endearingly thick—after more than forty years in the States—Hungarian accent through the phone. "It's me. Mama."

Mia smiled. The concept of caller ID was lost on Magda Vaccaro. She set the phone on speakerphone and laid it on the table.

"Hi, Ma. What's up?"

"I could ask ze same of you, you heffen't called since I cannot remember ven. Your father, he worries, that you hef fallen off ze face of ze earth."

"Nope. Right here in good old Greenwich."

"You are okay?"

"I'm fine, Ma." Relatively. "Busy."

"Making money?"

"Enough."

"You are sure?"

Mia shut her eyes at the worry, and disappointment, in her mother's voice. "I'm sure."

"How do I know you are telling me ze truth, that you are not just saying zis so I vill not vorry? You could still go back to Hinkley-Cohen, yes?"

Giving up on the star, Mia leaned her elbows heavily against the tabletop. "I'm not going back, Ma," she said gently, softly, for the hundredth time. "I told you, I was unhappy there."

"And you are heppy now?"

"Yes." More or less. When not faced with twelve-year-old she-devils. "I love what I'm doing, Ma. I really do."

Silence. Then her mother asked, "You hef new man in your life?"

All over the world, mothers were exactly the same, weren't they? Unbidden, Grant's scowl came to her thoughts. Mia smacked it away. "Nope, sorry. Still single." *And likely to remain that way for the rest of my life,* she thought morosely.

More silence. Never a good sign. But finally her mother said, "So how is ze little girl doing? Better?"

In an earlier conversation, since she did have to explain why she was suddenly living in somebody's guesthouse in Connecticut, Mia had filled her parents in on the situation. Naturally her mother went all soft-hearted and grandmotherly the instant she heard about Haley, never mind that she had more than a dozen grandchildren of her own. Fertile bunch, the Vaccaros.

"Yes, actually," Mia said. "In fact, I'm working on her birthday party right now. Which is tomorrow. In fact, not to cut you off or anything, but I need to get back to work."

"Efter midnight?"

"Yes, after midnight."

"Okay, then I vill say goodbye. But you're coming for Thanksgiving, yes? I think I vill make my cold cherry soup zis year."

Oh, God—sweet-sour cherries floating in a sour cream "soup." Heaven in a bowl. "I am so there," Mia said, and her mother laughed.

"Good. Because I am sure you are too skinny."

After more than a month eating Etta's cooking? "Not a problem, Ma. Trust me."

"And…Kevin? You hef not heard from him?"

What was that bible story? About the shepherd who'd lost one sheep, who left the rest of the flock to go looking for the stray because he couldn't rest until he'd found him? That was her parents with Kevin. They'd never rest until they knew their youngest was safe.

"No, Ma. I haven't. Sorry. But I swear, if I do, I'll let you know."

"Even if he makes you promise not to?"

"Even if. And now I really do have to go, someone's knocking on my door."

"At zis hour? Who could that be?"

One guess, Mia thought as she disconnected the call and went to her door. Surprise, surprise, there stood Grant on her doorstep. Glowering.

"Would it kill you to actually admit you needed help?" he said, and a chill scampered all the way down to her toes.

Grant matched Mia glare for glare as she crossed her arms and leaned against the doorjamb. Her hair halfheartedly clipped up, dark circles bloomed underneath those huge olive green eyes. She wasn't wearing a trace of makeup. Or, Grant thought, a bra. An old flannel shirt drooped from her shoulders, grazing her breasts; her legs—at least, what he could see of them—were sheathed in something that looked like tights, but without the feet. Because the feet were out-fitted in huge, green Kermit-the-Frog slippers. From inside, hip-hop blared, the pulsing beat reaching inside him, goosing his own heartbeat into overdrive.

"What makes you think that?" she said.

"Let me see…first I find my housekeeper drowning in enough pink glittery fabric to outfit every production of *The Nutcracker* on the eastern seaboard. Then she tells me you're planning on pulling an all-nighter to finish up for *my* daughter's birthday party. But God forbid you tell me you're in a bind."

"I'm not," she said, pushing herself away from the doorframe.

Except if Grant's hand hadn't shot to her shoulder, she would have tipped over.

Nothing said he'd had to leave his hand on her shoulder, though. Or gently squeeze her tense muscles through the soft fabric.

They locked gazes for a couple of intriguing seconds. "Is this you being gallant?" Mia asked, and Grant's gaze slipped to her naked mouth, and *gallant* wasn't exactly the word that first came to mind.

"Call it whatever you like."

One eyebrow arched before Mia twisted unsteadily around, presumably to take stock of the cluttered dining table, then twisted back. "Okay," she said, not even trying to stifle a yawn, "knock yourself out. Coffee's on, cups are in the cabinet above. But if you don't like the music, tough." She started toward the dining room, flapping at the table. "So sit. Glue. Make like an elf."

Grant sat, surveying the fluffy, glittery, over-girlified chaos spread over every square inch of the table and wondered what he'd gotten himself into.

Then he stole a glance at the anything-but-girly girl seated across from him and wondered pretty much the same thing.

"So," he said, rubbing his hands together. "What's first?"

"You glue those doohickeys to these doohickeys," she said, pointing to first one pile of...doohickeys, then another. "And you get this." She wiggled an assembled whatever-it-was. "Then you glue the whole shebang onto a wand, and ta-da! Fairy princess accessory to die for."

Grant picked up the first doohickey, feeling about as dexterous as an elephant. Without a trunk for backup. "Why couldn't you just buy all this crap ready-made?" he grumbled.

"Hey. No grumbling. You volunteered. And because I couldn't find exactly what I wanted. There were wands with stars, and wands with feathers, but not wands with stars, feathers *and* glitter."

"Glitter?"

Mia lifted a large jar filled with what looked like crushed glass and shook it. When Grant groaned, she shrugged. And grinned, clearly enjoying the moment.

"You think this is bad," she said, "you should see me at Christmas. Nothing brings out my inner Martha Stewart like the holidays, boy." She picked up a glue gun. "Armed and dangerous, that's me."

He shot her a dirty look, then squeezed a blob of glue in the middle of a silver star and plopped a feathery hot-pink fluffball in the middle. Except some of the glue stuck to his finger. Consequently, so did the fluffball. Which, he discovered when he tried to remove it, had clearly bonded to him for all eternity.

"Don't you dare laugh," he grumbled again.

"Wouldn't dream of it," Mia said, chewing on her bare bottom lip as she assembled one...two...three wands, her hands a blur. "Welcome to the world of little girls. Ultraprissy little girls who take after their ultraprissy mothers. And you might as well give up and go wash your hands," she said when he'd finally divested himself of the nasty feather. "And on your way back," she called after him, "wouldja mind grabbing the Hobby Lobby bags off my bed?"

Shaking his head, Grant de-glued himself, then did as she asked, feeling even weirder about being in her bedroom than he had when he'd moved the furniture in without her knowledge. He'd always had a thing about the sanctity of one's private space, whether his own or anyone else's. For that reason, and by mutual agreement, he and Justine had had separate bedrooms from day one. Even though—at least at first—they'd freely gone back and forth between the adjoining bedrooms. But never without the other's permission.

Never.

Now it struck him how absurd his and Justine's arrangement would seem to somebody else. Like Mia, for instance. Then again, maybe she already knew.

The room was neat to the point of spareness—no clutter on the dresser, no clothes scattered hither and yon, a single book on the nightstand. A complete contradiction, he realized, to Mia's customary dishevelment.

But when he went to grab the bags, he saw, in the middle of the tautly made bed, a long-limbed, black-and-white stuffed cat listing slightly to one side against her pillows, wearing the slightly embarrassed smirk of a drunk who hoped to hell no one else will notice.

Smiling, Grant returned to the dining room, dumped the bags on the floor by the table and resumed his attack on the wand…thing.

"Who's your friend?" he said. Mia looked over. "The cat? On the bed?"

"Oh! That's Sammy. I was in a toy store picking up yet another birthday present for a niece or nephew and he jumped right off the shelf and into my basket." A piece of hair tumbled loose; she shoved it behind her ear. "My one concession to froufrou."

"So I noticed." Grant scanned the inordinate amount of froufrou in front of them. "Do you think Haley's having this party as some sort of homage to Justine?"

Mia's eyes flicked to his before she shook her head. "No, I think Haley just wants a fairy princess party. That she would have wanted a fairy princess party whether Justine was here or not. Oh, for pity's sake…" Mia lunged across the table and grabbed the mangled feather and bent star out of his hands, tossing the feather into the garbage can by her side, kneading the star back into shape with the heel of her hand. She glanced up at him, her eyes twinkling more than the jar of glitter at her elbow, her mouth twitching at the corners. "Some elf, jeez. Can't even assemble a lousy wand."

Grant leaned back, his arms folded over his chest, his own mouth doing some pretty good twitching of its own. Through a thousand tiny cracks and crevices in his armor, her gentle teasing oozed through him, warmed him. Worried him.

"But no wonder," she was saying, setting aside the finished wands, then getting up to dig inside a cardboard box a few feet away. A minute later, she returned to the table, her arms loaded with—of course—tiaras. "I mean, really, what self-respecting elf wears black all the damn time?"

Caught off guard, Grant glowered at her, down at his outfit, then back at Mia. "I do not wear black all the time."

"No, sometimes you go wild and ratchet it all the way up to charcoal-gray. Or various shades of brown, navy or bottom-of-the-duck-pond green."

"So I like neutrals," he said, still glowering. "Would you rather I wear yellow cords with tiny Labradors all over them…what's so funny?"

"I knew somebody who actually had those pants! Bernie Lieberman, he lived next door to my parents until about five years ago, when he and his lovely wife, Doris, headed for the land of gators and hurricanes." She dumped out a packet of fake jewels and began to glue them one by one onto the shiny cardboard headpieces. "He was quite partial to pastel plaids in the summer, too. And he had this lime-green leisure suit you could see from the end of the block. In the dark. We called it his toxic-waste suit."

"We?"

"My brothers and I. I have five. One younger, four older. Believe me," she said, carefully setting a gaudy pink stone in the center of one tiara, "I didn't dare do fairy princess stuff when I was a kid, they would've creamed me. This may be hard to believe," she said, swiping a stray hair off her cheek, which had bits of feather fluff and glitter on it, "but I was the quintessential tomboy."

"No."

"Yep. My mother had to practically tie me down at fifteen to make me wear a bra. I still hate the damn things." When Grant's eyes dropped to her chest, Mia burst out laughing. "Well, whaddya know…you *are* human."

"You have no idea," he muttered, then got up to both get a cup of coffee and put some space between them. As he poured the brew into a mug that said Don't Make Me Get the Flying Monkeys, he thought about Haley, about how Justine hadn't exactly been lacking in that department, either, and his blood ran cold, thinking about the inevitable day when his little girl would suddenly not be little anymore.

In a daze, he drifted back to the table.

"Grant?"

He lifted his eyes to hers. She seemed…bemused.

"It's okay, big guy. Really."

"No, it's not that. It's…" He scrubbed a palm across his jaw. "How old were you when, ah…" When she looked over, frowning slightly, he gestured toward her chest.

"Got breasts?" Her brow wrinkled. "Eleven? Twelve?" She shrugged. "I don't really remember. My brothers were *horrified*. And went on the defensive like you wouldn't believe." She set aside the first completed crown, picked up another. "God help any boy foolish enough to come sniffing around when any one of them was home. And with five, at least one of them being there was pretty much guaranteed."

"Not a particularly fond memory, I take it?"

She snorted. "You might say. I think one of the reasons I went away to college was so I could finally actually be by myself with a boy. Except here's the thing…every time I went on a date, all those dark, disapproving glares went right along with me. Then I got so busy with classes and everything, and then straight into Hinkley-Cohen…" The second tiara joined its mate in the "done" column. "I didn't lose my virginity until I was twenty-five."

The comment was tossed off with no more weight than if she'd been telling him what she'd had for dinner the night before.

"Why on earth are you telling me this?"

"Hey. You asked."

"Not about that, I didn't."

She shrugged. "Blame it on sleep deprivation, then. The more tired I am, the more I tend to say whatever pops into my head. Go ahead, ask me anything." Her gaze flicked to his, along with a sly grin. "I dare you."

Her honesty was intoxicating. And extremely arousing. The CD had changed to sixties jazz, molten and sensuous. Grant leaned back, toying with his mug, his forefinger sliding up and down the inside of the handle. Mia noticed, glanced at him, then averted her eyes. Grant's lips curved.

"Was it worth the wait?" he said softly, and this time, when their gazes met, they held.

"Not really, no," she said. "In fact, I didn't bother again until I met Christopher."

Just hearing the name sent a shiver of annoyance through him. But Mia was the one promising honesty tonight. Not him.

"And how long was that?"

Her shoulders hitched. "Two years, maybe?"

"A long time."

"You're telling me." But then she added, on a soft laugh, "What can I say, I'll take quality over quantity any day."

"And did Christopher provide that quality?" When her brows lifted, Grant shrugged. "You said I could ask anything."

Mia smiled. "Then…yes. He did." She set another finished crown on the pile, picked up the last one. "In fact…"

"What?"

"I sometimes wonder—now, I mean—if a good part of the attraction was that I was just grateful to finally have a sex life. God knows we didn't really have time for much else. I mean, thinking back…" Her mouth pinched closed.

"You're still hurting."

"No," she said on a breath. "Not exactly. More… puzzled. That I still don't really know why we fell apart. Unless he simply got bored with me."

"Then the man was an idiot." When Mia's eyes zinged to his, he added, "You're aggravating as hell, and unpredictable, and borderline crazy, but if it's one thing you're not, it's boring. And you need to…to get over the jerk and get back out there and find someone who…who *appreciates* you."

She stared him down for a second or two, then grabbed her empty cup and stormed back to the kitchen. "Yeah, I'll do that. First chance I get."

"Why are you angry?"

Her coffee poured, she whipped around, apparently not caring when the liquid splashed over the top. "Excuse me, but where do you get off doling out relationship advice? You're not exactly batting a thousand here, either, in case you haven't noticed."

"I can't voice a simple observation, that you've got a lot to offer someone who'll appreciate you for who you are?"

"By that, I take it you mean some nutcase who's into aggravating, unpredictable, borderline insane women?"

"Damn it, Mia, stop twisting my words! I mean someone with the good sense to hang on to one of the most giving, honest women he's ever likely to meet! Some men actually *like* aggravating, unpredictable, borderline insane women."

"Even if you're not one of them!"

Shock exploded in her eyes before she wheeled around again, shakily setting the dripping cup on the counter. On a soft groan, she covered her face with her hands, then let them fall to brace herself against the edge of the counter. "It's the glue-gun fumes, sorry."

Grant stilled, realizing—whether it had been Mia's intention or not—the ball was in his court, hovering in time-stop suspension, waiting for him to swing.

He got up, went to her. Lifted his hand, letting it, too, hover suspended for a moment, before touching the back of her neck; she tensed, the ripple setting off a reciprocal reaction that shot through him like high-octane whiskey. Gently, he forced her to face him, hoping she could see the conflict in his eyes that he seriously doubted he could put into words. In a gesture at once innate and unfamiliar, he stroked a stray hair away from her face, letting his knuckle linger against her temple.

"As I said…someone with sense."

Her own eyes held his, huge with something a little more sharp-edged than annoyance. Then she blew out a sigh. "Look, thanks for the help—or at least the company—but maybe you should go now."

"I can't leave you with all this to do—"

"For God's sake, I'm giving you an out! Just take it already. I'd never planned on your helping anyway, so what's it to you?" When he didn't move, she pushed out another clearly exasperated breath and stepped around him, returning the dining room and giving him her back. "Just *go,* Grant. Please."

Torn—and irritated beyond belief—he watched her for another moment, then walked out the door.

Chapter Nine

"You didn't," Venus said, handing Mia the last of a dozen glittery, star-studded mobiles to hang from the dining room's coffered ceiling.

"Yep. Opened my mouth and out it fell."

"Out what fell?" Etta said from clear across the thirty-foot-long room, the birthday cake balanced in her hands.

Venus and Etta had met for the first time an hour ago. And instantly bonded. Even in Mia's sleep-deprived state, she knew this would not bode well. A supposition more than verified when Venus called out to her new best buddy, "This fool child went and told your boss she liked him."

"That is *not* what I said—"

"Nothing like showing your hand," Etta muttered, trudging over to set the cake on the silver-lamé-draped table.

"I didn't say I liked him!" ·

"As good as," Venus said, and Mia gave up. Arguing semantics on two hours of sleep wasn't exactly her strong suit.

But she had, hadn't she? Showed her hand. Hell, the instant Grant touched her she'd been ready to show him a lot more than that. So now he knew she had the hots for him. Whoopee. Of course, the good news was, since he didn't exactly take the bait—that little erotic handle-caressing deal notwithstanding—now at least *she* knew where she stood. In Alaska, as it happened, but still.

Although, once he'd left the building, she'd gathered her wayward hormones close again and reassured them it was just as well, that he hadn't taken advantage of them. Of her. By four in the morning, she almost believed it.

Mia climbed down off the ladder, turning her attention to the cake. The cake large enough to feed a bridal party of a hundred. Okay, so maybe they'd all gotten a little carried away.

"You made those roses yourself?" Mia said, her mouth watering at the dozens of perfect pink blooms scattered across what she already knew was pure buttercream frosting. A dozen little kids would barely make a dent. They'd be eating leftover cake for days. Pity.

"Yeah," Etta said, beaming. "They came out pretty good, huh?"

"They came out great. It's gorgeous."

"Good thing, 'cause those roses are a bitch."

Mia chuckled. "You know how much you could get for a cake like this in the real world? A thousand, maybe. At least several hundred."

"Dollars?" Etta said, eyes bugged out behind her glasses. "Get *out!*"

"I'm serious—"

"Oh, for crying out loud—" Venus smacked Mia in the arm. "Who the hell cares about cakes? You cannot get me all hot and bothered about you and Grant and then just drop the subject. I mean, honestly—it amazes me how people can be so adult about every other aspect of their lives, but when it comes to matters of the heart, twelve seems to be the cutoff."

"Ain't that the truth," Etta put in.

"Oh, right," Mia said, flicking one of Venus's hoop earrings. "This from the woman who couldn't wait to share Mia's Most Mortifying Moment with the first person to walk into the room. Like that was so mature."

"And was it me who brought up the subject? I don't think so. And anyway, it depended on who the first person was. I do have some scruples—"

"Hey," Etta said. "I'm flattered as hell. Thanks."

"You're welcome, honey." Venus turned back to Mia. "Although I was wondering how long it was gonna take you to finally admit you had a thing for the dude."

"Yeah," Etta said. "Me, too." Mia glared at her. "Oh, come on—there's been more hormone-buzzing in this house since you've been around than there was the whole time Justine was here."

"Really?" Venus asked Etta as Mia tossed her hands up in the air.

"Cross my heart," the brunette said, making an X over one mammoth bosom.

"Then you probably wouldn't be surprised to learn," Venus said to Etta, "that this all started way before he married Justine."

Mia squawked as Etta's eyes went wide. "You're not serious—"

"Excuse me? I'm right here?"

Venus's head swiveled in her direction. "Now I *know* you aren't gonna be dumb enough to deny it, are you?"

"Eat poop and die," Mia said, and Venus grinned. And Etta poked her, saying, "This, I gotta hear. But make it fast. I've gotta get the cheese straws outta the oven at exactly two."

Short of molecular disintegration, Mia realized, there was no way out. So, telling herself she really was going to feel better for finally owning up to something she'd kept bottled up for far too long, she perched on the edge of the velvet-cushioned throne, slapping her hands on her knees. "Okay, the first time I saw Grant—"

"Which would have been when he came into the law office where Mia and Justine worked, about six years ago," Venus told Etta, who nodded. Mia glared.

"Sorry."

"*Any*way…I have to admit my interest was piqued. I found him…intriguing. Scary as hell, but intriguing."

"In other words," Venus said, "the child nearly combusted, she was so hot for him."

"I was not—"

"So…what happened?" Etta said. To Venus.

"Justine happened," Venus said, not even trying to hide her disgust.

Etta looked to Mia for confirmation. "Oh, I'm sorry," Mia said, pressing one hand to her chest. "Is it my turn now?" When both ladies rolled their eyes, she said, "It's true. For a long, long time, I didn't want to admit that's what happened, but…" She pressed her lips together. "Justine was coming around the corner, noticed my momentary mental meltdown—"

"And the hussy went after him," Venus said, poking Etta. "Big as you please. Now *there's* somebody who wouldn't have known a scruple if it bit her in the butt."

Etta's head whipped around. "The bitch *stole* him from you?"

"That would imply there was something to steal," Mia said, thinking a defense of the woman she'd thought of as her best friend wasn't exactly leaping to her lips, here. "And anyway, she didn't make her move until Grant's second appointment." She turned to Venus. "You weren't in that day. Norm had been busy so he asked me to offer Grant coffee, keep him company for a minute. But when I came out of the kitchen, Justine literally snatched the coffee out of my hand and took it to him instead."

"And you didn't smack the child?"

"Smack, hell," Etta said, rearranging one bosom inside her bra. "I would've pulverized the skank."

"Boy," Mia said, "you really did not like her, did you?"

"Not much. But the point is…here you were, attracted to the man then, and that little—"

"Let's be real, I was barely twenty-two and fresh out of law school, I was *attracted* to pretty much anything in pants that didn't have a comb-over or bad breath. But that's all. I didn't *know* him. Or anything about him. Which is probably why I stepped aside and let Justine have at him. Then, after they got married… Well, I realized it was just as well. As far as I could see, he was pretty much made of stone."

"Or so you told yourself," Etta said softly, and Mia sighed.

"Or so I told myself," she admitted. "But by then I'd moved on, I'd gotten engaged, and after Grant and Justine broke up…" She shrugged. "I guess I just bought into everything she told me about him. But the thing of it is…"

She got up to mess with one of the sparkly bushes at the base of the "magic" bridge that Haley would cross—amidst much "fairy dust"—to mark her passage from three to four. Grant was right—she was borderline crazy.

"The thing is, I must have seen something in him then. That first time, at H-C. Buried really deep, but I saw it. Some faint glimmer of humanity that attracted me to him. Now that I've gotten to know him a little, I can see more. A lot more. But who's got the energy to go digging for it—"

"Mia!"

As one, the three women turned at the sound of Haley's delighted squeal as, in a blur of pink tulle, she barreled over to them, only to come to a dead stop in the middle of the room. Two doll-like hands clamped over her mouth, the little girl slowly turned all the way around, before running over to hug Mia's thighs. "It looks like…like magic!"

"It really does," Bitsy Braeburn said from the doorway, a stunned overlay to her normal you-may-bow-at-my-feet voice. Her fresh-caught designer pumps went from *click-clack* to *shush-shush* as she passed from polished wood floor to deep carpet. Which was going to be a bear to clean after a dozen little girls had ground cake and whatever into it. But far less of a bear than being stuck in a vast, high-ceilinged room with nothing to absorb a dozen high-pitched little voices. Bitsy's off-white gored skirt twirled slightly as she, too, did a slow turn in the middle of the room, her expression nothing short of awestruck. "It really, truly does." Her gaze slid to Mia's. "*You* did all this?"

"Of course she did, what do you—"

"Not *all* of it," Mia said, laying a "down, girl" hand on Venus's wrist. "I have an in with someone who runs a children's theater, they'd just done *Once Upon a Mattress* and let me borrow pieces of the set. And Etta and Venus helped a lot with the odds and ends. Including the cake."

Bitsy minced over to the cake table. Mia half expected

her to whip out a pince-nez to get a better look. "This looks almost…professional."

"Geez, don't hurt yourself," Etta muttered, then said in a louder voice, "Thank you, Missus Braeburn. Coming from you, that's high praise."

Bitsy's eyes narrowed almost imperceptibly as Haley yelled, "Daddy," her ballet-slippered feet thudding on the floor as she raced back toward the arched doorway.

"Oh, my!" Bitsy said, clutching the space where her bosom should have been. *"Grant?"*

"Holy you-know-what," Venus muttered, while Etta sucked in a breath and Mia basically felt a thunderbolt *ka-boom* inside her head.

Grant's eyes met hers. "You ordered a prince?" he asked, and she thought, *Hell, yes.*

Where he'd gotten the dress uniform—the white double-breasted jacket with stand-up collar, the banded pants, the royal blue sash bedecked with medals and other assorted princely regalia—Mia had no idea. Nor did she care. But honey, put six-feet-plus of tall, dark, brooding male in an outfit like that and…

Uh, boy.

One side of Grant mouth's tilted. Oh, he was so pleased with himself. And she wanted to say, *Excuse me? Last night you sure as hell weren't looking at me like that.* Only she knew down that path lay madness, so she closed her mouth and tucked her eyeballs back into their sockets and said, off-handedly, "It'll do."

The smile broadened, a little, and one eyebrow arched, slightly, and all at once the air was choked with a whole boatload of unspoken somethings, and suddenly the path to madness was looking not so bad.

The doorbell rang.

"Come on, little bit," he said, his eyes lingering on Mia before finally lowering to his bouncing daughter. "Let's go greet your guests."

After the Braeburns left, Venus muttered, "Whatever that man told you? Don't believe it for a second."

"What she said," Etta put in, then reached over to snatch a spoon off the cake table, smacking it into Mia's hand.

"What's this for?"

"So you can go digging," she said, and a chord of doom sounded inside Mia's head. Especially when Etta added, "He needs you, doll. And I'm not talkin' about for the kid, I'm talkin' about for him." Etta let go, folding her arms across her chest. "And somethin' tells me you need him, too."

Helplessly, her eyes slid back to Venus, whose shrug set off a second round of those damn doom chords. "What've you got to lose, baby?"

"My self-respect?"

The two older women looked at each other and burst out laughing, leaving Mia staring at the spoon, not knowing whether to join in the yuk-fest or go stick her head in the oven.

"C'n I pleeeease stay in my dress?"

Welcoming the tug of connection that he now knew couldn't ever be broken, no matter what, Grant smiled down at his impossibly cute little girl, her bejeweled crown askew in a cloud of fairy-dusted curls, her dimples on full display as she made the full skirt of her sparkly pink dress swish from side to side.

"Don't see why not." Squatting in front of Haley, he smoothed away a smear of glitter-flecked icing from her chin. Microscopic bits of silver dotted her nose and cheeks, as well, as they probably did the dozen very happy little princesses, full of birthday cake and ice cream and laden with more goodies than the Head Princess herself, who'd just left. "As long as you like. Now why don't you help Nana carry your presents up to your room, while I help with the cleanup?"

"'Kay." Haley leaned forward and planted a butter-cream-scented kiss on his cheek; Grant grabbed both little hands before they could inflict damage on his rented outfit. "I had fun today," she whispered, but he could hear the sadness trembling at the edges of her words, see the un-spoken "but" in her eyes.

"That was the idea," he said, then added, "That's what Mommy would have wanted."

"I know," she said, nodding, hard enough to dislodge the crown for good. Grant caught it as it headed south, handing it back to her. She stared at it for a moment, then spun around and ran out of the room.

Grant watched her go, then went back into the dining room, still wearing its fairy-tale finery. As was Mia, traips-ing around in something befitting Glenda the Good Witch, a satin top with sheer puffy sleeves and a voluminous skirt studded with thousands of silver stars, in a shade of pink so hideous no self-respecting flower would be caught dead in it. She looked ridiculous, adorable and sexy in a strange-dream kind of way, and Grant hauled in a mammoth-sized breath, clutching the hilt of the sheathed sword dangling at his hip.

For hours after he'd returned to the house last night, he'd sat in his dark office, Mia's challenging accusation—that he wasn't one of those men who could appreciate her unique qualities—ringing in his ears.

Not true, he wanted to say. Had wanted to, at the time. With an intensity that had shaken him to the core. But habit was a bitch. Years of deadening any hint of emotion that might cloud his vision, hamper his business decisions, had, ironically, left him petrified to take the one risk millions of human beings willingly took every single day. He could move around millions of dollars of other people's money without batting an eye, yet the thought of risking his heart…

Terrifying.

And, Grant now knew, completely out of his control. Because sometime in the middle of that long, sleepless night, he finally admitted to himself that the very *idea* of anybody else appreciating Mia Vaccaro—or doing anything else to, for or with her—made his stomach turn. That he wanted her all to himself.

And would do pretty much anything to make that happen.

"Hey. Prince Charming," she yelled from across the room. "Get your royal buns over here and help."

"Wand's at the shop, is it?" he said as he walked toward her, feeling a bit like he'd just taken a bungee jump without first checking the cord.

A half-full tray of munchies in her hands, she made a "ha, ha, very funny" face at him before tromping over to the serving window between the dining room and the butler's pantry. The late afternoon sun streamed through the trio of French doors, bathing the room in a luscious golden light…and shining straight through all those layers of tulle. Hmm.

Grant grabbed another tray, reaching the serving window just as Mia turned around, nearly colliding with him. Her cheeks went nearly the same color as her dress, and his brain said, *Back up, fool,* while his body said, *Yeah, right.*

Judging from the weird expression on Mia's face, he guessed her brain and her body were having much the same argument. He reached behind her to set down the tray, noticing exactly how low the neckline of that silly dress dipped. And that its original wearer had clearly not been as…blessed.

"You look edible," he said, and the *O-kay, what are you up to?* lights went on in her eyes.

"Yeah, there's an original line," she said. "Although I have to say, you don't look half-bad yourself in that getup. The commanding presence look suits you."

He smiled. "As does the see-through look, you."

"See-through?!"

"But only when you stand directly in front of a light source."

"Oh, well, then…" Directly below his gaze, bosoms heaved. Although from pique, caution or sexual interest, he couldn't say.

"Where's everybody else?" he said mildly, looking at her mouth. Which today—in honor of the party, he supposed, or at least the dress—glistened prettily in some sheer, rosy gloss.

"Venus had to get back to the city, she's doing a gig by herself tomorrow. And Etta's in the kitchen. On the other side of that door."

"I know where the kitchen is."

"Yes, but do you know where your hand is?"

"Your waist, I believe."

"And why is that?"

"Because it's generally easier to kiss someone when you're holding on to her."

Momentary confusion gave way to something close to panic in her eyes; a heartbeat later, she'd sidestepped him and returned to the table, dumping unused plasticware into a tub she pulled out from underneath the floor-length tablecloth.

"*Damn it,* Grant!" she muttered over the clattering. "This is *so* not fair! I'm so sleep-deprived I'm an inch away from hallucinating. Which is all this probably is, anyway—"

"You're not hallucinating."

"You expect me to believe that you'd do a complete about-face in one night?"

"Not one night, Mia. This has been building for a while."

"And what, exactly, is *this?*"

"I didn't think I was exactly keeping my interest a big secret," Grant choked out past the bottleneck at the base of his throat. "I just wasn't sure it was such a hot idea to act on it."

"Boy, you're really bad at this, aren't you?"

"I'm really *new* at it. For God's sake, Mia—I'm trying to change! You *make* me want to change. And I know you've been hurt, and that you're probably still shaky, but the thing of it is, I've grown to care about you more than I would have thought possible. Not two months ago, not *ever,* for anyone. I'm crazy about you, actually, and I'm damned tired of pretending I'm not, and…and, well, that's it, really."

"Wow," she breathed out after the dust settled. "I sure didn't expect that."

Grant pushed out a sigh. "That makes two of us."

After a moment, Mia whirled around to sink with a *whoosh* onto the edge of the throne, dropping her head into her hands. He couldn't quite tell, but it sounded as though she was muttering an interesting variety of swear words.

"Mia?"

"I can't believe I'm about to say this," she mumbled, then knotted her hands on her lap, her mouth pulled tight. "Okay. Obviously, since I wasn't exactly the most subtle person in the world last night, I've got feelings for you, too. Feelings *I* would have never, in my wildest dreams, thought possible two months ago, either. I don't know if it's that you've changed, or—more likely—that I was laboring under a serious misconception. But, see…" A pained look crossed her face. "I guess I never really thought they'd be reciprocated."

"Surprise," Grant said, and she quietly groaned.

"And after my reaction last night," she then said, "this is going to sound really nuts. But in the clear light of day— and the absence of glue-gun fumes—you're right. I *was* hurt. Hell, Grant—my trust was stomped on, shredded and hung out to dry in a freezing wind. And despite *some* people's insistence that I put myself out there," she directed, loudly, toward the kitchen before returning her gaze to his, "I'd like to think I've learned a thing or two about not jumping in without finding out how deep the water is first."

Deep inside him, a surge of concern took most of the edge off the sting of disappointment. Her words were at clear odds with the longing in her eyes—that whatever she'd wanted before, with Christopher, she still wanted. Badly. Only now she was gun-shy to a fault. Even more than Grant was, most likely. Sure, his ego had taken it on the chin, when he'd so badly miscalculated Justine's needs, needs she looked to another man to fulfill. *Failing* was not part of Grant's job description. Still, he didn't know what it felt like to have his heart broken.

Mia did. And if there was some way, any way, Grant could have taken that burden from her, he would have without a second thought.

Slowly, deliberately, he finally closed the space between them, pulled her to her feet. "So you *don't* trust me," he said gently, so gently, curling his fingers around the back of her neck and pressing a kiss into her hair.

"I don't trust myself, Grant," she whispered. "Not yet. And then I think about Haley, about how awful it would be for her if we started something we couldn't finish, and she ended up getting caught in the middle...."

"Of course we wouldn't say anything to Haley. Not until we were sure."

Mia seemed to take that under advisement for a moment, then pulled away. "Still. Even if Haley weren't an issue—and anyway, kids pick up on stuff, she'd figure it out whether we told her or not...." Slowly, she shook her head.

"Are you saying...no?"

Something close to agony contorted her features. "I'm saying...it's too soon? I'm sorry, the timing just seems... off."

"Then good thing for you this isn't one of those horrid dating reality shows where a decision has to be made by the end of ten weeks." When she hiccupped a little laugh, he said, "So what now?"

"Now? Now we get out of these ridiculous outfits and get this mess cleaned up. After that..." Another shrug. "I don't know."

"You don't know what you want?"

"Oh, believe me, I know exactly what I want. Whether I could have that with you...?" Shaking her head, she turned and started out of the room, and the old lightbulb went off over Grant's head.

"I have to prove myself, don't I?" he called after her.

The star-studded skirt glittered in the waning light when she faced him again. "Somebody has to," she said with a sad smile, then walked away.

Chapter Ten

"Girl, what *are* you so afraid of?" Venus boomed in Mia's ear as she pulled up in front of the guesthouse. Mia held the phone away from her ear—no need for a speakerphone with Venus, boy.

God knows, Mia wouldn't have minded in the least keeping her assistant in the dark about the latest chapter in the Grant-and-Mia saga. But Etta had indeed been right on the other side of the wall that day, and the housekeeper cum blabbermouth had wasted no time on giving Venus the lowdown. Two weeks later, both of them were still ragging on her about it.

"Because from where I'm standing, it sure doesn't look to me like Grant Braeburn's the blowing-up-your-skirt type. *Get* up your skirt, maybe—"

"Venus, sheesh—give me a break, already."

Not that her assistant's question wasn't a valid one. In

fact, until that particularly choice turning point in their relationship, Mia'd had no idea exactly how unready she was to trust someone again. She also should have known better than to issue Grant Braeburn a challenge. Even unintentionally. Because in that split second before she'd walked out of the dining room, she'd seen his eyes narrow and his lips curve and thought, *Oh, hell*.

If nothing else, at least those two miserably damp, cold weeks had allowed little time for ruminating about unexpected declarations of…whatever. During the day, at least. At night was something else again. Bone-tired though she may have been, the instant Mia's head hit the pillow her brain started humming a refrain that was one of many variations on the *oh, hell* thing.

Really, *really* irritating ditty, that.

"And Etta says watching the two of you dance around each other is better than the soaps," Venus said. Speaking of irritating. "Without the fake tans and blinding teeth. Unless she's feeding me a line…?"

"No," Mia said on a sigh, watching the rain slither down the windshield. She was seriously beginning to worry about mold in very inconvenient places. And she didn't mean the house. "Okay, yeah, in those odd moments these days when we're actually in the same zip code, he really seems to be trying awfully hard to let me see under his hood. That didn't come out right," she said when Venus laughed. "Into his head, then."

And indeed, Grant had opened up to her—about his childhood, his investment business, even his previous relationships—with an almost raw sincerity that was definitely wearing her down. "But even if I've moved past the impulse to check for fangs, what are the odds of Grant and me making something work? I'm beer and brats, and he's champagne and caviar, and—"

"And if you go any further with that cliché I'm going to have to hurt you. Honey," Venus said, more gently, "I know that scumbag fiancé of yours did you dirt, but Grant ain't him. And you really, really need to move past this."

"And how do you propose I do that?" she said, banging her hand on the steering wheel, her stomach churning with annoyance. "If I'm not ready, I'm not ready. I thought I was, but apparently I was wrong. So sue me. And anyway, we've been so busy—"

"And do not tell me the business is your life because that is just too sad to even contemplate. Yeah, at the beginning when you were trying to get established, I know you couldn't afford not to take every event that came your way unless there was a scheduling conflict—"

"That hasn't changed, Vene. Especially since that jerk stiffed us."

"The hell you say. You forget, I do the books. You've been in the black for a solid six months now—"

"The business is in the black," Mia said softly. "*I'm* not. It'll be years before I pay back my student loans, my parents, reestablish my retirement account…" Venus grunted in her ear. "Okay, so maybe I've used the work as a substitute for therapy—or pointless drunken binges—a time or six over the past year and a half. But trust me, I've needed every dime we've pulled in." When her assistant didn't reply, the hairs raised on the back of Mia's neck. "What?"

"Oh, nothing. Other than the fact that you've got one of the richest men on the eastern seaboard trying to get into your…good graces. And don't you dare give me some song and dance about making it on your own. You've done that, baby. But, hell, if some fairy-tale ending smacks you upside the head, what's so bad about going for it?"

Her phone beeped—an incoming text message. "Gotta go, someone's texting me," Mia said, grateful for the interruption. Not so grateful when she saw who it was from.

Mom coming 2 c u!

Frowning at Grant's message, she climbed out of the van, barely getting her umbrella popped open when a "Yoo-hoo! Mia!" nearly gave her a heart attack.

She whipped around to see Bitsy, booted and trench-coated and, despite a flower-strewn umbrella large enough to shield Mars, about as weather-worthy as a paper boat, making a beeline for her from Grant's back patio.

"I need you!" she practically shouted over the constant thrum of rain on their umbrellas. "Desperately!"

Mia blinked at the frantic, blurred image on the other side of the waterfall separating them. "Excuse me?"

Bitsy gestured toward the guesthouse. "Can we go inside? These boots aren't waterproof!"

Not even bothering to question why someone would wear weather-wimpy footwear when it had been raining for two days straight, Mia said, "Uh, okay, sure," and led Bitsy inside, too late remembering Grant's mother didn't know about The Great Furniture Heist.

"How odd," Bitsy said, taking in the living room as she dumped her drenched umbrella into the stand beside Mia's. "I had a sofa exactly like that…." She clickity-clacked farther into the room. "And a chair…*and my Aubusson!*"

"Don't look at me," Mia said when Bitsy wheeled on her. "I came home one day and it was all just…here. But I make sure the guys on the team remove their shoes whenever they come inside, so it's all okay."

"The guys on the— Oh. A joke." Her gaze swept the

room again, then she swatted her hands. "Oh, what does it matter, it wasn't as if I using it. Anyway," she said, with another abrupt turn, "the reason I wanted to see you—I'm hosting a charity thing on December nineteenth. Fancy buffet, silent auction, the usual. Only the gal I'd hired backed out on me." Cold fingers clamped around Mia's wrist. "So please, please, please say you'll fill the gap!"

Setting aside for the moment the earth-shattering revelation that Bitsy Braeburn was begging to hire her, Mia said, "Wait. *This* December nineteenth?"

"I know it's short notice, but I'm really in a bind."

"And *I'm* already booked." When the blonde looked blank, as though the message had taken a detour on its way to her brain, Mia added, trying her level best to look sincerely disappointed, "I'm *so* sorry, Bitsy, I'd love to, but…" She shrugged. "If you like, though, I could see if one of my competitors is free—"

But Bitsy was shaking her head. "Noooo, I want *you*. After what you did with Haley's party…it *was* magic, Mia. And I want magic."

A small, but blindingly bright, lightbulb went off in Mia's brain. "Ohmigod. Your planner didn't leave, you fired her, didn't you?" When Bitsy's face blanched underneath the layers of Lancôme, Mia sighed. "Call her back. Maybe if you really grovel—"

"I can't. She said…well, never mind what she said. Oh, come on—surely that assistant of yours could handle the other affair?"

"Honestly, Bitsy—has anyone, in your entire life, ever told you no? I said I can't, and that's that. And I refuse to feel bad because you fired your planner without checking to see if I was available first—" Her cell rang. Venus. She clicked open the phone. "Sorry, Vene, I'll have to call you back—"

"No, it's okay, just wanted to let you know the Stanfords backed out. She said she knows the deposit's nonrefundable, but her mother found out about the party and had a hissy fit. My word, not hers. Said the last thing she needs is a bunch of people reminding her that she's ninety."

"Too bad. When was that date again?"

"The nineteenth. Saturday before Christmas."

All the blood left Mia's face. Especially when her eyes cut to Bitsy, who—beaming—had clapped her hands together like a little girl.

Yo, God. So *not funny.*

"Don't free up that day just yet," she muttered to Venus, and hung up.

"You could have said 'no,' you know," Grant said, his back to Mia as he laid a log on the fire in the living room. Since Etta had gone to see a movie, he'd plied her with pizza and the promise of crunchy, gooey, toasted marshmallows, and between Bitsy's ambush and feeling as though she hadn't been dry since August, Mia had been powerless to resist.

Okay, so despite her innumerable protests, both to herself and Venus, maybe it was *Grant* she was becoming more powerless to resist as the days went by. Loath as she was to admit it, she *liked* the man, her reservations about their long-term compatibility notwithstanding. It was a hoot, watching him shed his emotional armor, bit by bit. Watching that tiny seed of something good and solid she'd recognized so long ago finally take root in his growing love for his little girl, and start to blossom. And the thought that maybe she had something to do with his metamorphosis…well, she did have to admit that made her feel good.

So of course she was *attracted* to him. What was she,

dead? Falling in love with him, however…uh, no. Not that his interest wasn't flattering, but neither was it real. Maybe they'd both been caught in the emotional crossfire after Justine's death, but once Mia moved back to Manhattan after the New Year she imagined Grant would forget all about her. In the meantime…

Wedged in the corner of the bottle-green velvet sofa, she tucked her sock-clad feet up underneath her, trying not to think too hard about how sappy-Christmas-movie it all was, the sight of a broad-backed man messing about with logs and pokers and things as his adorable child lay on her tummy a few feet away, coloring pictures, the firelight glinting off her tousled curls….

"I know I could have said 'no,'" she said, in answer to Grant's comment. "And fully intended to, right up until the moment your mother offered to double my usual fee, because it was last-minute. Oh, Haley…" she said when the child shoved her latest artistic triumph onto her lap. Mia's heart clenched. "It's beautiful, sweetie."

Grant stood and dusted off his hands, then a smudge from one knee of his coffee-colored cords, before coming over to admire Haley's masterpiece. Underneath a tan, suede-cloth shirt, a dusty blue Henley hugged his chest. Still straight out of a high-end catalogue, but at least no black. Progress.

"Wow, honey," he said. "That's really…something."

Henry clamped to her side in an indelicate choke-hold, the little girl beamed up at her father, whom she clearly adored, once again reminding Mia of her inevitable obsolescence. Haley seemed to have accepted her mother's death as well as could be expected, even though she still hadn't cried. And might not, the therapist had said, adding that they shouldn't worry about it.

"It's Mommy in heaven," the child said, pointing to the smiling stick-figure Justine, floating in the clouds, surrounded by…shoes. Lots and lots of shoes. And purses. Because Etta had told Haley that heaven was filled with everything you loved best. "You can have it, Daddy. For your office."

"Thank you so much," Grant said, and Mia smiled despite the twinge of melancholy, wondering where in the art-gallery-formerly-known-as-his-office Grant would proudly display *this* offering. "And now somebody needs to get ready for bed," he said. "Henry's looking very sleepy."

"But *I'm* not!"

Grant chuckled, then pointed toward the door. "March, little girl," he said, trying to sound stern. "Right now. Come get me when you're in your jammies."

"O-kay," she said on a dramatic sigh and trudged from the room, dragging Henry by his tail.

Grant watched her go. Then, picking up his mug of coffee from an end table, he deliberately sat in an overstuffed plaid chair across from Mia, letting his eyes settle on her face, and her heart started hoppity-skipping in her chest.

Yeah, about that…

Not once in these past two weeks had he tried to touch her, let alone seduce her. But not, she knew, because he wasn't interested, or didn't care. He may have been keeping his distance—to earn her trust?—but there was nothing even remotely distant, or paternalistic, or—God knew!—*safe* in the look he was giving her at the moment.

Unreal, illusionary or temporary though it may have been.

Somehow managing not to squirm, Mia pretended to take a sudden and profound interest in the room's furnishings. Which, despite the collection of oriental rugs scattered throughout and the eclectic, original artwork, was much less formal than it had been when Justine had been in residence. Some of the furniture she'd taken with her for the Manhattan apartment. What he'd done with the rest, she had no idea. And wasn't about to ask.

She was, however, curious about the house itself. Of which, alas, she'd grown quite fond. "What made you decide on this house? Of all the properties you could have bought, I mean?"

"Because I'm insanely rich, you mean?"

His candor about his wealth was strangely refreshing. He didn't flaunt it, or act the entitled braggadocio, but neither did he assume a faux modesty that only served to make people even more aware that he was, as he said, insanely rich.

"Yes. I mean, really, how do you make do with only a six-car garage?"

"We all have to make sacrifices in an uncertain economy," he said, and she laughed. "Actually, the house had belonged to friends of my parents, who'd inherited it from the wife's grandfather when he died. We used to visit a lot, when I was a kid. It always…" He raised his mug to his lips, a slight frown wrinkling his forehead. "Margie and Jacob were completely devoted to each other, and their children. Two boys and a girl. And they weren't afraid to show it. I always looked forward to coming here, knowing there'd be smiles and laughter and joking around. I used to think—"

"What?"

He smiled. "That all those good feelings had somehow permeated the walls. After the Richardses' deaths, when their kids didn't want the house, I bought it. Only the minute I walked in after closing, I realized my mistake. It wasn't the house that had made me feel wanted, it was the people in it. Whatever had been so clear and vibrant when the Richardses had been in residence had faded, gone out of focus, leaving only…an empty, soulless building."

"So why didn't you sell it?"

"Because I couldn't stand the thought of some numb-skull tearing it down, imprinting the property with his own ego. Although I've certainly had offers—"

"All ready now," Haley said as she reentered the room in a new pair of ruffled, footed flannel pajamas Mia had gotten her for her birthday. A second later, she'd climbed into Grant's lap, molding to his chest and stuffing her thumb in her mouth. Grant looked down at her with that slightly stunned look that hits every parent now and then, then back up at Mia, and her heart turned inside out.

"Now the house is beginning to feel the way it did when I was a boy. Not completely, not yet, but…" He brushed back a shock of curls from Haley's temple, stroking her soft cheek with his thumb. "But as though whatever had been here before is beginning to come back into focus." His eyes lifted to hers again. "Especially when you're around."

"Grant, I—"

His head shake cut her off. "No response necessary," he said, getting to his feet with Haley in his arms. Mia stood as well.

"You're making this very hard."

His gaze raked her face for a moment before a slight smile touched his lips. "Good," he said softly.

After he carried Haley up to bed, Mia gathered her things, running into Etta, who was coming in through the back door as Mia was leaving.

"Good movie?" she asked, winding her scarf around her neck.

"Eh," Etta said, propping her open, dripping umbrella on the cement floor of the mudroom. "I've seen better. Any pizza left?"

"Tons. Grant still hasn't figured out that little girls don't eat, they nibble."

"Too bad big girls don't," the housekeeper muttered, then frowned at her. "You okay?"

Manning her own umbrella, Mia yanked open the door. "Actually…no. But thanks for asking," she said over the pounding rain as she and her freaking ambivalence headed out into the cold, wet night.

"Could you please read to me?" Haley said as Grant lowered her to her bed.

His musings about Mia and her continued resistance shattered, he nearly dropped the little girl. After all these weeks…*finally.*

"Sure, honey. Let's see…." This was big. Bigger than big. And even as he lifted from her nightstand a collection of Beatrix Potter stories she must have pulled from her bookcase earlier, he thought, *Wait until I tell Mia.* "This?"

Haley nodded. "But you hafta let me pick which story," she said, motioning for him to hand her the book. Which he did, then sat beside her, filled with a sense of wonder as he watched her intently turn the pages, this amazing, funny, frighteningly bright little person he'd fathered. "This one," she finally said, and returned the book to him, opened to a story about three kittens, all decked out in turn-of-the-century clothes.

Grant started to read, only to be immediately interrupted by, "Dad-*dy.*"

"What?"

Snuggling closer, Haley breathed, "You hafta read the voices."

"The voices?"

She huffed a tiny sigh. "You know, because everybody

sounds dif'rent when they talk? I have a little voice, and
Etta has a big, boomy voice, and Gramma Bitsy has a
voice that sounds all squeezed up, and Mia has…" She
thought. "Mia has a voice that sounds like happy."

Yes, Grant thought, his heart squeezing. *Yes.* Haley
tapped her finger on the page. "So you hafta make the
kitties all sound dif'rent, too."

"And what kind of voice do I have?" Grant asked.

Haley scrunched up her face. Then shrugged. "Just a
daddy voice."

Good enough, he thought. Good enough.

So he read, about Mittens and Moppet and Tom, and
their mother's exasperation with them, making each one
sound different, and when he'd done, he asked, "So how'd
I do?" and Haley said, "Okay," but she didn't sound particularly okay.

At some point during the reading, she'd crawled under
her covers. Now, as Grant set the book back on the nightstand, he noticed she'd rolled onto her side, hugging Henry.
Seized with a sudden premonition, Grant reached over and
brushed her curls away from her cheek.

"What is it, sweetheart?"

After a moment, she looked up at him, her eyes glisten-
ing with tears, her lower lip trembling. "It's not fair!" she
said on a choked sob. "It's not *fair!* God has lots and lots
of old people He c-could take if He's lonely, why'd He have
to t-take *M-M-Mommy?*"

On a soft moan, Grant scooped his now bawling, incon-
solable little girl into his lap, holding her tight despite her
best efforts to wriggle free, as though his touch actually
hurt her. But damned if he was going to let go, he thought
as tears crowded his own eyes. Ever.

And so he held her, rocked her, letting his embrace

convey what he had no words for, his child's emotional release unlocking something inside him, as well, until exhaustion eventually overtook the wracking sobs and she went limp in his arms, still sniffling in her sleep.

Carefully, Grant tucked Haley back in bed, making sure Henry was there to greet her when she woke up. He stood over her for several moments, considering, then turned off her lamp and crawled onto the bed beside her.

She burrowed into his chest, easing deeper into sleep.

Giving up the night as a lost cause, Mia made herself a cup of cocoa and crawled into bed to read or make notes for one of her gigs, anything to drown out the sound of the relentless rain, like packs of snarling wolves, lashing ferociously against the—thankfully—storm-proof windows. Except naturally the *moment* she opened the novel she'd been trying to read for the past month, her cell rang.

She checked the caller ID, recognizing the Manhattan area code but not the number. If this was a client, it was one with neither the sense nor courtesy to think, *Hey, maybe it's too late to call.*

"This is Mi—"

"At least you've still got the same cell number!"

The forsaken novel slithered onto the floor. *"Kevin?"*

"Where *are* you?" they said at the same time.

"I'm in the booth across the street from your building," her brother said. "Totally soaked. Not in a good mood."

"Wait a minute—you're in *New York?* Never mind, obviously that's where you are. But why the hell didn't you call me before you arrived, dumbbell? I don't live there anymore!"

"Yeah, I kinda figured that out when some strange chick answered your door and said she had no idea who you were. So what's your new address? And I hope to hell you aren't in Brooklyn or Staten Island or something."

"You want to stay with *me?*" The last word came out on a squeak.

"Uh, yeah? Since the aforementioned chick wasn't exactly amenable to the idea?"

A whole slew of thoughts tramped through Mia's head, most of which involved wondering when, *when,* her brother was ever going to grow up. "Well, Kev, the good news is, I don't live on Staten Island. The bad news is, I'm not even in the same state."

Silence. "Are you at least in the same time zone?"

"More good news." When he groaned, she told him to go to Grand Central and get the train to Greenwich—no, she was not driving into the city at this hour, in this weather, to get him. She'd pick him up at the station in two hours.

So much for her early night. Lucky her, to have such a considerate brother.

Two more cups of cocoa and a surfeit of barely absorbed late-night TV later, she hauled on jeans, boots, two sweaters and her vest, grabbed both her umbrella and her resolve and sallied forth to do what she'd been doing for more years than she cared to admit.

Only to let out a yelp when she opened her door to find Grant standing there in a hooded black raincoat, looking like the Grim Reaper's sexy cousin.

"Where the hell do you think you're going?" he said over the rain pounding the cement walk behind him.

"I'm off to pick up my brother at the station," she said, sounding more than a little agitated, then frowned. "And why is one side of your face all creased?"

"What?" Grant lifted a hand to his cheek. "Oh. Right.

Because I've been asleep on Haley's bed for the better part of the last two hours. Actually, that's why I came over. Because it finally hit. About her mother." He swallowed, remembering. "I had no idea a child could cry so hard."

"Oh, Grant…" Mia bit her bottom lip as tears welled in her eyes, too. "Is she okay now?"

"I don't know," he said on a rush of air. "I mean, I think so, but she's asleep."

Her head tilted, she asked softly, "And how's Dad doing?"

Grant let out a tired laugh. "I have no idea. But we got through it. At least, we got through *that*. What this means for the future, though…"

"She's going to be fine, Grant. She's got you. And Etta. And…and she'll be fine," she repeated, sternly, almost as if to reassure herself more than anything.

Grant decided to let it lie. For now. "So. What's this about your brother?"

Her mouth screwed up again. "He showed up at my old place, no warning, nothing. I hope it's okay if he stays with me for a while?"

"Of course. Although I'm guessing it's not so fine with you?"

"Yeah, well, welcome to Sibling Support, Inc. And as I said, I have to get to the station to pick him up—"

"And you're not seriously thinking of driving down there at this time of night by yourself? Let me grab my keys and I'll drive you."

The look she gave him was equal parts pissed and pitying. "After seven years of riding the New York subway alone after midnight, I think I can handle the mean streets of Greenwich. Besides, whatever's about to go down between my brother and me is in all likelihood not going to be pretty."

It was patently ridiculous, the pang at being shut out, even though there was no reason for him to be included in Mia's family business. Even more ridiculous was the jolt of concern about her driving by herself, in this weather—God knows he'd never felt that way about any other woman. Not even Justine—

"Grant?" she said, making a shooing motion. "Move?"

When he did, she sidestepped him, her umbrella *whooping* open as she strode out to the van. Grant followed, his thoughts a muddle. He'd hated when Justine had played the helpless card, her oft-used ploy for attention whenever she'd felt neglected. So why the equally sharp stab of irritation at Mia's insistence on taking care of herself? Was this just the residual effect of the earlier scene with his daughter? Or was this how a man was supposed to feel about a woman who'd gotten to him the way Mia had?

After Mia climbed behind the wheel, Grant rapped on her window. She lowered the window a scant two inches, enough for him to see her glower.

"You have your cell?"

"Yes, Grant. I have my cell. And an emergency kit. And, believe it or not, some common sense. So go to bed. I'll be fine."

She disappeared behind the raised window and backed out of the drive, her windshield wipers groaning. The ice-cold rain mercilessly pummeled Grant as he stood in the drive, disgustingly aware that no way in hell would he be able to sleep until he saw the van once again safely parked in front of the guesthouse.

This part of caring about people, he decided, he could do without.

* * *

"So who, exactly, is this dude again?"

Huddled in her fleece robe across from her brother at her kitchen table, Mia desultorily poked at her instant oatmeal. Bad enough the ark-worthy downpour had dragged out the twenty-minute drive from the station to more an hour without dealing with a buzzed brother who'd wanted to stay up and chat for another two hours after they finally docked back at the guesthouse. However, since Mia had a job in the city this evening, playing the lazy bum and staying in bed until noon wasn't in the cards. And, unfortunately for Kevin, exhaustion tended to make her even less tolerant of dumb-ass younger brothers than usual.

"Grant was my best friend's ex-husband," she croaked out. "I'm close to his little girl, Haley." She forced a spoonful of oatmeal past her lips, trying not to gag. "After her mother died, I offered to stay for a few days until she was through the worst. In the meantime, I lost my apartment, and this place was available, so…" She shrugged, thinking, *If only it were that simple.*

That Grant's chest-thumping had annoyed the hell out of her was no surprise. That it also kinda thrilled her, however, was. Especially since the testosterone-drenched nightmare that was four older brothers—not to mention a father who still treated her as if she were made of spun glass—had in large part fueled her desire to leave home to begin with. So what was up with all the female fluttering, for God's sake?

Wearing a navy blue hoodie a lot cleaner than she would have expected and jeans with only one small hole—that she could see—at the knee, her brother crossed his arms, his hands tucked in his armpits, and frowned at her. Mia lowered her coffee mug and frowned back.

"What?"

"You don't want me here, do you?"

Mia forked a hand through her still-matted hair. "I've had less than four hours of sleep," she muttered. "Right now I wouldn't want Gregory Peck here."

"Who?"

"Never mind," she said with a limp wave. "But to answer your question, while it's good to know you're still among the living, knowing you've become a productive member of the still-living would be better. Since, you know, it's been some time since you were a clueless nineteen-year-old."

"Yeah," Kev said on a sigh, leaning back in the kitchen chair. "I know." His mouth flattened, and she thought, okay, she guessed he was pretty good-looking. In a spiky, scruffy, shipwrecked kind of way. At least his hair was back to its natural caramelish brown. As opposed to the assorted crimson/cobalt-blue/bleached/Goth phases it had gone through over the years. But he'd inherited their mother's Slavic cheekbones and strong jaw, and his eyes were soft and gentle and the rich brown of expensive tanned leather, and Mia supposed he could even be pretty presentable, given a lot more patience than she had.

Those eyes were fixed in hers, at the moment, more clear and intense than she could ever remember, and she thought, *Huh.*

"I've changed," he said, and she snorted. "No, I mean it this time, Mimi." He looked so stricken she overlooked the much-loathed baby name. "I've done a lot of stuff I shouldn't've, and I know I've put a lot of people through hell these last few years, but…I dunno, it was like one day I woke up and realized this was the only life I was gonna have, and watching it go down the drain wasn't nearly as much fun as it used to be."

One wrist on the edge of the table, Mia kept her gaze

locked on her brother's. Kev had been "her" baby, born when she was about Haley's age. She'd helped feed him and dress him and taught him to walk, protected him from getting creamed by his boisterous older brothers. In elementary school, she'd been his champion; in middle school, she'd been his tutor, having far more patience—and academic wherewithal—than their parents, with Kevin's academic struggles.

Mia's leaving for college, however, before Kev entered high school hadn't done her younger brother any favors. He was smart, God knew, but without her cheerleading, his motivation to succeed, to overcome his handicaps, nosedived in her absence. He'd gotten in with the wrong crowd, started drinking and doing drugs, and the bottom fell out. Eventually, in frustration and defeat, he left high school; shortly thereafter, unable to stomach their parents' muchvoiced shame and disappointment, he left home.

"So," she said softly, "what exactly does this mean?"

"I've been sober for six months, for one thing," he said with the same angelic grin that used to make old ladies swoon in the grocery store when he'd been a toddler. "And I've been learning how to fix things. You know, restoration crap? Furniture, houses, whatever." The smile dimmed. "I'm never going to match you in the brains department, but I'm good at it. And I enjoy it. So I'm thinking maybe one day I can open up my own business. Who knows?"

His sincerity broke through her early-morning fog, dissipating years of frustration and heartbreak. "I take it you haven't talked to the folks yet?"

He shook his head. "I'm working up to it. In fact, I'm working up to a lot of things. The substance abuse program I was in? They're real big on getting you to face your past, making peace with the people you've hurt or wronged along the way. And I know I hurt Ma and Pops—"

"They let you down, Kev," she said quietly. "We all did. I should have kept up with you more after I left for school—"

"That's bull, Mia. You had your own life to live. You weren't responsible for me. And I knew what I was getting into, believe it or not." His gaze rested on hers. "You were so damn trusting. I got away with some serious crap with you."

Her forehead knotted. "What are you talking about?"

"I was messed up, really messed up, long before you left home. I was smoking pot by the seventh grade—a couple of the other kids and me, we'd ditch school and go smoke out by the railroad tracks. And those nights I'd spend at somebody's house?" He shook his head. "I'd get so plastered I couldn't even stand up. And you never knew."

Mia watched her brother's face for several seconds, then stood, carrying her uneaten goop over to the sink. She would have been sixteen, seventeen at the time. Still young, yes, but for God's sake—who the hell was that naive in the nineties? Had she loved her brother too much, wanted so badly to believe in him, to see him overcome the obstacles nature had thrown in his path, that she'd been blind to those he was throwing in his *own* path?

"Of course I knew," she said, not looking at him. The bowl rinsed out, she turned, her arms once again folded over her ribs. "But what good would nagging have done? If I'd thought you were in serious danger—"

"Mia." A half grin pulled at her brother's mouth. "You're trying to B.S. the champion. There's no way in hell you could have known and kept your mouth shut. The way you always came to my rescue? Get real."

She waited out the flare of heat in her cheeks, then said, "So what now?"

"Major damage control. Starting with you. If it's okay, I'd like to hang out here for a couple of weeks—I have money, I'll chip in for food and gas if I borrow the van—so you can see for yourself I've changed. After everything you did for me…" He stood, shoving his hands in his pockets. "I owe you."

"And I can trust that you're not going to sit here all day while I'm gone and get stoned? Or drunk? Because this isn't my house, I'm only here as Grant's guest, and even if it were—"

"Mia. I swear. And I know you have no reason to trust me, but hell, if you want I'll take a drug test. You can even come with me, watch me pee in the cup."

She barked out a laugh. "Oh, God—if it comes down to that, just kill me." Her smile faded. "Okay, okay…you can stay. But one slipup—"

"Got it," he said, smiling. "You going to the folks' for Thanksgiving?"

"Um, yeah, I suppose—"

"Good. I should be ready to face them by then." He sighed. "This is a one-day-at-a-time journey back. And you're the first stop. If that's okay."

After a moment, Mia closed the space between them and drew her brother into a hug. "Yeah," she whispered. "It's definitely okay."

Grant wandered into his kitchen, hoping to score lunch, to find the male version of Mia sitting at his kitchen table devouring a sandwich the size of an aircraft carrier as Etta, clearly entranced, looked on. The young man immediately rose, however, proffering one hand. After he wiped it on his jeans.

"You must be Grant," he said, his handshake firm and

brief. "I'm Kevin, Mia's brother. Hey, thanks for letting me crash in the guesthouse, I really appreciate it."

Was I ever that young? Grant thought wearily, even as he said, "The house is Mia's to do with as she wishes while she's here. You're more than welcome to stay for as long as you like."

Etta shot him a glance, which Grant ignored.

"Cool, thanks. Listen, I noticed some of the upholstered pieces in the living room over there could use some repair. Mia said they're your mother's, but maybe I could fix them for you. As a way to say thank you? I'd need to pick up some supplies, but I've got my tools with me."

"You're an upholsterer?"

The young man's face broke into a proud, enthusiastic grin. "Among other things. Of course, if you don't feel you can trust me with your mom's stuff—since it's not like I can exactly show you any samples of my work—I'll completely understand. I just thought—"

"No. I mean, yes, that's fine," Grant said, smiling despite himself. Earnestness clearly ran in Mia's family. "But don't even think about doing the work for free, I'll be happy to pay you."

"Cool," Kevin said, the grin even broader than before.

A hour or so later, they stood over an upended wing chair, Kevin pointing out the frayed webbing, the sagging coils. "You get somebody weighing more than a hundred-fifty pounds in this puppy, she's gonna give right out on you. But the frame's still solid. Fixed up, you could get another twenty, thirty years' use out of it, easy. Of course, people like you," he said, righting the chair again, "it's probably just as easy to throw it out, get a new one."

Grant's gaze swung to Mia's brother. "People like me?"

"You know." The warm brown eyes met his dead-on. "Not exactly indigent."

Although Grant caught the accusation in Kevin's voice, he suspected it was fueled far more by testosterone—and filial devotion—than any resentment over the difference in their economic standing.

"Your sister can take care of herself," he said mildly, and the young man's pupils expanded, just for a second.

"Sorry?"

"This isn't about furniture, is it? It's about checking me out."

"Whoa," Kevin said on a nervous laugh, then rubbed the back of his neck. "Look, man, I have no idea where you got that—"

"From Mia, actually. From what I gathered, the Vaccaros tend to be a bit on the overprotective side."

Kevin stared him down for a moment, then released a breath. "I know it's none of my business if you guys have anything going or not. So it's not like I'd actually say anything, okay? Well, unless I got the feeling you were a real scumbag, like that jack-ass fiancé of hers. Which I don't, by the way."

"Glad to hear it. But why—"

"It's the look on her face, man. Whenever she talks about you. And the kid. You ask me, she's got it bad. And she'd kill me if she knew I'd said anything so—"

"Not to worry," Grant said, clapping a hand on Kevin's shoulder. "I won't say a word. You know…why don't the two of you join us for dinner tonight? Mia often does, anyway, so you're welcome to join us."

"Cool, thanks. I don't know if Mia's cooking's improved any, but I can't cook worth squat."

Grant smiled. "Then we'll see you around seven." As he started to leave, however, Kevin called him back.

"So, is this a two-way thing or what?"

"I'll keep you posted," Grant said, chuckling softly to himself as he closed the door behind him.

Something was up. Mia had no idea what, but she was pretty sure her brother was somehow involved. And judging from the way every nerve ending she possessed had been on full alert from the moment they arrived for dinner, so was Grant.

"So," Grant said, passing her the rolls, "other than working on my mother's party, your schedule should free up a bit after the weekend, right?"

And there it was, that I've-got-you-in-my-sights look that was making the skin melt off her bones. But why? What on earth had happened in the past ten hours to his normal *I want you* expression to warrant tacking a loud *Now!* onto it? She'd searched her brain a dozen times over, but she knew she hadn't said anything to Kevin he could use as ammunition—a lesson she'd learned the hard way by the time she was twelve—and she sure as hell knew she hadn't said anything to Grant. So what the heck?

"Other than that, yeah," she said, pulling her roll apart and her gaze away from Grant's. "But at least no parties until after Thanksgiving."

"Speaking of which," Kevin said, digging into Etta's homemade potatoes au gratin, "you know yet when we're going up to the folks'? The night before or on Thanksgiving Day itself?"

Mia shot him a shut-your-pie-hole look. "I don't know yet," she said.

"What's Thanksgiving?" Haley said.

"It's this holiday where everybody eats turkey and four kinds of dessert," Kevin responded, "and sweet potatoes with marshmallows and our mom makes these fat little Hungarian noodles and cold cherry soup, and our grandmother always brings lasagna or manicotti or something, and there's tons of kids, so it's noisy as hell—"

"Kevin!"

"Daddy, c'n we go to Mia's and Kevin's house for Thanksgiving?" Haley asked, and Mia dropped her fork. The little girl's curls vibrated when she tossed Mia a brief "don't interrupt" frown, then turned back to her father. "'Cause Nana's going away, and so's Etta, an' I don't think you know how to cook a turkey, do you? *Or* four kinds of dessert."

"Your mother's not going to be here for Thanksgiving?" Mia asked.

"No, as it happens. But that's okay, Haley, we can go to a restaurant—"

"Forget it," Kevin said. "There's always like five times more food than even our family can eat. And Ma loves taking in 'strays'—"

"Oh, gee, Kev," Mia said. "It's always so noisy and crazy and crowded—"

"And my brothers, they bring extra TVs so there's a different football game on in practically every room of the house. And there's a huge tree fort out back," he said with a wink at Haley.

"She can't go into the fort, Kevin! For heaven's sake, she's only four!"

Amazing, the silence reverberating inside the trap she'd just walked into. Because what was she going to say now? That Grant and Haley *couldn't* come?

"Aw, come on, sis," Kevin said, grinning. "As long as one of the bigger kids is with her, she'll be fine."

Mia turned to Grant, who, yes, looked as though butter wouldn't melt in his mouth. "I'm sure the folks would be thrilled to have you," she said, even though she knew she'd been set up. Besides, ever since she could remember, there had always been at least a half dozen extras at her family's Thanksgivings. In fact, some years it had taken her the better part of a half hour to ascertain whether or not she was in the right house.

Grant looked over at Haley, who beamed and nodded enthusiastically. Just like the kid's mother, Mia thought. Always up for a good party.

"We'd love to come," he said, and Mia sank into a very bad mood, indeed.

Chapter Eleven

On Thanksgiving Day, Mia got out of Grant's Lexus in front of her parents' house and froze. Not from the frigid temperature, but the familiar roar of assembled Vaccaros from inside the two-story house, a sound at once comforting and absolutely terrifying. The unassuming, tree-lined street—studded mostly with comfortably large sixty-to-seventy-year-old houses built not to impress but to accommodate the fertile Catholic families who'd once lived in them—had changed little over the years, even if the neighbors' languages and cooking smells had. Many had been converted into apartments, of course; others, however, were still the proud bastions of older, grateful, mortgage-free couples like her parents, whose kids were grown but not completely gone, who would hang on to their home until age, infirmity or said kids forced them to give it up.

Speaking of kids—Kevin was already up on the porch, wrapped in their mother's boa-constrictor-like grip, no mean feat since she was nearly a foot shorter than her youngest son. Mia, however, hung back, mentally arming herself. A small, gloved hand slipped into hers; she'd no sooner smiled into Haley's slightly apprehensive eyes when a stocky yellow Lab and a white, unclipped toy poodle shot off the porch and made a beeline for The New Kid.

On a squeal of delight, Haley instantly let go of Mia's hand and gave herself up to unbridled doggy love, the quivering little poodle sending her into helpless laughter as he slathered her with nonstop kisses.

"And just wait until my mother gets hold of you," Mia said as Grant came up behind her, close enough she had to dig her feet into the sidewalk to avoid getting sucked into his gravitational pull.

"What's the matter?" he said softly, settling his hand on the small of her back, and she thought, *Where would you like me to start?* But then her mother let go of Kevin long enough to notice three more chicks needing to be gathered into her roast-turkey-and-pumpkin-pie-scented nest.

"Mia!" she said, her breasts bouncing underneath her fuzzy, fitted, off-the-shoulder tunic sweater as she carefully negotiated the front steps in four-inch-heels. Once safely on the sidewalk, bangles jangled as her arms swung wide.

"*That's* your mother?" Grant said, as her father appeared on the porch, the sunlight glinting off his full, white beard. Haley's eyes—large as dinner plates—swung to Mia's.

"*Santa* lives at your house?"

"Don't I wish," she muttered to no one in particular, moments before she was swallowed up in angora, Wood-hue and way too many childhood memories.

* * *

"So," Mia said to Grant some hours later, as they stood at the dining table trying to choose between, yes, four desserts. "On a one-to-ten scale, how's your pain?"

Deciding on the pumpkin pie with the slightly charred crust, Grant gazed at Mia's back, then leaned over to whisper, "At the moment? About an eight."

Her plate already crowded with slices of both apple and cherry pie, Mia's eyes cut to him before she went after the pumpkin. "Not what I meant," she mumbled.

"I know," Grant said. Then he chuckled.

Fork poised, still standing, Mia frowned at him over her loot. "What?"

"Oh, nothing," he said, turning away. Smiling.

"Hey. I've been on my feet ever since we freaking got here," she said, shoving a very unladylike forkful of cherry pie into her mouth and saying something that sounded like "I'm entitled" around it. "And I meant, how are you holding up—" she fought to regain her balance when a gangly-limbed nephew elbowed her aside to get to the goodies "—with the family thing?"

His hand on her elbow, Grant steered her away from the madness and toward the only slightly less crowded living room. Since Mia's older brothers were all cops, each on a different shift, dinner had been more or less an all-afternoon affair, with food appearing, disappearing and reappearing on the dining table at regular intervals.

"Compared with the dinner-promptly-at-two, over-at-two-thirty torture I endured throughout my entire childhood?" he said, his words nearly drowned out by a burst of good-natured arguing as her two oldest brothers simultaneously went after the last piece of cherry pie, over her mother's, "Is okay, is okay, there is more in ze kitchen!" "What do you think?"

Mia's eyes caught in his, followed by a sigh. "So what you're saying is, short of offering up live animal sacrifices, there's not much my family can do to put you off."

"That's pretty much it. Look sharp," he said, nudging her to the right, "two spaces over on the sofa."

Not that Mia had exaggerated, Grant thought as they threaded through a clot of bodies to reach the worn, rust-colored, early-American sofa. En masse, they were certainly scary. And definitely an acquired taste. But as far as he could tell, everyone seemed to accept Grant's and Haley's presence with the equanimity of people accustomed to regularly seeing strangers at their dinner table. Or feeding trough, in this case. And Haley was thoroughly enjoying her status as Cousin for a Day—he'd barely even seen her in the past two hours, except when she'd fly in for a moment now and then to check in, only to immediately fly off again, lost in a jumble of loud, laughing little Vaccaros.

But he could deal with this, he thought. He could definitely deal.

With a sound that was half-groan, half-sigh, another of Mia's brothers—the biggest and scariest-looking of the lot, buzz-cutted, beard-hazed and massive-shouldered—dropped into the armchair across from him. Grant felt a slight flush of embarrassment that he couldn't remember his name.

"Rudy," Mia mumbled around a bite of something. "Two years older than me."

Surprisingly gentle blue eyes, permeated with good humor, met Grant's from a few feet away. "Yeah," he rumbled, grinning, "the one who was *really* pissed with our folks for having a girl instead of finally giving me my very own younger brother to pick on. Hey!" Rudy said, laughing, when Mia's foot shot out to clip him in the thigh.

Before the siblings came to blows, however, a very pretty girl around twelve or so leaned one hip on the arm of Rudy's chair, pilfering a cinnamon-infused chunk of apple. "This is Stacey. My little girl."

"Da-ad!" She whipped long, dark hair over her shoulder and snatched another piece of apple. "I'm not *little,* I'm in the seventh grade!"

Chuckling, Rudy held the plate out of her reach. "Get your own pie!"

"Yours is better," she said, brazenly helping herself to the entire top crust, and it dawned on Grant how young Rudy must have been when the kid was born. And that, as far as he could tell, there was no mother in evidence.

Licking her fingers, Stacey said to Grant, "Your little girl is like, so adorable!" Then she frowned slightly. "She said her mother's dead?"

"Geez, Stace—"

"No, it's okay," Grant reassured Rudy, then nodded. "Yes, Haley's mother died in September. But we'd been divorced more than a year by that point."

"So *that's* how come you're here with Aunt Mia, huh?" she said, and beside him, Mia nearly choked.

"Stace!"

"Oh, come on, Dad—it's not like everybody isn't dying to know, anyway."

Mia recovered enough to get out, "No diplomatic career for you, boy," then added, at Stacey's "Huh?" expression, "Haley's mom and I were good friends—"

"And Mia's been a huge help the last couple of months," Grant put in. Patting Mia's knee. Ignoring her glare.

The young girl looked from one to the other, then snatched

another apple slice from her father's plate. "Well, I don't care what anybody else says, *I* think you're nice." Then she flounced off, as, groaning, Mia collapsed back into the sofa.

"Is that what I have to look forward to?" Grant asked, and Rudy chuckled.

"Can't *tell* you how much I'm looking forward to her teens. Man…it's been a bear, doing this by myself. Raising a kid, I mean."

"The whole time?" Grant carefully prodded.

"Pretty much. Stace's mother was only eighteen when she was born, I was barely twenty. She walked out when Stace was six months old, and that's all she wrote. Of course, Stace has always had my mother—and once my brothers started getting married, her aunts—but it's not the same. I mean, she says she's cool with things the way they are, but sometimes, I wonder." He took another bite of pie. "And sure hope she remembers that when we move—"

"Move?" Mia said, just as Kevin appeared—with a plate of gravy-drenched seconds—to motion Mia to move closer to Grant so he could sit down. Close enough for their thighs to touch. She stiffened. Grant tried not to grin *too* hard.

"I finally found a place," Rudy was saying, his eyes sparkling. "A small inn up north, coupla hours from here. The widow who owned it died, her daughter couldn't wait to unload it. Except she didn't want to pay to fix it up, so it wasn't moving. I made this ridiculously lowball offer and she accepted. Closing's next month, so we can move during winter break."

"Oh, wow," Mia said, chewing. Resting his empty plate on one knee, Grant stretched his arm along the back of the sofa, behind Mia's neck, knowing damn well she couldn't say or do anything and not draw attention to herself.

"Let me guess," Kevin said. "You haven't told the folks yet."

"Are you kidding? Pop is going to have a cow. So's Ma."

"They'll get over it," Mia and Kevin said at the same time, Mia adding, as she leaned forward to touch his knee, "It's about damn time you get a place of your own. Not to mention a *life* of your own."

"You're tellin' me." He glanced around, then said to Grant, "I hate bein' a cop. But it's what all of us boys did, so…" He shrugged. "So, yeah. This feels good. It's also gonna be nice to be able to make my own decisions about how to raise Stace without five million opinions."

"How's *she* feel about the move?" Mia asked.

Rudy flushed. "I haven't told her yet, either."

"*What?* Rudy!"

"Oh, unknot your panties, the deal just went through yesterday. I'll tell her tonight—"

Mia signaled her brother to hush, presumably because their father had just come up behind him. One of the tinier Vaccaros perched on one arm, the older man clapped his free hand on Rudy's shoulder, then grinned at Grant through his full beard. A more perfect Jolly Old St. Nick, you couldn't find, the Robert De Niro aura notwithstanding. He even wore suspenders over his plaid shirt to heighten the effect. "You get enough to eat, Grant? Don't want you goin' away hungry, now."

"Honestly, Pops," Mia started, but Grant said, "I certainly did, Mr. Vaccaro—"

"Please. Benny." Oblivious to the baby in his arms poking tiny, undoubtedly food-caked fingers in his beard, Benny's smile slid to his youngest son. "This is so great, havin' all my kids together again. You just got the one, right?" he directed to Grant. "The little Shirley Temple with all the curls?"

"Yes, she's mine."

"The kids, they're the ones who know what it's all about. Isn't that right, sweetheart?" Benny said to the tiny girl, who nodded with enthusiastic adoration.

"So when do you have to be at the mall tomorrow?" Mia asked as Benny set the child down to go find her cousins.

"Not until nine, thank God. Santa doesn't have to show up at five a.m. like the rest of the suckers."

"You play Santa?" Grant asked.

"Ever since I retired, yeah. Five years ago. I did it as a lark one year for some police shindig, and getting swarmed by all those kids…" His belly actually jiggled when he laughed. "I was hooked. And I don't suppose it hurts that I bring in a little extra cash so I can keep this pretty lady—" he snagged Mia's mother as she walked by, hauling her against his side for a one-armed hug "—in all those fancy shoes she likes so much."

"Is true," she said in her husky, and thoroughly charming, East European accent. The woman had to be at least sixty, but between her showgirl makeup and Marie-Antoinette hair, she wasn't going down without a fight. "I *love* shoes," she said. "Especially with ze high heels. Because I hef such short legs, you know? In ze circus, I hed to perform barefoot, my femily used to joke I could valk underneath ze elephant vithout stooping ofer."

Grant blinked. "You were in the circus?"

She grinned. "I vas. Until some big, strong policeman shows up efter one show vis flowers, begs me to go out vis him. At least, this is vat my brother said, my English vas not so good then. I vas horrified! *No, no, no,* I say—" she looked fondly at Benny, before turning back to Grant "—but vill he give up? No! He even tries to learn Hungarian so ve can go on date. I do not even finish high school, but my baby girl, she is smart enough to become a lawyer—"

"Hey, Ma, Pops!" one of the others called from the next room. "You gotta come see this!"

"That was close," Kevin said, finishing off his last bite of stuffing after Benny tugged Magda away, and Mia grunted her agreement.

Rudy stretched and linked his hands behind his head, weight-lifter muscles bulging underneath his sweatshirt. "At least when the you-know-what hits the fan about my move, I can take solace that the two of you have been there before me."

"Still," Grant said, watching the older Vaccaros roar with laughter over one of their grandkid's latest antics in the next room, "you have to admit they're great parents."

"Easy for you to say," Mia said. "Pops never let us get away with *anything*."

"Oh, come on," Grant said, grinning. "Santa Claus? Mean?"

"Santa, hell," Kevin said. "More like Attila the Hun."

"Boy, is that the truth," Mia said, relaxing back into the sofa again. Not even flinching when her head landed on Grant's forearm. "And he took that whole naughty-or-nice thing *way* too seriously." But then she rolled her head to the side and met Grant's gaze and he could tell she understood exactly what he wasn't saying.

"It's not that we don't appreciate them," she said, more softly. "They *are* great, even if what they want for us and what we want for ourselves doesn't always mesh. I mean, listening to Pops talk about playing Santa…" She shook her head. "It breaks his heart, when a little kid comes in all by himself, asking 'Santa' for things he knows they'll never get—"

"Or worse," Rudy said, "when what they want *is* a parent. Somebody they don't have to leave in six months or a year."

"Oh, God…." Mia's voice lowered to a whisper. "Do you remember when that little boy asked Santa to make his stepdad stop hitting him? My chest hurt for days after he told us that."

"What did he do?" Grant said, his own chest not feeling so good right then.

"Since he couldn't exactly get up and go call child welfare services, he tried to convince the kid to tell somebody who could help him, like his teacher. Right after that, though, Pops joined this organization that works with abuse victims. Turns out he's a great fund-raiser. Except with heating-oil prices the way they've been, it's been harder and harder to get what they need—"

"Mia, Mia!" Haley popped into view, grabbing Mia's hand to tug her off the sofa. "Nobody'll go up into the tree house with me, will you come, pleeease?"

One hand on her obviously full tummy, Mia groaned. "Oh, sweetie—"

"Pleeease?" Haley said, wrapping her hands around Mia's neck, nose-to-nose, and Mia laughed, cupping the little girl's cheeks. "How can I resist this cute little face? How? Okay," she said, letting the little girl haul her to her feet. "But you might have to push me up the ladder…"

As Grant watched them go, Rudy said, "Don't do what I did."

His gaze swung back to the other man's. "Pardon?"

One side of Rudy's mouth turned up. "Take it from someone who's been there—the excuses are a bitch. Every year, it's been something, why the time wasn't right to start a new relationship. Then one day I turn around and damn, the kid's twelve years old, it's always only been the two of us, how the hell could I introduce a third party into the mix now? So I'm telling ya, don't wait for some 'perfect' time, because there's no such thing. You just gotta go for it, man. While she's little. Before it's too late."

Grant smiled. "I know," he said softly, then stood, scanning the sea of heads for Mia's father.

One very frigid hour later, Mia convinced Haley to abandon the tree house for the much warmer house on the other side of the yard. "And anyway," she said as they trooped across the dry grass, "we need to get going soon."

"Awww...do we hafta?"

"Yes, we hafta. As it is, it'll be way past your bedtime by the time we get back."

"C'n I play with Brandi and them for just a little while longer? Please?"

"A few more minutes," Mia said as they entered the unheated, enclosed back porch that served as a combination laundry and mudroom. "Your dad or I will come find you when we're ready to go."

That is, Mia thought as Haley took off to find *The Vaccaros: The Next Generation,* providing she could locate said dad. Or, come to think of it, the brother who'd come with her.

She walked into the kitchen to find her father, all alone, standing in front of the decimated turkey carcass with what was left of a wing in his hand and a very satisfied look on his face. "Hey, Pops—you seen either Kevin or Grant?"

"Yes to both," he said, then waved the mangled wing at a vacant kitchen chair across from him. "Sit. I want to talk to you."

"Whatever it was, I didn't do it."

Pops chuckled. "Sit, anyway." When she did—suspicion running amok in her brain—her father wiped his hands on a napkin, then folded his arms over his belly. "First, Kevin's not going back with you. He's decided to hang around here for a while, probably through Christmas."

"You're kidding?"

"I know, you coulda knocked me over with a feather, too." Then he frowned, not looking much like Santa anymore. "Then I'm gathering he's goin' with Rudy when he and Stacey leave."

"Oh. So…Rudy told you?"

"Your brother didn't tell me squat, I overheard 'em makin' plans. So you knew? About this inn or whatever it is Rudy's bought?"

"I just found out today, I swear. But don't you dare come down on him, this is something he wants to do and—"

"And he hated bein' a cop. I know." Shaking his head, her father unfolded his arms to stick his hands in his pockets before looking at Mia from underneath hooded lids. "You, Kev, Rudy…all of you, you just gotta march to your own drummers, doncha?"

"Yeah. We do. But that doesn't mean we don't love you and Ma. Or respect you—"

"Your mother, she took a boatload of flack from her family when she told them she was leaving the circus. To marry an *Italian,* no less. A *stranger.* She walked away from everything she'd ever known, took a huge risk, trusted me not to let her down…" He cleared his throat. "That took guts. Far more guts than I ever had, that's for sure. Yeah, I was a cop, but right in the same town I grew up in. Big deal, right? Now I see the three of you, and I'm thinking how much like your mother you all are. Even if she's forgotten about that gutsy young woman she usedta be. So you guys, you go do what you've gotta do. Long as you make me proud, okay?"

Tears stinging her eyes, Mia nodded. "Deal." But when she started to get up, he said, "Not so fast, I'm not finished with you yet. So this young man of yours—"

"What is this, high school?"

"Whatever. Anyway, he comes to me a little while ago, says he heard about how donations are way down for the program. Asks me how much we need." Her father reached into his shirt pocket and pulled out a check, and Mia nearly choked. "Yeah, that was pretty much my reaction, too. Especially since that's twice as much as I told him we were short. I know you said he was well-off, but…" Her father shook his head. "You wouldn't think, somebody that rich, he'd fit in as good as he did. He really seemed to be enjoying himself. His kid, too."

"Despite my best efforts to convince him how insane we all were."

That got a big laugh, following by one of those wise-Daddy faces a daughter both loves and dreads. "You know, your mother and me only met that guy you were gonna marry a coupla times. Your mother got one of her weird feelings about him, and I just plain couldn't stand the guy. So we weren't nearly as upset as you were when he cut bait and ran. This Grant, however…we both like him. I'm just sayin'," he said when she started to protest. "Not that I'd dream of telling you what to do—" she rolled her eyes "—but maybe you should pay more attention to the way he looks at you."

"Geez, Pops—did he ask for my hand, what?"

"For that much money? I'd tie you up, toss you in a sack and dump you on the man's doorstep."

"Good to know," Mia said over her father's chuckle,

then went looking for the man who'd just won her father's stamp of approval.

Which, oddly, wasn't sitting nearly as badly as she might have expected.

In borderline desperation, she searched—with the Lab's eager help—both the front and back yards, until the dog planted his big yellow paws on the elm's trunk out back and barked up at the tree house. Mia squinted, trying to pick out man from shadow. "Grant?"

"It really is nice up here," floated down. Wistfully.

"Yeah, until the butt-frost sets in. I just spent an hour up there with your daughter, remember?"

"I never had a tree house," he said, even more wistfully, and she thought, *Oh, hell,* and climbed back up. There was just enough light to see that his expression was even dopier than the wistful voice. Damn.

"Escaped, did you?" she said.

"Just needed some air," Grant said, looking up at her with a funny little smile. He patted the space beside him. "Sit. Look at the stars with me."

"It's cloudy; there aren't any stars."

"Imagine them, then," he said, and she sat, and he looped one arm around her shoulders and tugged her close, and he smelled like everything you want your man to smell like, and she sagged against him, too tired to fight whatever this was anymore, finally accepting that the inevitable madness at the end of this particular path couldn't be any worse than the inevitable misery of refusing to go down it. "Now," he said. "Can't you see the stars?"

"No," she said, and he sighed. Then she said, "Did it ever occur to you we might have been setting you up for a major con?"

"A con— Ah. I gather your father told you about my contribution?"

"Told me? You'd've thought you'd offered two goats and a hut for my hand. Well?"

"As it happens, we agreed that I'd postdate the check, so I could run it by my attorney and accountant. But no. I didn't. He wasn't supposed to tell *you*, though."

"As I said. Two goats and a hut."

Grant chuckled into her hair, and her hoo-hah went whoo-hoo, so, to distract the little bugger, she said, "By the way, Kev's not coming back with us."

"I know," Grant said, in that way that puts a woman who survived five brothers on instant alert, and she twisted out of his arms to gawk at him. "Okay," he said, "when he asked if he could toss his gear into the trunk, I kind of figured it out. But I don't think he'd made up his mind until after he got here."

"You might have warned me."

Now he shrugged. "If Kevin had wanted to let us in on what he was thinking, he would have. Since he didn't, what was there to tell?" As she chewed this over, Grant sidetracked her by saying, "I really like your family."

"That's the tryptophan talking," she said.

"I'm serious."

"So'm I." She laid a hand on his chest, and he covered it with his own, and it felt really weird and really right all at once. "I know you've got family issues, but this ain't Norman Rockwell time, either, believe me. We fight too much, over stupid stuff. Some of us drink too much. And we all get up each other's noses about things that are none of each other's business."

"And you want what your parents have so badly it hurts." In the void left by Mia's sudden inability to speak, Grant said, very softly, "I know what it is, to bad-mouth the very thing you really want. And why. And anyway, as someone raised by a pair of androids, I'd say your family's *humanness* is a huge improvement. They *care,* Mia. That trumps some impossible ideal of perfection any day." He pulled her close again. "So I repeat…I like them."

"So do I," she said. "But I like them more with at least fifty miles between us."

His soft laugh warmed her temple as he gently stroked her shoulder through her jacket. "Your mother was really in the circus?"

"She really was. The Beautiful Miss Magda, that was her, performing her death-defying aerial act three performances a day, thirty feet in the air. Pops was a rookie cop working what passed for security back then. It was love at first split." Then she got quiet, thinking about everything her father said, about the huge risk her mother had taken, about how she'd trusted him. Not that her mother hadn't already regaled her countless times about how she'd trusted what she'd seen in Mia's father's eyes, that he'd keep her safe, that he'd never hurt her.

"I've never been to the circus, either," Grant said.

She slapped his chest. "Get out! Never?"

"Can you see my mother at the circus?"

"Point taken," she said, snuggling closer.

"You know what else I've never done?" he said, and she expected him to say something kinky, like "Make love in a tree house," but just as she braced herself he said, "Sat with my arm around a girl, just enjoying the moment," and he sounded both so sad and so content that this huge lump rose in her throat and she thought if she didn't kiss him that very instant, she'd die.

When she lifted her face, however, apparently he was thinking much the same thing because his hand curved around the back of her neck, warm and firm against her skin, and whatever lingering thoughts she might have entertained about his being cold scattered to the four winds the moment their mouths touched.

Touched, hell, try *blended,* because that's what was going on here, that fitting-together-perfectly thing that rarely ever happened in real life because, frankly, most men didn't have a clue. And she thought, as their mouths opened so their tongues could get acquainted and all manner of *delicioso* tingles Gene Kellyed over her skin, that maybe, under certain circumstances—like, say, this one—control's not such a bad thing. Especially not when exerted by a man who actually *knows what he's doing,* who's somehow figured out that masculinity and gentleness were not mutually exclusive concepts.

"Ummm," she said when they finally pulled apart. She scraped her fingertips over his scratchy cheek. "I'm guessing we don't hate each other anymore?"

"No," he said, chuckling and kissed her again, and if the tree house had had windows, they would have started to fog up, because some things you don't realize how much you miss until faced with the prospect of maybe having them again, especially when Grant's hand deftly slid underneath her coat and sweater, clearly contemplating more than caressing her bare back.

So she moaned into his mouth, hoping he'd take the hint, almost weeping with joy when he unhooked her bra one-handed, palming one breast before it even had a chance to bounce.

"Okay," she whispered, panting slightly. "I've got one

for you—I've never…gotten turned on in a tree house before."

She'd almost said "fallen in love," but for once her brain's filter was working and the words sounded lame, or precipitous, or silly, or something. But this…this was lovely, the kissing and the touching—oh, *yes*, the touching, she thought, smiling, as his thumb gently teased her nipple—the chill of the breeze keeping them from combusting and setting the poor tree house on fire. Then she stilled, savoring, touching her forehead to his as he continued to torment her poor nipple, back and forth, back and forth, feeling the delicious ache build between her legs.

And build.

And build.

And—

Okay, so maybe she was a bit more ready than she'd realized.

"Did you know," she said, an inch away from gasping, "that some women can climax just from…th-this?"

"Yes," he said, and he lifted her to her knees so he could suckle her, hard, then harder still, and her fingers tangled in his hair, as the sweet suction changed to something even sweeter, even more amazing, and damned if a second later she didn't see those stars after all. Galaxies previously undiscovered, in fact.

"Well," Mia said, sometime later, after she'd regained faculty for speech and Grant had tugged her sweater back down over her breasts so they wouldn't fast-freeze. "I sure as hell didn't expect *that* to be on the menu today. And you can wipe that smug look off your face."

"Why?" Grant said, grinning like a man who'd just made a woman see stars on a cloudy night. Grinning as she'd never seen him grin before, which made her feel all warm and mushy inside. Yeesh. "Sounds to me as though I gave you something to be very thankful for."

Men, she thought, but she didn't slug him because for one thing, it was true, she was very, *very* thankful, and for another, she didn't want to mess up her chances of it happening again. Because solitaire is fine, as far as it goes, but there's a lot to be said to have somebody else's hand to play against.

"By the way," he said, pulling her against his side again, "I never hated you. I thought you were weird, maybe, but I never hated you."

"Oh, and now you don't? Think I'm weird?"

"One can learn to love weird."

Silence.

Followed by more silence.

"That wasn't just a figure of speech, was it?" Mia finally said.

"No," Grant said, kissing her temple. "And *I* can't even blame it on post-orgasmic glow."

She slugged him. Not hard. "Jerk."

He laughed. *Really* laughed. And the more he laughed, the more the tightly woven little cage she'd kept her heart in for more than a year crumbled away....

"Daddy?"

After jumping at least five feet, Mia's hands flew around to her back, clumsily trying to rehook her bra. Grant, however, calmly stood and looked over the rail at his daughter. "Yeah, honey?"

"S'Mia up there with you?"

"She is."

"Whatcha doing?"

"Just hanging out," he said, dodging Mia's kick to the back of his foot. "You ready to go home now?"

"Yeah. Everybody's leaving, anyway. Mia?"

"Uh-huh?" Having given up the bra rehooking as a lost cause, she scrambled to her feet, too, extremely grateful for the darkness.

"C'n we come back sometime?"

"Sure, baby. Why don't you go find Benny and Magda, tell them we're about to leave?"

"'Kay," she said and scampered off. But before Mia could turn to climb down the ladder, Grant pulled her into his arms again and kissed the stuffing out of her. When she whimpered, he said, "Hold that thought," and she damn near *fell* out of the tree house.

Chapter Twelve

Integrity could be a real bitch, Grant mused several days later, hitching himself up on his elbow to wake a softly snoring, and very naked, Mia beside him. Because doing the right thing wasn't always as cut-and-dried as the world might have you believe. In some cases, *many* cases, the line between being honest and being kind was too blurred to call.

In response to his caress—on her shoulder, a relatively safe spot—she stirred, then burrowed deeper underneath the down comforter. Her obvious unwillingness to leave provoked, as it always did, the thrill of satisfaction—if not awe—that came from realizing she wanted not just him, but to be *with* him. However, they'd both agreed it was probably better that Haley not find her in his bed. Not yet.

"It's nearly four," he murmured, moving aside the covers to place a kiss on that same shoulder.

"What it is, is cold," Mia said, yanking the edge of the comforter out of his hand and back over her head.

Only to immediately thread a long, smooth, warm, wicked leg over his, chuckling when her knee made contact with his erection. "Oh, yeah," he heard from under the covers. "I can tell, you really want me to leave."

"Hussy," he murmured, pulling her on top of him, her sex-tangled hair curtaining them both when she buried her face in the crook of his neck, her cold-hardened nipples pressing into his chest. She never wore perfume, but she smelled of shampoo and sex and him and fireplace smoke and something indefinable that made his heart feel too tight for his chest.

"Got a problem with that?" she whispered in his ear, and he gave up, gave in, letting his hands slide down her back to cup her soft, cushiony backside.

"What do you think?" he said a split second before their mouths met, even as *tell her, tell her, tell her!* clanged louder and louder inside his head.

"Don't go away," she murmured, getting up and padding into the bathroom, far too conscientious to let a little thing like lust deter her from properly replenishing her birth control, as Grant stared up at the ceiling, thinking, *And exactly what purpose would it serve?*

What, indeed? The affair was over, had been over since before Justine's death, from what he could discern. It wasn't as if there was anything to warn Mia about at this point, to alert her to potential heartbreak. That had already happened. And as awful as it had been for Grant to discover the truth, he couldn't imagine Mia's reaction to it. Not that she couldn't handle it—of course she could *handle* it, the woman could probably *handle* anything—but why put somebody through that kind of unnecessary pain, to make her relive her agony all over again? Justine had apparently been a good friend, someone Mia could trust—and no, the irony was not lost on him. He liked to think he was Mia's friend, too, as well as—now—her lover. But what kind of friend destroys the memory of another?

"Hey," she whispered, the word a butterfly across his cheek as she climbed back into bed, whipping back the covers to straddle him, the thread of moonlight trickling through the window snagging on her dark, erect nipples. "Thought you were cold?"

"Something tells me I'll warm up soon enough," she said, taking him inside her in as matter-of-factly as she did everything. He watched her face as he filled her, his own tremor of contented anticipation mirrored in her satisfied smile.

Grant slowly, lightly, scored the space between her breasts with the side of his thumb, deliberately avoiding touching her nipples. Turns out her main complaint about sex had been that, like a grilled cheese sandwich, it never lasted long enough.

"A grilled cheese sandwich?" he'd said that first night, not sure whether it was okay to laugh or not.

"Yeah," she'd said, lying in his arms. "Okay, first you have to understand I've got a *serious* thing for grilled cheese sandwiches. You can keep your cheesecake and chocolate, but a perfectly grilled cheese sandwich—in butter, not margarine!—with all that gooey melted cheese…now *that's* heaven. Except it takes like thirty seconds to eat the damn thing, and then it's gone."

"You could always have another grilled cheese sandwich," he'd said, and she said, pointedly, "Yeah, well, that only works if there's more than one slice of cheese. Or at the most, two," and he got it.

So although it was now even later, and they were

supposed to go buy God-knew-what sort of Christmas stuff in barely five hours, he'd do his best to make her grilled cheese sandwich last, letting her savor each lingering bite…and nibble…and taste…and lick…and every time he started to move inside her she shook her head.

"Not yet," she said, her eyes closed, her breathing shallow, controlled, and Grant thought, *I'm going to die,* only he knew he wouldn't because they'd done this a time or six before and he hadn't died yet, not in the literal sense, anyway. Then her eyes opened and their gazes locked, even more than their bodies, and a rush of amazement swept through him, bittersweet and a little frightening, that she trusted him enough to let him be inside her, *see* inside her, the first man to do that since—

You have to tell her, you have to, you have to, you have to…

His heart aching, he reached over to stroke where they were joined, and she bit her lip, fighting so hard not to let go. Not yet. But he saw, and smiled, and fingered her again, shouldering aside his conscience in the name of giving her everything she'd never had before, praying it would be enough.

"Not. Yet," she said, grimacing, her breathing betraying her, and he said, "Yes. Now," and thrust, and she gave up, gave in, gave back. Gave him…everything.

Everything.

Except she left the bed almost immediately afterward, grabbing his discarded Oxford shirt off the chair and shrugging into it as she moved toward the window.

"It's starting to snow," she said softly, and Grant could practically feel the room tilt from the shift in the relationship. He got up and came to stand behind her, wrapping her in his arms. After a slight pause, she leaned into him, his own shirt rough-soft against his chilled, damp skin.

He released a breath. "So you're not angry?"

"About what? Oh. You, uh, winning that round? No," she said, the word almost a laugh. Shaking her head, she scrubbed the heel of her hand over his forearm. "No."

He paused. "Afraid I'll break your heart, then?"

"You could, you know."

"But I won't. Not if I can help it."

"You wouldn't mean to, no."

Pressing his cheek to her temple, he murmured, "I don't want you to go."

"We agreed, I shouldn't stay overnight—"

"I don't mean that. After the New Year."

Grant could hear the snow barely ticking against the glass. Finally, Mia said, "I already promised to take the apartment. I can't back out now."

"Sure you can. How hard can it be to find someone to babysit a garden apartment in the West Village? Hell, if push comes to shove, I'll *pay* somebody to watch the damn thing for the year."

"Because money solves everything, doesn't it?"

Outside, the snow fluttered aimlessly, like tiny, confused insects, glittering in the lights along the path leading to the guesthouse. "Obviously not everything," he said, nestling his chin on her shoulder. "But it definitely has its uses."

She laughed softly, then set free another sigh. "I have to be completely honest with you, Grant. I'm a thirty-year-old woman who really isn't interested in a dead-end affair. So if—"

"Neither am I," he said, cutting her off. "At least, I'm not interested in a dead-end affair with *you*."

Several beats passed before she said, "And you want a mother for Haley."

"Only if it's you."

He could hear her breathing, feel her heart beat. "You've changed your mind?"

"About marrying for the wrong reasons? No."

She seemed to take a moment to absorb this, then said, "I shouldn't trust you, you know. Especially considering my track record."

"But you do. Trust me, I mean."

Another pause, the longest one yet. "I *love* you," she said, and electricity shot through him, followed by a second, more potent jolt when she added, "And you've certainly never given me a reason *not* to trust you."

"But…?" When she shrugged, Grant's hold tightened. "You're still scared."

"I'm sorry," she whispered.

The uncharacteristic insecurity in her voice burned a hole in his chest. Asking why, or what happened to change her mind, would be pointless. So instead Grant combed her tangled hair off her face with one hand, the other dipping inside the unbuttoned shirt to cover her breast, the gesture as protective as it was possessive. "I won't hurt you, Mia. I swear. I also swear I'm not in this just for the sex."

"Your hand on my breast notwithstanding."

"You know the truly wonderful thing about your breasts? They're attached to *you*."

On another soft, almost sad laugh, she twisted to snake her arms around his waist, and Grant wondered why he'd never noticed before how simple and wonderful and good and right it could be, to simply stand pressed together, naked-to-naked.

"The thing is," she said, her eyes searching his, "I've trusted before, and…" She shrugged.

"Christopher?"

"Yeah. He seemed so…normal. Safe."

"Hate to point out the obvious, but I'm not Christopher."

"Yeah. I noticed."

Grant gently stroked her back under the shirt. "So why didn't you ask him? Why he broke up with you?"

"Because what would have been the point? It was finished. Why poke around in the wound for answers I couldn't have done anything with, anyway? Chewing over the past...not my thing. Sure, the pain hung on for a while, but once I'm over something, I'm over it."

"You're sure about that?"

"Positive." Her fingertips traced his jaw. "I don't look back, Grant," she whispered. "Ever. Sometimes, maybe it's just better not to know, right?"

Was this his absolution, unwittingly given though it may have been? That she wouldn't *want* to know about Christopher and Justine? If so, then why didn't he feel more relieved?

Apparently misreading his silence for censure, Mia gave him a quick, meant-to-lighten-the-moment squeeze. "Hey, I'm the bizarre, aggravating, weird chick, remember? I never promised you logical."

She moved away then to finish dressing—she never bothered putting her underwear back on to trek back to the other house. Practical for her, incredibly erotic for him. Grant grabbed his robe from the back of the bathroom door as, one hand braced on the wall, Mia tugged on one of those hideous boots that looked like something a Sherpa would wear.

"Do you think Christopher had a problem with your going into business? Some men do," he said when she frowned in his direction.

"I don't know," she said, shifting to yank on the second boot. "Although he'd been my biggest supporter, at the start." Instead of replacing his shirt with her own sweater, she buttoned it up, her breasts shifting underneath the fabric. "He and Jus, both."

Grant's hands stilled on his robe sash. "So they knew each other? Aside from dinner here that one time, I mean?"

"No, not really," she said, frowning, and Grant realized he'd had no reason to link their two exes simply because they'd both supported her career move. Apparently not picking up on his gaffe, however, she then said, "My attempts at getting them to be friends bombed, big-time. Generally not a good idea to put a defense attorney and an assistant D.A. in the same room. All they did was argue. I could tell Justine was just as glad when he dumped me. Still, it stung, realizing I'd fallen in love with an illusion."

"You're hardly the first person to do that."

"I know, but…" Mia walked back to him, slipping the fingers of one hand behind the sash's knot. "The problem is, with a few notable exceptions, I've trusted the wrong people all my life."

"Those exceptions being?"

She smiled. "My parents. *Most* of my brothers. Venus. Justine. Please don't make a face, Grant…I know she wasn't perfect. I do. She was driven to a fault and did not take kindly to being thwarted. And yes, she married you under false pretenses. *Her* pretenses, not yours. But I never knew her to be disloyal. Not to me, at least. And certainly never to Haley."

"No," Grant said, the truth lodging at the base of his throat. "Never to Haley."

He caught the barest flash of curiosity in her eyes before she patted his chest and whispered, "And if I don't go now, I won't."

Grant followed her as she crossed the room, the trapped words searing his throat as he watched her cautiously open the door, peer down the hallway. He grabbed her hand, a slight frown marring her brow when she faced him. "So tell me…am I one of the wrong people, or one of the exceptions?"

Instead of answering, she smiled slightly, then pointed at him. "Ten a.m. sharp, my place. Bring Haley and credit card, leave good sense—and taste—at home. Home Depot ain't gonna know what hit 'em!" Then, grinning, she disappeared.

But when Grant returned to bed—the jumbled sheets infused with Mia's scent and presence and insanity—he realized he had no idea what had hit him, either.

Or that being clobbered could feel so damn good.

Thonk! Thonk! Thonk!

Mia pried open one eye and glared at her clock: seven-thirty. "Fuggedaboutit," she muttered, rolling over.

THONK! THONK! THONK!

Muttering many naughty words, she threw back the covers and snagged her robe off the chair, pinballing off the walls as she tromped down the short hall to answer the door. "Swear to God, Kev," she muttered, "if this is you finding your way back like a lost dog…"

However, when she threw open the door, there was Haley, still in her pajamas and the goofiest bunny rabbit slippers ever—provoking an instant, bittersweet memory of Justine's laughter, the spark of delight in her eyes, when she'd spotted the slippers in a children's store on Madison Avenue—precariously balanced on an upended flowerpot so she could reach the knocker.

"For heaven's sake, Haley!" In one move, Mia snatched the child off her perch and whisked her inside before she either fell off or froze to death. Although the snow had barely frosted the grass and trees, the meat-locker effect left a lot to be desired. "What on earth are you doing here?"

she asked, slamming the door shut with her foot since her arms were full of shivering little girl.

"I w-wanted to m-m-make sure you were up. So we c'n go get the tree and stuff. C'n we get one of those really, really *big* Santas that's as tall as the house?"

"You're on," Mia said, imagining the look on Grant's face. Not to mention his mother's. Was this going to be the best Christmas ever or what? Then she caught sight of their reflections in the mirror by the front door, each of them more wild-haired than the next—a look only cute on a four-year-old—and her good mood deflated like one of those house-sized Santas.

Haley twisted to look up at her. "An' c-c'n you help me write a letter to S-Santa?"

"Uh, sure," she said, doing more whisking—no sense depressing herself any more than necessary—this time to the kitchen, where coffee, or in Haley's case, hot choco-late, awaited. She plunked the little girl down in one of the kitchen chairs, wrapped the vibrating child up in the throw until nothing showed but two pink cheeks and a small, red nose. Then she tromped over to the refrigerator for coffee and milk, punching on the radio along the way. *"Jingle Bell Rock!" Yes!* "Does anybody know you're over here?"

Curls sproinged out from the top of the throw, vigor-ously bouncing from side to side. Great. Mia grabbed her cell phone and punched in Grant's number, just as Haley said, "How come you're wearing Daddy's shirt?"

She was staring at Haley, willing brain and tongue to work with each other, when "Please tell me you've got her!" blasted in her ear.

"Yes, she's here, she's fine, we're having breakfast, then we're apparently writing a letter to Santa. Then we're all getting dressed and going to *buy* a Santa as big as a house."

"I suppose it's too much to hope that you're kidding?" Grant said as Haley crossed her arms over her chest and said, again, *"How come you're wearing Daddy's shirt?"*

"You're not," Grant said.

"I am," she replied, then smiled for Haley. "I, uh, spilled hot chocolate all over my sweater after you went to bed, so your Daddy lent me his shirt, and then I fell asleep with it on."

"Good save," Grant said, followed by, "For that, you owe me breakfast." Then he hung up, leaving Mia staring at the phone wondering, one, where Etta was and two, how he'd translated *her* save into *his* breakfast.

Thinking, *Men are so strange,* she resumed her coffee and hot chocolate-making, realizing she was now committed to more than sticking a Pop-Tart in the toaster. Happy, happy. "Your daddy's coming over to have breakfast with us," she said, rummaging through the fridge for she-knew-not-what. Eggs, maybe. Past that, it was anybody's guess.

"But I don't want him to see my letter to Santa!"

Funny, how she'd resisted accepting heaven as real—or Humpty Dumpty—but she'd bought in to the whole Santa thing without a second's hesitation. "Why? You planning on asking for a car?" Then Mia's blood ran cold: *Oh, God, please don't let her ask for her mother back.*

More curl bobbing. "Uh-uh. A fam'ly. Like yours."

Mia's heart had no sooner resumed beating when Haley's words stopped it cold. Again. That couldn't be good. "What do you mean, a family like mine?"

"Where there's more people than house. So I wouldn't get lonely."

"You get lonely?" she said over the sharp, all-too-familiar pang.

"It's too quiet. My toys don't talk to me."

And thank God for that, Mia thought, clicking on the

coffeemaker. "Take it from somebody who would have killed to have some space to myself growing up," she said as she poured milk into a mug, then set it in the microwave to nuke, "all those people around…it gets old fast."

"Huh?"

"I mean, sure, it's fun on holidays—well, sometimes—but day in, day out?" She shook her head. "You know what it's like when you're on the subway or the bus and there's no place to sit because there are too many people? Now imagine living like that all the time."

"We always took taxis."

Of course. "Whatever. Anyway, trust me. You've got it pretty good."

Except even as the words spilled out of her mouth, she thought of the ones that had spilled out of Grant's the week before, about her bad-mouthing the very thing she most wanted. And okay, so maybe there was a reason Mia had avoided being alone in her apartment, why she'd so readily accepted Grant's invitations to join them for dinner. Why the prospect of moving back to the city—and into another apartment by herself—wasn't exactly thrilling her to her toes.

Why the idea of being able to legitimately wake up in Grant's bed every morning, maybe with Haley snuggled between them, was sounding alarmingly more appealing by the second.

The microwave beeped. Mia retrieved the hot milk, stirred in two tablespoons of Nesquick and handed it to the little girl, who frowned at it.

"I like mushmellows in mine."

"Sorry, kiddo, fresh out. Buuuut…" Mia stuck her head back in the fridge and pulled out a can of whipped cream. "Ta-da!"

Haley grinned. Mia topped the kid's hot chocolate with

the Mount Everest of whipped cream; a minute later, however, her nose whipped-cream-frothed, Haley sank back into serious mode. "Could I at least ask Santa for a *couple* more people in my family?"

Thinking maybe they should make this a joint letter, Mia brought her cup of coffee to the table and sat down. "Got anybody specific in mind?"

Haley shook her head. "I can't say, else it might not come true. But Santa will know," she added with an emphatic nod.

"Ah. Would this be the same thing you couldn't tell us when you blew out your birthday candles?"

"Uh-huh," she said, then disappeared behind her whipped cream, just as Grant walked in, which is when Mia realized she was still bed-headed and in her robe and his shirt, and that this was not the morning-after of her fantasies.

Until—*hel*-lo!—one smoldering look, stage right, provoked instant recall from every single place on her body he'd touched or kissed or done assorted other things to the night before. Hell, a scant four *hours* before. Yeesh, she half expected the electric charge to interfere with the radio reception.

Grant hadn't shaved yet—or, it would seem, combed his hair—but he was dressed, of course, in black again, or at least in shades of dark brown that might as well have been, cords and another one of his many, many sweaters, and she thought, *What am I thinking, he should wear pastels?* Then he strode over to the table to bring his face within inches of his daughter's, love and anger and relief and fear all mixed together, and Mia's heart did everything but rip itself out of her chest and run over to him, begging him to take it.

"Don't you *ever* disappear like that again!" he said. "You scared me half to death!"

For a second, the child's lower lip trembled, until Grant scooped her out of the chair and hugged her to him, and Mia turned away, stunned to realize her hands were shaking. For weeks, she'd been fighting the truth—that she hadn't been wrong about that first tiny spark of recognition five years ago, that in this case, at least, her intuition had been dead on. Because from the moment Grant made up his mind to heal the breach between him and his daughter, whatever bill of goods he'd bought about who he thought he was, *what* he thought he was, didn't stand a snowball's chance in the face of his child's pure love.

And what was left after all the crap had melted away— the *real* Grant, warm and caring and even funny, when he put his mind to it—Mia knew she could trust.

Even more important, though—she could trust herself.

"Mia?"

She turned. Haley was strangling his neck, repeatedly kissing his cheek. She caught the concern in his eyes. The love. Yes, it was shiny and new and untried, still in its original wrapping. But did that make it any less real?

Mia let out a long, slow breath. "How hard *could* it be to find someone willing to babysit a garden apartment in the West Village?"

Almost instantly, realization—and something deeper, richer, more wonderful—flared in his eyes. "Consider it done," he said.

Smiling, she turned back to the counter to crack four eggs into a glass bowl.

Chapter Thirteen

"I have to admit," Bitsy said as she surveyed Mia's handiwork the day of the charity event, "after seeing what you and Grant did to his house…" She shook her head. "I was worried. But this is gorgeous."

"Thanks," Mia said, tweaking a crystal garland on the nine-foot-tall flocked tree standing majestically in the bay window in Grant's mother's living room. Of course, Haley was absolutely thrilled with the Santa That Ate Greenwich camped out in *her* front yard. Not to mention the Vegas-Strip-worthy lighting display that had taken Mia, Etta and Grant a full day to put up. But poor Bitsy had been duly appalled, comforted only by the fact that since the house was set so far back from the road, virtually no one would see it.

By contrast, Mia had turned Grant's mother's house into the snow scene from the Nutcracker Suite, with yards of frosted silver garlands, dozens of white topiaries and thousands of tiny white lights to coordinate with the soft blue and ivory decor of the main rooms and large foyer.

Oh, yeah—she'd truly outdone herself this time, she thought, inwardly chuckling at the image of the smaller, live tree in Grant's family room, decked with the obligatory red-and-green construction paper garland, the hodgepodge of ornaments Haley had randomly tossed in the Home Depot cart, the four strands of multicolored M&M lights. Neither Justine nor Grant had ever bothered with a tree before, let alone monster Santas, so this year it was all about Haley. Plenty of time in future years to work in other people's druthers.

A future, Mia was beginning to let herself believe, that might even include her. A thought that stole her breath. Could it really be that, for the first time in her life, all the pieces of her life were fitting together? Heck, Grant had even come through with someone to take over the Abrams's apartment. How could she not trust that? Trust *him?*

"Grant tells me he enjoyed Thanksgiving at your parents' house immensely," Bitsy said, looking too-too in a starkly simple tube of silver panne velvet with long sleeves. As usual, her hair was pulled back, her makeup exquisitely done, her only jewelry a pair of diamond studs the size of blueberries. *Large* blueberries.

"He certainly seemed to," Mia said, heading toward the kitchen for a last-minute check, only to flinch slightly when Bitsy, who'd followed, laid a hand on her arm before she reached the door. From inside, Mia could hear Venus barking orders at the catering staff like it was their first day in boot camp.

"I take it you and Grant are…an item?"

She could lie, but what would be the point? "We are. You got a problem with that?"

One narrow eyebrow arched. "Would it make any dif-ference if I did?"

"No," Mia said, then pushed through the kitchen door.

A few minutes later, she headed upstairs to quickly change into her Hotshot Party Planner getup, a little black sheath, pearl earrings and a pair of black pumps left over from her Hotshot Young Attorney days. Basically, though, her part was pretty much done—Bitsy was only hosting the bash, the charity's officers were actually running it. But Mia would stick around to keep an eye on the food and such, staying alert to any opportunity to whip a business card out of her pocket and press into a prospective client's hot little hand.

She was just finishing taming her hair into something less likely to scare people when someone knocked on the guest bedroom door. Before she could say, "Come in," Grant did, all breathtakingly handsome in a dark, pin-striped suit a shade lighter than black, a white dress shirt and a crimson jacquard tie.

"Wow," they said at the same time, then laughed. She rose from the velvet-covered seat fronting the vanity, shi-vering slightly when his hands landed on her waist.

"God, I love your legs," he said, craning his neck to get a better look.

"Uh-huh. This morning it was my—"

"I'm nothing if not adaptable," he said, and kissed her neck, and she pushed him away—reluctantly—and said, "Not while I'm on duty, sorry."

Grinning, he slid his hands into his pants' pockets. "The place looks terrific. Mother is beside herself. And for once, in a good way."

Mia fished in the bottom of her tote bag for the lip gloss she only wore when she was working. "Actually, your mother's beginning to grow on me," she said, slicking it on. She capped the gloss and dropped it back in her bag. "And God knows she's no more bonkers than my family."

Actually, more and more Mia was getting the feeling Bitsy wanted to break out of her pod, if she could only figure out how. What Mia wondered, however, was what had made her crawl into the pod to begin with.

"Mia? Mr. Braeburn?" one of her helpers said at the open door. "Mrs. Braeburn said to tell you the guests have started to arrive?"

"We'll be right there," Mia said. But when she got to the bedroom door, Grant grabbed her hand.

"Grant, I've got to go—"

"I get what you do," he said, all earlier playful leering banished by a look of such sincerity, such tenderness, her heart nearly stopped. "You make people happy. No small talent, that."

Then he kissed her on her forehead and went off to help his mother do the gracious host thing, while Mia launched into facilitator mode, making sure the food table never looked picked over, the waitstaff kept those drinks and nibbles coming, the music never stopped and nobody landed in the tree. On her third or fourth pass around the living room, however, she nearly fell into the tree herself when her gaze snagged on a familiar male back, clad in a navy suit jacket she'd picked out her very own self.

Not six weeks before the wedding-that-never-happened.

"Hell, girl," Venus said, rapidly transferring hot stuffed mushrooms to a Lenox platter when Mia flew through the swinging door into the kitchen, nearly taking out a waitperson in the process. "You look like you just saw a ghost."

"Close. Christopher's here."

Venus let loose an appropriately pithy comment just as Grant's mother appeared. "Mia? Is everything all right?"

"Her dirtwad ex-fiancé's in the other room," Venus supplied, handing the filled platter to one of the servers and moving on to the next tray. She frowned at Mia. "Who's he with?"

"I have no idea, I was too busy having a coronary to notice. Not that I'd probably know who it was, anyway. Oh, God," she said, clutching her stomach. "I think I'm going to be sick." Venus snatched up the nearly filled platter and held it well out of range. "I can't go out there," Mia said, more to herself than anyone else. "I can't…"

"Of course you can't," Bitsy said in a voice that had probably reduced more than one Saks salesgirl to tears. "Venus, you'll have to take over."

"No problem," Venus said, removing the apron she wore over her black top and pants and wiping her hands on a towel. "Although if you've got a really sharp paring knife handy, I could probably find a good use for it while I'm out there. Oh, don't look at me like that," she said to both ladies. "I'd be discreet. He'd never know they were missing until he tried to go pee. Just *kidding*," she said, patting Bitsy's arm. "Anyway, everything seems to be under control here, the next courses are all ready to go." She headed out the door, only to turn back around. "You sure you don't want to give me that knife?"

"No!" both ladies said at once, and Venus vanished. With something like genuine concern in her eyes, Bitsy faced Mia again. "So what happened? In twenty-five words or less."

"He dumped me. Six weeks before our wedding—"

Another server yelped and leaped when Grant burst through the swinging door, in full-out protective mode. Mia held up one hand.

"I know, Christopher's here." Then she thought, *And look at me, acting like the mature adult.* "I just need a moment, but I'll be fine."

Bitsy frowned. "But you just said—"

"Momentary freak-out," she said, smiling bravely. "All good now."

"Who's he with?" Bitsy asked Grant.

"I'm not sure. Some short redhead in blue velvet with an avaricious gleam in her eye." He looked over at Mia. "Not pretty. Not pretty at all. Downright homely, in fact."

In spite of herself, Mia smiled, warmth flooding her at his earnest—if misguided—attempt to make her feel better. He was such a man. And God, how she loved him for it. "News flash, honey—I don't care."

Bitsy sort of groaned, and Mia thought, *Crap.*

"Potty break," she said brightly, and vamoosed, hotfooting it up the back stairs to one of the upstairs bathrooms, only to mutter a bad word when she found it *occupado.* As she stood there, however, two women came up behind her...one of whom was a short redhead in a dark blue velvet dress.

A short, extremely pretty redhead in a dark blue velvet dress.

Nice try, Grant, she thought, only to immediately plan her escape route in case the not-ugly redhead's companion decided to come looking for his date. Then she thought, *No, I'm not some lily-livered wimp. If Christopher shows up, I'll deal—*

"So anyway," the redhead was saying, "the last few weeks haven't exactly been a picnic. I mean, I really thought he was over her—at least, he swore he was—but then she died in that awful car crash and I guess he wasn't as over her as he'd thought. Or admitted, at least."

Every one of Mia's bodily functions came to a sudden, painful halt as the other woman—some tallish, crop-haired blonde with a penchant for noisy jewelry—*tsked*. "How long had they been together, do you know?"

The redhead smirked. "He wasn't exactly open and aboveboard about that, but I did some snooping. Turns out she was still married when they'd started. She had a little girl. A toddler. But after the divorce, she apparently lost interest and broke it off. From what I gathered," she said, somewhat bitterly, "he wasn't exactly happy about it."

Ms. Clanky Bangles *tsked* again. "And what did I tell you about taking on somebody with that much baggage?"

"Oh, please, everybody has baggage. He's straight, passably good in the sack, just bought a house and has damn good political prospects. For all that, I'll deal with a little baggage."

"Somebody told me," the other woman said conspiratorially, "that this is her former mother-in-law's house."

The redhead sounded as though she was choking on her martini olive. "Are you *serious?* Ohmigod! When I told him where the party was, he never said a word—"

About to choke herself, Mia mumbled something incomprehensible and backtracked, her heart about to pound out of her chest—

"Mia!" Grant grabbed her at the bottom of the stairs before she barreled over him, tugging her into the pantry and shutting the door. "What happened?"

"They were having an affair! Christopher and Justine! I just overheard his date and another woman talking about it!" She clapped her hand over her mouth, then lowered it, her stomach dropping at his tortured expression. "Oh, God, Grant—I'm so sorry! I'm not thinking, the shock—"

"It's okay, honey," he said, wrapping her in his arms. "It's okay…"

Okay, something about that "okay" wasn't *okay* at all….

Mia struggled out of Grant's arms, taking a step backward, the harsh, unflattering overhead light in the pantry doing nothing to disguise the truth in his eyes.

"You knew," she said, barely able to get the words out. "You *knew*."

After the longest moment in history, he nodded.

"Mia! Wait!" he said, grabbing for her when she pushed past him to get away. "Stay put, damn it, and let me explain!"

But she slipped out of his grasp and bolted through the door, his shouted curse ringing in her ears as she ran.

Grant finally caught up to her outside, in the gazebo in the middle of the his mother's formal garden. The very spot, in fact, where Grant and Justine had exchanged worthless vows more than five years before.

She was quaking like a Chihuahua. Shrugging out of his jacket, he came up behind her to drop it over her shoulders, clamping her arms to keep both jacket and woman there.

"In that skimpy dress you'll freeze in ten seconds flat."

"As h-hot as I am r-right now?" she said, wriggling free. Although she kept the jacket. "Not bloody likely. So what was the reasoning, Grant? Were you worried that I'd go all hysterical on you if you told me? That it would make you *uncomfortable*? And don't you *dare* tell me I'm overreacting."

"I wouldn't dream of it. And that wasn't the reason."

"Then what?" She swiped at her cheek, then huddled more deeply into his jacket. "I mean, *God*—d-do you have *any* idea how big a fool I feel right now?"

The wind bit through his flimsy shirt, whipped his tie

up and over his shoulder as he crammed his hands into his pockets.

"For what it's worth," he said quietly, "I didn't know Justine was cheating on me for a long time, either. Not until it served her purpose."

Mia's head twitched slightly in his direction. "What do you mean?"

"I guess she figured an affair was her ticket out. Of the marriage."

The wind snatched at Mia's hair; impatiently, she tucked the runaway strand behind her ear, then half turned. Her eyes cut to his, then darted away again. "When did you find out about Christopher?"

"I'm not sure. Much later. After you two were no longer together."

He saw her swallow. "But before Justine's death."

"Yes."

"So you knew, when I came out here to live."

He paused. "Yes."

Now her gaze met his dead-on. "And this mildly important piece of information just, what? Slipped your mind?"

"Hardly," he said on a harsh laugh. "You have no idea how torn up I was, knowing I had to keep this from you—"

"Ex*cuse* me? You *had* to keep it from me? I can't believe you deliberately *chose* not to tell me that my fiancé had been screwing around with my best friend! For crying out loud, Grant, after everything I said about being afraid to trust—"

"No, after what you said about not asking Christopher why he broke it off with you, I honestly thought you wouldn't *want* to know! And what was that about never looking back?" She faced away again. Grant hauled in a breath and tried again. "Mia—I swear to God, you can trust me. I would *never* betray you. But not only was I following *your* lead…think about it. If I'd told you the truth, how would that have made me look?"

"Oh, I see—so this is about how *you* would look!"

"No, damn it! It was about not hurting you! It was about deciding there was no point in destroying your memory of your best friend! Not because of how you'd react, but because I didn't want to cause you pain! Whatever differences and problems Justine and I might have had, she'd clearly been something very real and good for you."

"Except for the cheating with my fiancé thing," she said bitterly.

"And up until you found out about that, you thought the world of her. I wasn't about to take that from you."

"So instead you left me wide open for humiliation?"

The wind howled between them. "Mia, believe me—it kills me that you found out the way you did, that I obviously screwed up. Even if I don't know whether I would have done things differently, given the chance. But it kills me more to know that two people you trusted were too selfish and short-sighted to realize what a precious gift that trust was. And then didn't have the decency to tell you the truth."

"And how does your keeping the truth from me make you any better than them?"

Grant shut his eyes against the sting. "Maybe it doesn't," he said after a moment. "Maybe, in their own convoluted way, Justine and Christopher both thought they were sparing you, as well. But there is a difference between telling a lie to save your own butt, and not telling a truth that would only hurt." When she glared at him, he added softly, "You have no idea how much you mean to me, Mia. How much I owe to you. I know it sounds corny, but you really have made me a new man. And Justine is gone. Whatever she did to either of us…it all died with her. And I suppose I figured if Christopher hadn't come clean by now, he never would. I simply saw no reason to hash over something that had nothing to do with us—"

"How can you say that?" she said, her cheeks streaked silver with her tears. "How do you figure that this has nothing to do with us? You kept a major, major secret from me, Grant. This has nothing to do with not looking back, or why I never felt compelled to ask Christopher what happened. This is about whatever you and I are trying to build together right now. How on earth can I possibly trust you after this?"

"Because I wasn't the one who cheated, Mia," he said in a low voice. "And if you can't see the difference, then we've got a serious problem here."

Hurt and confusion swarmed in her eyes for several seconds before she turned her back on him again. "Yeah. We do," she said sadly. "Please…please, just…leave me alone."

After a long, horrible moment, he did.

"Haley's all ready for bed," Etta said to him when he came in through the kitchen two hours later. "But she fell asleep on the sofa, looking at the tree." Sitting in the breakfast nook thumbing through a magazine, the housekeeper made a big show of trying to see past him, then frowned over her reading glasses. "You lose somebody?"

Grant let out a ragged sigh, sinking onto the chair across from her as he loosened his tie. After he'd filled her in on the night's events—including that Mia had decided to go home with Venus rather than returning to Grant's—Etta shook her head.

"And here I always figured *you* were the one with the serious issues."

Although Mia and Grant had still kept Haley in the dark about their relationship, Etta had been well aware of it for weeks. Partly because they'd made no secret of it, partly because Etta was Etta and would have figured it out, anyway. Now Grant pulled a face. "Do *you* think I screwed up?"

She flicked a page, her mouth thinned, her eyes averted. "I suppose you did what you thought was best. But…"

"But what?"

Her eyes lifted to his. "If you want my opinion, it sounds to me like she took a giant leap of faith, and in her mind, you let her fall."

Glowering, Grant yanked his tie out of his collar. "Got any advice?"

Another page flicked. "Groveling probably wouldn't hurt. Punching the creep in the nose might not be such a bad idea, either."

"Believe me, the thought occurred to me. But I never got the chance. They'd already left by the time I got back inside. Somebody must've told him Mia was there."

"Too bad. Did everything go okay otherwise?"

"Yeah," Grant said, getting to his feet. "The silent auction raised nearly a hundred grand. And mother was beside herself with Mia's work. So at least that." Pressing the tight muscles at the base of his neck, he nodded toward the family room. "Haley's conked out on the sofa, you said?"

"Last I checked, yep. Mr. B.?" He turned. "It's gonna work out, you'll see. Mia's too smart a gal to toss everything into the crapper because of some dumb misunderstanding."

"Yeah, I'm sure you're right," he said. But as he walked back to the family room, he wasn't so sure. Was this simply a "dumb misunderstanding"? A lover's tiff? Or had his severe underestimation of Mia's insecurities led him to commit an unforgivable sin? At least, in her eyes.

He stopped in the family room's wide doorway, his spirits lifting a little at the sight of his very *awake* daughter squatting in front of the outlandishly decorated tree, Henry smashed to her chest.

"Hey, chipmunk. It's way past your bedtime."

"S'okay, Henry 'n' me had a nap. How many sleeps to Christmas again?"

"Six," Grant said, hauling her up into his arms and starting toward the stairs. Haley frowned at him.

"Where's Mia?"

Grant's insides turned over. "She decided to spend the night with Venus."

"How come?"

Because your father's an idiot. "I guess because she thought it would be fun. When you get bigger, you can have friends come spend the night, too."

"Why?"

"Because that's what little girls do?" he said, carrying her into her room and tucking her into bed.

"Oh. Will Mia be back tomorrow?"

"I don't know, baby," Grant said, somehow holding everything in until he'd endured five minutes' worth of hugs and kisses and drinks of water, after which he went outside and kicked the crap out of a twelve-foot-tall Santa.

Chapter Fourteen

"Oh, don't take everything away yet!"

A topiary in each hand, Mia turned at the sound of Bitsy's voice. Damn. The plan had been to get in, get stuff, get out, before Bitsy could snare her. Whole reason she'd arrived at 7:00 a.m. However, coiffed and fully made-up, but still in her nightgown and robe—a nude charmeuse, very fetching, undoubtedly pricey—Grant's mother now swept across her living room, one hand on her chest, the other outstretched in supplication.

"The display place charges by the day," Mia said. "I have to get them back by this afternoon."

"I'll pay the difference. Leave them. Yes, all of them. And come have a cup of coffee with me. We need to talk."

"I don't think so," Mia said, putting back the poodle-ized bushes.

"It wasn't a suggestion, Mia," Bitsy said, and Mia

sighed, then trooped into the large, blindingly sunny kitchen behind the older woman.

More than twelve hours after The Bombshell, the shock—not just of the discovery itself, but of Grant's part in it—not only hadn't worn off, it had burrowed even further into her soul. And damn, it hurt. The kind of hurt one isn't inclined to share. Especially with the mother of the person who caused the hurt.

Bitsy pulled two china cups and saucers down from the cabinet, saying as she poured, "You took off before I could thank you properly last night. You did a fabulous job. Sit," she said, nodding toward a wrought-iron-and-marble table in the eating alcove.

Not meeting Bitsy's gaze, Mia sat. "You're welcome."

"I don't suppose you've talked to Grant yet this morning?"

"I…no."

"Helluva way to find out," Bitsy said sympathetically, lowering the filled cups to the table before settling in at her own seat in a ripple of silk and high-end body lotion.

"I really don't want to talk about this, Bitsy."

"Nonsense. Drink your coffee before it gets cold."

Succumbing to the irresistible force that was Bitsy Braeburn, Mia sipped her coffee, then said, "Did *you* know?"

"About the affair?" The blonde shook her head. "Oh, I knew Justine had been having one—Grant had told me about it some time ago. But not the particulars." She was quiet for a moment, then added, "You deserved better than that. So did my son." Then she sighed. "So did I."

"So did…? I'm sorry—did I miss something?"

Bitsy set her cup down on its saucer, her diamonds flashing in the morning sunlight. "Say what you will, being a trophy wife isn't all a bed of roses. Especially once the initial shine starts to dull. Not that I entirely blame Patrick—as you may have noticed, I'm not exactly the warmest person in the world. But we had an arrangement, when Patrick promised me far more than a life as a glorified bank teller could offer. And I lived up to my side of the bargain. Patrick, on the other hand…" She reached for her coffee again, smiling before the cup reached her lips. "You thought I came from money, didn't you?"

"Um, well…"

"Nope. I was just a plain old Jersey girl. My father worked for the post office, my mother was a receptionist in a doctor's office in Paramus. They're both gone now. I don't think they ever got over it. My marrying up, I mean." She reached over to adjust the blinds, probably thinking, *Keep out of direct sunlight.* "They were here exactly once, for the wedding. They never came back."

"And you're telling me this why?"

Bitsy laughed, a soft, sad sound. "Because even though I'm guessing our backgrounds are similar, our personalities aren't. From everything I've seen, your feet are far too firmly planted on the ground to ever let all this—" she waved one hand to indicate the house and everything it represented "—go to your head. *You* wouldn't let money or position or social standing change you, because you already know who you are. I didn't. The fairy tale isn't likely to suck you in, like it did me. And my former daughter-in-law."

Mia rose to refill her coffee cup. "So…you don't think I'm scum anymore?"

"Oh, don't be so dramatic, I never thought that. Exactly. I just…" Mia turned back to see Bitsy's mouth thinned. "Despite all outward appearances, I do love my son, Mia. Who happens to be very wealthy. And, I'd thought, somewhat naive when it comes to women. Women with…agendas."

One side of Mia's mouth hiked up. "You thought I was a gold digger."

"The possibility was not lost on me. Especially after Grant's last debacle."

"Meaning Justine?" When she nodded, Mia added, "You never got on with her, did you?"

Bitsy snorted softly. "Please. The first time we met, it was like looking into a mirror. I wasn't at all surprised it didn't last. It's a bitch, you know, marrying an illusion. Which is what I suppose I was to Grant's father, why, after an embarrassingly short time, he looked elsewhere for… whatever it was he decided he didn't, or couldn't, have with me." She paused. "I'm sorry, I know Justine was your friend."

"*Was* being the operative word here," Mia muttered over the gouge of pain. "Speaking of illusions. God, it kills me that—"

"What?"

"That knowing the truth negates everything else. You can forgive a friend for blowing off a shopping date, or forgetting your birthday, or even never returning your favorite sweater. But stealing your man? Uh, no."

"So now maybe you understand why Grant didn't want you to find out."

"It wasn't his place to keep it from me."

"Neither was it his place to tell you. No, you listen to me—yes, right now you're upset that he knew and you didn't, but you're really angry with Justine, and that bastard, for lying to you. Not with Grant for wanting to protect you."

"I'm pretty pissed with all of them, if you must know."

"But Justine is dead and Christopher had, for all intents and purposes, fallen off the face of the earth, so Grant was the only one left to bear the brunt of your hurt."

Hating that the woman was probably right, Mia leaned against the counter, her arms tightly folded over her middle. "That still doesn't exonerate Grant."

"Who was hurt far more by Justine's cheating than he let on. Especially since he'd thought he'd been doing everything he was supposed to. Just like I did with his father. In fact, it was only because I'd been there, so I knew the signs, that I had any idea how much pain he was in. One learned to be stoic in Grant's father's presence," she said acerbically. "A habit not easily broken. But not showing emotion doesn't mean it's not there. And as much as Justine's betrayal stung Grant, I imagine Grant felt it would be a hundred times worse for you."

"But—"

"My son loves you, Mia. In a way he never loved Justine. Or anyone else, other than his daughter. I know you feel he betrayed your trust, but trust *me*...whatever he did, however misguided it may have been, his heart was in the right place."

"It's not that simple, Bitsy." Mia saw a crystal platter sitting on the counter from the night before; she snatched a lint-free towel off the counter to buff out imaginary streaks. "When I was a little girl," she said, her voice perilously close to breaking, "my brothers teased me constantly for being so gullible, for believing everything they told me, good or bad, no matter how preposterous. Eventually I smartened up. Somewhat. But not entirely. Even after I'd been through college and law school, I—"

Her nostrils flared as, her voice snagging in her throat, she shook her head, unable to continue.

"You what?" Bitsy said gently.

The now sparkling platter rattled against the counter when Mia set it back down. "My brothers were right, I am gullible. Horrendously. But I just couldn't…" She swiped at an escaped tear trickling down her cheek, then let out a short, rueful laugh. "You know, I always used to pity those sad, embittered cynics who never trust anybody. But these days…I don't know. Sometimes I really, *really* envy people who can shield themselves from getting hurt."

Bitsy almost laughed. "You really think that's true? That putting up barriers keeps you safe? There's a joke! The wall might keep the pain from getting out, but it sure as hell doesn't keep it from getting *in*."

"Maybe not, but—"

"Mia! For God's sake, wake *up!* Whatever Grant's faults—and God knows I take the blame for many of them—trustworthiness isn't one of them. And I think you know that. And come on, we all have secrets, we all soft-pedal the truth from time to time. Often to save our own skins, true, but more often to save other people unnecessary pain. Unfortunately there's a huge gray area in there where it's all too easy to screw up. I mean, be honest— would you tell Haley the truth about her mother? Would you expect Grant to?"

Mia started. "That's different, she's just a little girl."

"When she's older, then."

She flushed, then sighed. "I don't know."

"You see? Gray area. But honey…Grant needs you. We *all* need you. If for no other reason than to keep us honest. Hell, to keep us *human*. Because you've brought something to this family that's been lacking for far too long."

"Tacky Christmas decorations?"

Bitsy smirked. "In a way…yes. It's called *genuineness*. The permission to not take ourselves so damn seriously. And yet you've slipped right into the very trap you've sprung the rest of us from, haven't you?" When Mia didn't—couldn't—reply, the older woman stood and came to stand in front of her. "You know, the pain stays as long as the splinter does. You're blaming the wrong person, here. And I don't mean Grant. *Or* you."

After enduring Bitsy's direct gaze for several seconds, Mia snorted another dry laugh. "And what good would it do to confront Christopher?"

"What good has it done *not* to?" She laid a hand on Mia's arm. "Do it for me, Mia. For all the women who've taken the crap their men dished out without ever fighting back."

Well, hell. Since she put it like that…

A house, the redhead had said. Christopher had apparently bought a house. But where? So go, her, for hitting paydirt with the first mutual acquaintance she called— *Yeah, that's right, Chris moved to Brooklyn Heights. Hold on, here's the address—*

Half-bemused, half-annoyed that he'd been so pathetically easy to track down, Mia scribbled the address on a napkin, then transferred it to her PalmPilot, fully intending to delete it as soon as this ordeal was over. True, she still had no idea what she hoped to gain by demanding answers to questions not yet fully formulated in her own mind. Except, perhaps, to dump the burden for their breakup back where it truly belonged—on her ex-fiancé's sorry head.

Of course, she mused as she gunned the Voyager's startled engine and pulled out of the driveway, she had no way of knowing if he'd even be home. But she seriously doubted he'd pick up once he saw her number on caller ID, and what D.A. on God's green earth was going to answer an anonymous blocked call?

So she'd just have to take her chances.

* * *

Grant watched Mia's van streak past the house, wondering where on earth was she going on a Sunday afternoon. He knew she didn't have any events—that, in fact, she was free until after the New Year. He also knew she'd been at his mother's that morning. Because he'd driven past, that's why.

In the middle of looking up Mia's cell number, he remembered she couldn't answer her phone while driving. So he called his mother instead.

"Okay, what did you do to Mia?"

"Oh, holster your weapon, hotshot," Bitsy answered coolly, tempting Grant to check to see if he'd dialed correctly. "I didn't do anything to her. We talked, that's all. And how do you know she was here?"

"Never mind that. What did you talk about?"

"As if I'd tell you. I like her, by the way. You could do worse. Hell, what am I saying—you *have* done worse. And let that be a lesson to you. So when she comes back, I think you should propose. Do you have a ring handy, dear?"

"When she comes back from where?" he asked, deciding to ignore the proposal part of her monologue altogether. For the moment.

"Well…I can't be sure, it's not as if she told me where she was going. But maybe…to see that pitiful excuse for a man she used to be engaged to?"

"She went to see *Christopher?*"

"You're bellowing, dear."

"What the hell is she thinking," he bellowed, "going to see him by herself?"

"The man may be an idiot, but I sincerely doubt he's capable of bodily harm. And Mia's a big girl, she doesn't need you—or anyone else—to hold her hand."

He stilled. "You put her up to this."

"I may have encouraged her to face her demons, yes." Bitsy paused. "Since it occurred to me perhaps she shouldn't wait forty years like I did. That maybe her turning into someone like *us* wasn't such a good idea. Now if you'll excuse me, I have to get dressed. I promised to take my granddaughter Christmas-shopping. And FYI, I already talked her out of getting you a horse."

"A hor— Never mind, I'll talk to you later."

But the instant he hung up the phone he called Venus, who was about as sympathetic as his mother had been. Although perhaps a trace more amused.

"Man, do you have it bad or what?"

"Yes, Venus, I have it bad. Now do you know where Christopher lives?"

"No, baby, I sure don't. And anyway, he could have moved, right?"

Feeling remarkably frustrated, Grant hung up to see a dressed-to-go-shopping Haley scowling up at him.

"Whatsa matter?"

"Nothing, honey, it's okay."

"S'not okay, your face is all mushed up."

"Okay, you got me. But it's nothing that affects you, I swear."

"Did you talk to Mia?"

"No," he said on a sigh. "But she's back. Well, she was back, I just saw her drive away. So she's okay." When Haley blew out a huge sigh of relief, he said, "So—you all set to go shopping with Nana?"

"Uh-huh. But she asked me to call her 'Bitsy,' she says Nana makes her feel old. But she *is* old, huh?"

The tension easing inside him, Grant chuckled, scooping Haley up into his arms. "Just don't tell her that."

"'Kay."

"Where's your hat? It's freezing outside."

"I left it at Mia's. C'n we go get it?"

"I don't know…I wouldn't feel right about going into her house when she's not there. Don't you have other hats?"

"I don't like any of them, they make me look like a baby. An' they don't match my coat. Please? I know right where it is, I left it there yesterday, it's on her kitchen table."

Grant hesitated long enough for a sly *Got 'im!* grin to slide across his daughter's mouth.

"Okay, in, grab your hat, and back out. I'll wait outside. Deal?"

"Deal."

But when, a minute or two later, he heard Haley's wail of "I can't find it!" from Mia's kitchen, Grant tromped inside, locating the hat almost immediately—on the counter, right beside the microwave.

He also found a napkin with an address, the felt-tippenned words slightly blurred. And beside that, a MapQuest printout with directions. Probably a client's address, right? Then again, maybe not. He entered the address into his BlackBerry, crammed the hat onto Haley's curls, then left. Soon after, having delivered his daughter to his mother, he brought up one of those "find anybody, anywhere" programs on his computer. Five minutes later…

Bingo.

Except for the Volvos and Beemers replacing the Studebakers and Buicks, Mia imagined the tree-lined street probably looked much the same as it had more than a half century ago—a row of handsome, unassuming three-story brownstones with tall, worn stoops. Some of the buildings were undoubtedly still carved into tiny apartments, a leftover legacy from the sixties and seventies. But others had been reclaimed, purged of redundant kitchens, bathrooms and microscopic bedrooms, brick exposed, woodwork stripped of twenty coats of cheap enamel paint.

Or at least, she thought as she checked the address, they were in the process thereof. Scaffolding clung to the face of the building, the top tier frosted with a single string of icicle lights. Underneath, the top third of the exterior appeared to be several shades lighter than the rest of the building, which over the years had dulled to the color of dry dog poop.

The remodel must be costing him a fortune, she mused as she eased into—wonder of wonders—a parking space a few doors down. The fire hydrant was a little closer than it probably should be, but at this point a ticket was the last thing on her mind.

She got out, locked the car, marched up to the house, climbed the front steps, rang the bell, all with less thought than she usually gave to going to the bathroom. Didn't even hesitate when Christopher's "Yes?" wheezed through the intercom.

"It's Mia," she said with remarkable calm. "We need to talk."

"Who?" a female voice said. The redhead, she presumed. Then again, with his track record, maybe not. The intercom cut off, but no buzzer. Just as she was about to ring again, the front door—recently restored to its stained-glass glory—swung open.

In some ways, he hadn't changed much. The neatly cut hair, the geeky glasses, were the same. The clothes had gone high-end, though—she sincerely doubted the sweatshirt hailed from Old Navy, nor did the jeans. And vanished entirely was the perpetually mellow expression she'd once thought was cute, replaced by one that might have made a lesser, less-motivated woman, go "Ooooh!" and quake in her Ugg boots. Of course, she had just bearded the man in his den, but whatever.

"Sorry to drop in like this," she said with a smile, "but I just found out you and my best friend were screwing around while you were both otherwise committed. Mind if I come in for a moment?"

"This isn't really a good time—"

"Yeah, real sorry for the inconvenience. Ten minutes, Christopher. And some honest answers. Then I'm gone."

"And if I say no?"

"Then I make your life a living hell." She shrugged. "Up to you."

He glared at her for several beats, reminding her—but not—of Grant, then backed up and let her inside. The redhead was right there, doing a little glaring herself. Mia stuck out her hand.

"Hi. I'm Mia. Christopher and I—"

"Are old friends," he supplied, and she laughed.

"Used to be engaged. Long time ago. Ancient history, nothing to worry about, I assure you. But I do need to steal him from you—" she swallowed down the ironic laughter threatening to break free "—for a few minutes. Although not to worry, I'm not here about a secret child or anything like that."

Red blinked at her, then over at Christopher as if to say *You sure I can leave you alone with the nutcase?* When he said, "It's okay, Cynth," she nodded and walked away.

Mia watched Cynth—sounded like a sneeze to her, but whatever—go, then turned to Christopher. Who, after an exasperated look, led her into the front room, a mélange of ladders, drop cloths and plaster dust. There was no place to sit. Just as well.

"Nice place," she said, scanning the rampant destruction.

"You said ten minutes," Christopher said, folding his arms across his chest. "So what do you want?"

She turned, wondering how she'd ever thought she'd loved this man. Then she realized, no, this *wasn't* the man she'd loved. That man had never really existed.

"Answers," she said at last. "At least, those I can get. Since Justine is dead, I can't exactly ask her why *she* betrayed me."

"See, I knew you'd see it that way—"

"How else was I supposed to see it?" Mia asked, tilting her head. "She was my best friend. And oh, yeah—you were my fiancé. You know, the man I'd trusted enough to say 'sure' when he asked *me* to marry him?"

"Okay, Mia, calm down—"

"Don't you dare tell me to calm down," she said, thinking if she was any calmer she'd be comatose. "And you know, forget answering that. Obviously the grass was greener on her side of the fence, or whatever, what does it matter? What I do want to know, however, is why you—either of you—never had the *cojones* to tell me."

He let out a short, harsh laugh. "You're kidding, right?"

"Let me think…" She paused. "Nope. Not kidding." Unbidden tears sprang to her eyes. "Especially since Justine had been my *friend*. I mean, you…" Her mouth screwed up. "Obviously, you and I had never really been right for each other. I knew it even before we broke up, even if I didn't want to admit it. What hurt was the *way* you broke it off—no explanation, nothing. You didn't even try to be kind about it. But Justine…"

Mia glanced out the dusty window, her heart bumping in her chest when she thought she saw Grant's Lexus cruise by. Telling herself she was hallucinating, she turned back.

"Knowing how little she obviously valued our friendship hurts far, far worse than anything you did to me."

"And what good would it have done, if you'd known?"

"Well, let's see...maybe I wouldn't have made a fool of myself defending her, defending our relationship, to her ex. A man who deserved better than a fickle opportunist."

Christopher's forehead knotted. "Justine left Grant because she was bored to tears, Mia. The man's a freaking *hermit*. You know how she loved to be in the limelight, to be the center of attention. She felt as if she'd been left to rot, out in the Greenwich house. She had no idea what she'd really gotten into. And finally she couldn't take it anymore."

Mia folded her arms. "And you left *me* because...?"

His fingers probed the back of his neck for a moment before he stuffed his hands in his pockets. "Because you turned out not to be the woman I thought you were, either. Talk about fickle! Throwing your career away like that, to set yourself up for failure when you—"

"A course correction isn't a failure, Christopher."

"Exactly what I thought when I started seeing Justine," he said coldly. "But if Justine had really been an opportunist, she would have stayed with Grant, who has far more money and social position than I'll ever have."

"But, alas, no political ambitions. As you said, she loved being in the limelight. And you're right, she would have never had that with Grant. Still, no matter how you slice it, she stole you from me—"

"It wasn't like that, Mia! It just...happened."

"Oh, please, spare me the tired clichés. Nothing just *happens*. At every point along the way, both of you had choices, not the least of which was that you could have severed your previous relationships before starting a new one with each other. It would've been weird, yeah, but at least it would have borne some resemblance to integrity. But no. You decided to cheat on the people who trusted you, then keep the whole thing a secret. So now I'm left with the knowledge that a relationship I truly treasured was nothing but a sham."

"I'm so sorry, Mia, I didn't mean—"

"I'm not talking about *our* relationship, you bonehead. I mean mine and Justine's."

His hands still in his pockets, Christopher walked over to a streaked, clouded window. Through the murk, Mia saw a few Christmas lights blink on across the street. "Believe it or not," he said tiredly, "Justine treasured your friendship, too, far more than I ever understood. She hated the lies, the subterfuge. Keeping up the pretense. But I said, no, telling you would only make it worse—"

"Wait, wait, wait—" Mia's forehead knotted as she forced her brain to catch up with his words. "She *wanted* to tell me?"

"We fought about it constantly. At the end, especially. When the guilt got to be too much for her. She knew you'd hate her, that you'd probably never want to see her again, but the secret was making her crazy, she said. *I* said telling you was a deal-breaker." A tight smile stretched across his face. "She said it was if she didn't."

He turned back, his expression grim. "The day before she died, she called, saying she was going to tell you when the two of you got together to go shopping. She never had the chance."

Through the roaring in her ears, Mia barely heard Christopher say, "Despite everything, Justine really did love you. Far more than I did, apparently. And God knows, far more than she did me."

A lump the size of a baseball lodged in her throat, Mia

simply stared at him for several more moments. "Thank you," she finally got out, then walked away, coming face-to-face with the redhead, who'd apparently been in the dining room across the hall. The other woman gave her a funny look, then briskly crossed the narrow space to the living room.

"Christopher?" she said, in a tone of voice that told Mia exactly how much she'd overheard.

Hey. Not her problem.

The cold air, bracing and welcome, chilled the tears clinging to her lashes, tracked down her cheeks. A few houses down, a man who'd been leaning against his car straightened. Still on the landing, Mia blinked, realizing she hadn't been hallucinating, that was definitely Grant, his face a study of concern and love and everything she knew she could trust, forever and ever, amen.

He met her halfway, wrapping her in his arms just as the first sob broke loose.

Grant held on tight, Mia's head tucked underneath his chin as she cried, her tears simultaneously cracking his heart and mending it, as he finally, truly understood how precious it was, having another human being trust you enough to keep nothing back. Then she lifted her tear-stained face and kissed him, almost hard enough to knock teeth, and Grant got the definite impression that whatever had gone on inside that house, he could at least put one or two major worries to bed.

Not to mention her, he thought when she backed up, giving him a shaky "it's okay" smile. She swung her bag around to dig inside for a tissue, mumbling, "How on earth did you know I was here?" as she blew her nose.

"Does it matter?" he asked, and she blew again, then shook her head.

"Not really, no." But when he tried to ask her what had happened, she shushed him with two fingers against his lips.

"When we get home," she said.

Home. Was that the most wonderful word in the English language or what?

Only when they got back—of course—Haley and his mother had returned from their shopping expedition, so naturally, Haley had to tell them about every single thing she'd seen or done, except for the presents, which, she announced in a loud whisper, she had to keep a secret, and how she'd gone back to Santa and asked him if he'd read her letter yet—

"Let's go see what Etta's up to in the kitchen," Bitsy interrupted, although Grant could tell she was dying to know what happened, too. "I think she's baking cookies."

"Cookies!" Haley yelled, and was off like a shot.

It had started to snow an hour or so ago, giant, feathery flakes that floated so slowly you could almost watch each one's lazy journey before its already landed comrades welcomed it home. At Grant's suggestion that they go for a walk, Mia popped off the sofa and grabbed her toggle coat off the chair, tossing Grant's to him.

The minute they got outside, she scraped a handful of snow off the driveway and made a snowball, hitting him square in the chest.

"Oops," she said, and took off up the road, Grant hot on her heels, both of them only stopping to re-arm, dissolving into helpless laughter each time their missiles hit their marks. Then, panting and breathless, he took her gloved hand in his to walk—or slide, rather—in the slippery powder, giving her whatever time she needed. And finally, quietly, she told him about her conversation with her ex-fiancé. About the tragedy of Justine's never getting to clear the air.

He slung one arm around her shoulders. "That's why you were crying, then? About Justine."

"Certainly not about Christopher. But yes. God, what a mess. On so many levels." She shook her head, apparently unable to be any clearer. She didn't need to.

"Would you have forgiven her?"

"I don't know," she said on a breath. "I really don't."

Grant took a deep breath of his own. "Have you forgiven *me?*"

Mia looked up at him, her cheeks, eyelashes, the brim of her hat dotted with snowflakes. "Don't get me wrong, I'd still rather you'd told me. But I know you got caught in the middle. And that you were only trying to spare my feelings. Not yours. Watching Christopher today, though, listening to him…it's total apples and oranges time. I trusted him, and Justine, because I wanted to. Needed to. But I trust *you* because I know I can. And if that still makes me naive and gullible—"

"And so what if it does?" Grant said, pulling her closer to kiss her snow-flecked temple. "Because if it hadn't been for *your* openness, I—" Overwhelmed with emotion, he simply tucked her hand in his and kept walking. And she squeezed his fingers, understanding.

For several minutes, they just walked, content to simply enjoy the deep, blue hush of the snowy night, until Mia said, "Until I finally faced Christopher, I don't think I realized exactly how much I blamed myself for the breakup. When all I'd done was follow my heart, with the business. So he would have never been the right person for me. Still, it would have been nice to know what had been really going on. Hell, I never could compete with Justine, not even—"

When she cut herself off, Grant stopped, tugging her around to face him. "Not even what?"

She fidgeted for a moment, before out came the most extraordinary confession, about how she'd been originally attracted to him, only to back down when Justine made a play for him. Grant stared at her for a long moment, then let out a sound that was half laugh, half groan.

"And if you hadn't backed down," he said earnestly, her gaze captured in his, "I probably would have never gone out with Justine to begin with."

Confusion muddied her eyes. "What?"

"I thought I detected a spark of interest that first day, too. But before I could act on it—I told you, I'm lousy at this stuff—Justine moved in. When you didn't do anything to dissuade her, I decided I'd been mistaken. Brother," he said on a half laugh. "What a cock-up."

Mia smiled. "It's okay. Because if you hadn't married Justine, there wouldn't be Haley, and neither of us would be who we are now. For all we know, if we'd gotten together then, it would have been disastrous."

"And now?"

"And now," she said, linking her hands behind his neck, "I think it's looking good for Santa to bring Haley exactly what she wants for Christmas."

"And what's that?"

In response, she laughed softly and kissed him.

Epilogue

The grown-ups all thought Haley was in bed asleep, but she couldn't get comfortable, her tummy was much too crawly and tickly. It was Christmas Eve, and Etta and Mia had cooked a big ham and lots of other yummy stuff, and Mia's mommy and daddy came, and Bitsy, too, and Venus, and after dinner everybody sat in the living room, talking and laughing and telling stories about Daddy and Mia when they were little, with no lights except from the tree and the fireplace. She hadn't wanted to go to bed while everybody else was having so much fun, but Daddy said Santa couldn't come until she was asleep.

But she was still awake, anyway, so she got up and put on her robe and slippers, got Henry and went downstairs to look at the tree for a little while. Most of the presents were already under it—because Santa couldn't possibly do it all himself, Daddy had told her—but the one thing she most wanted couldn't fit underneath the tree, anyway—

Haley stopped when she got to the living room doorway, 'cause Mia and Daddy were still in there and they'd probably send her back to bed if they saw her. So she and Henry backed into the shadows, just as Daddy got up and walked over to the tree. He reached way inside it and pulled out a little box, then turned around, his face all happy in a way that made Haley feel happy, too. Only Mia made a funny sound, and Haley felt her forehead get all bunched up.

But Daddy just laughed, then went back over to the sofa and opened the box. Haley couldn't see what it was, but it sparkled almost as much as the lights on the tree. Then Mia said a kind of bad word—but not like she was mad, more like she was surprised—and put the cup she'd been holding on the end table.

"Not fair," she said. "I only got you a scarf. Cashmere, but still."

Haley thought a scarf was a pretty dumb Christmas present, but Daddy didn't seem to care.

"Hand, please," he said, and Mia lifted her hand, and now Haley could see that the sparkling thing was a big shiny ring, like the one she sorta remembered Mommy wearing a long time ago. Then she got real still, waiting for the sad feeling that happened when she thought about Mommy…except it didn't come, not really. Because all the happy thoughts crowded it out. She frowned, then decided maybe Mommy wouldn't mind.

Then Daddy got down on one knee in front of Mia and put the ring on her finger, and they were both laughing and acting silly, not like grown-ups at all. And Daddy said, "Make us a family, Mia. You, me, Haley… Marry me and make us whole," and then Mia said, "Yes," in a funny voice, and all that happiness wouldn't stay inside Haley a *second* longer.

"Santa answered my letter!" she yelled, making Mia's and Daddy's heads turn at the same time. "He did, he did, he did! Hot *damn!*"

Mia and Daddy looked so surprised Haley started to laugh, and then they looked at each other and starting laughing, too, Daddy laughing harder than Haley had *ever* heard him. Then Daddy held out his arms and she ran into them, and everybody else came into the room to see what was going on—and Daddy said something to Etta about their needing to have a little talk—and then Mia showed them the ring.

Then everybody was hugging everybody else and making so much noise that nobody even noticed when Daddy looked into her eyes, smiling really, really big, so big she couldn't even remember anymore what it had been like when she'd thought he'd looked scary.

"Merry Christmas, sweetheart," he said, and Haley snuggled against him, her heart completely filled up, forever and ever and ever.

* * * * *

And watch out for
YOURS, MINE...OR OURS?
the next story in Karen Templeton's
GUYS AND DAUGHTERS *miniseries,*
available January 2008
from Silhouette Special Edition.

Brad shoved the truck into gear and drove to the bottom of the hill, where the road forked. Turn left, and he'd be home in five minutes. Turn right, and he was headed for Indian Rock.

He had no damn business going to Indian Rock.

He had nothing to say to Meg McKettrick, and if he never set eyes on the woman again, it would be two weeks too soon.

He turned right.

He couldn't have said why.

He just drove straight to the Dixie Dog Drive-In.

Back in the day, he and Meg used to meet at the Dixie Dog, by tacit agreement, when either of them had been away. It had been some kind of universe thing, purely intuitive.

Passing familiar landmarks, Brad told himself he ought to turn around. The old days were gone. Things had ended badly between him and Meg anyhow, and she wasn't going to be at the Dixie Dog.

He kept driving.

He rounded a bend, and there was the Dixie Dog. Its big neon sign, a giant hot dog, was all lit up and going through its corny sequence—first it was covered in red squiggles of light, meant to suggest ketchup, and then yellow, for mustard.

Brad pulled into one of the slots next to a speaker, rolled down the truck window and ordered.

A girl roller-skated out with the order about five minutes later.

When she wheeled up to the driver's window, smiling, her eyes went wide with recognition, and she dropped the tray with a clatter.

Silently Brad swore. Damn if he hadn't forgotten he was a famous country singer.

The girl, a skinny thing wearing too much eye makeup, immediately started to cry. "I'm sorry!" she sobbed, squatting to gather up the mess.

"It's okay," Brad answered quietly, leaning to look down at her, catching a glimpse of her plastic name tag. "It's okay, Mandy. No harm done."

"I'll get you another dog and a shake right away, Mr. O'Ballivan!"

"Mandy?"

She stared up at him pitifully, sniffling. Thanks to the copious tears, most of the goop on her eyes had slid south. "Yes?"

"When you go back inside, could you not mention seeing me?"

"But you're Brad O'Ballivan!"

"Yeah," he answered, suppressing a sigh. "I know."

She rolled a little closer. "You wouldn't happen to have a picture you could autograph for me, would you?"

"Not with me," Brad answered.

"You could sign this napkin, though," Mandy said. "It's only got a little chocolate on the corner."

Brad took the paper napkin and her order pen, and scrawled his name. Handed both items back through the window.

She turned and whizzed back toward the side entrance to the Dixie Dog.

Brad waited, marveling that he hadn't considered incidents like this one before he'd decided to come back home. In retrospect, it seemed shortsighted, to say the least, but the truth was, he'd expected to be—Brad O'Ballivan.

Presently Mandy skated back out again, and this time she managed to hold on to the tray.

"I didn't tell a soul!" she whispered. "But Heather and Darlene *both* asked me why my mascara was all smeared." Efficiently, she hooked the tray onto the bottom edge of the window.

Brad extended payment, but Mandy shook her head.

"The boss said it's on the house, since I dumped your first order on the ground."

He smiled. "Okay, then. Thanks."

Mandy retreated, and Brad was just reaching for the food when a bright red Blazer whipped into the space beside his. The driver's door sprang open, crashing into the metal speaker, and somebody got out in a hurry.

Something quickened inside Brad.

And in the next moment Meg McKettrick was standing practically on his running board, her blue eyes blazing.

Brad grinned. "I guess you're not over me after all," he said.

REQUEST YOUR FREE BOOKS!
2 FREE NOVELS PLUS 2 FREE GIFTS!

SPECIAL EDITION®
Life, Love and Family!

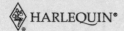

American ★ Romance®

Kate Merrill had grown up convinced
that the most attractive men were incapable
of ever settling down. Yet the harder she
resisted the superstar photographer
Tyler Nichols, the more persistent the
handsome world traveler became.
So by the time Christmas arrived, there
was only one wish on her holiday list—
that she was wrong!

LOOK FOR

THE CHRISTMAS DATE

BY

Michele Dunaway

**Available December
wherever you buy books**

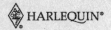

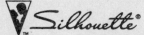

COMING NEXT MONTH